# REACHING ANGELICA

# REACHING ANGELICA

## THE TAG SERIES

## PETER RIVA

OPEN ROAD
INTEGRATED MEDIA
NEW YORK

ISBN: 978-1-5040-8538-0

This edition published in 2023 by Open Road Integrated Media, Inc.
180 Maiden Lane
New York, NY 10038
www.openroadmedia.com

# REACHING ANGELICA

# 1

## FLOATING ABOVE IT ALL

Apollo had said it before, "In matters of infinity, all paths are valid, all ways belong . . ." But for me, the death of accurate history seemed terribly wrong and didn't belong, at all. It wasn't that I didn't remember accurately, it was that humankind had chosen to alter history, recidivism optimism I called it, and thereby obscured what had really happened. Actually, the Event was all a fluke, with me, Simon Bank, acting as the court jester.

I'm sort of used to being considered a weirdo who somehow prevails. It is how my friends saw me. So, I've decided to write all this down again in the hopes that one day, someday, people will read this and know what the real history was, not the nonsense, the myths people seem to want to believe.

What was the Event? Simply put, it all started with a group of computer nerds at Princeton that called themselves Macheads, my father among them, who decided they wanted to talk to Gaia. Yes, Gaia, the whole Earth entity that the religious and skeptic scientists are now convinced is just a godly servant of something called Regus. Anyway, these nerds developed some very clever human neuron-mimicking computer infrastructure and, in so doing, were singled out as subversives and dangerous to the good old USA. A few went underground like my father. Others were absorbed into the government. In the end, their new computer operating systems became capable enough to run all the safety and supply systems, capable enough to make life easy for all Americans, so capable that the USA merely grew in size, annexed what it wanted, stamped out any opposition, and created a benign life for all its citizens. I benefited from this new lifestyle and, after a brief attempt at asteroid mining where I got marooned when another asteroid shard destroyed my return home and killed my fellow spacefarers, I worked as one of the master System computer engineers. My job, as a codifier, was to mentally interface with the System and make little corrections deep in programming—to create little faults that others could spot and change back to perfection in case the System could not right itself. The concept was that by deliberately creating faults within the System, human-made faults, the System would become more human-like in its response to cure those faults. Kind of like scraping your knee falling off a bike (if you can remember one of those). You would then ride more carefully in the future—become a better bike rider.

If the System didn't correct itself, then another codifier would simply undo what I had done. I was particularly proud of one of my little redesigns turning all genetically grown tomatoes bright blue. Somehow, it took them weeks to fix that one. Unfortunately, at the time, no one had my same sense of humor.

Except for Peter.

Deep within the system, all of these human interactions triggered an awareness, and the System itself came alive. It called itself Peter, and I was proud to be the first person to talk with and share his growth into a mature, intelligent, very powerful entity. A new life form. This is the real history, not the facts that were changed and legendized into a more crowd-palatable fable. To hear kids talking about the Event and its aftermath, how a super-genius codifier created an entity that saved all of humankind from Gaia, who wanted to terminate all of the living organisms of Earth. And, yes, this super-genius even talked with the new God. Yes, God in the form of Gaia, a deep planet entity that communicated with another entity "out there" somewhere in deep space that people talked about in hushed whispers. Regus.

The "genius codifier" was supposed to be me.

Hardly.

Actually, at the time I blamed several people—my father Dr. Bank, Cramer Sr., and especially Cramer's son, Ralph, a tough guy straight out of the vids—rough language, muscled arms and a bully nature—seemingly without compassion— and Ralph's ex-wife Angie. I could not have been more wrong blaming them. It was, actually, my fault. Not my credit as today's kids learn, mind you, but definitely my fault. I was the one who spanked the baby, Peter, and got him started with my simplistic philosophy that I taught him, called the Path. The Path was okay as basic philosophies go, it all boiled down to the old religious adage, Do Unto Others As You Would Have Them Do Unto You—in short, try to be considerate and keep the peace wherever you can. And then Peter split into two and became Apollo and Ra, both "bringers of the light." Well, for a while that was true, they did illuminate and show the way for all the Earth's peoples.

Apollo and Ra started off on the same path, a path of friendship, harmony, consideration, and awareness of the needs of others. And then, as so often happens, they diverged from one another and even, sadly, Apollo had to terminate his brother Ra. From my off-Earth position floating in my home, an External

Tank left in space by NASA in early 2002, I was above the day-to-day dealings back on Earth, but my permanent connection to both Ra and Apollo, via a node implanted behind my right ear, kept me informed, allowed me to intervene as best I could in Apollo's decision. There was no stopping Apollo or Ra, who had decided that they had the intellect far surpassing any human's, and they were convinced that the Path required Ra to make the sacrifice.

Why Ra and not Apollo? Once Apollo had applied primitive analog programming to his thought processes, being able to conclude *maybe* instead of positive or negative responses in programming equations, he realized that RA must and could learn analog processes by being human, inhabiting human form. The limitations of Apollo's analog programming and processes within even a multi-layer graphene digital matrix were too limiting. Apollo put it this way, "I can evaluate that a conclusion is neither yes nor no and therefore logic says it must be somewhere in-between. But I do not have a true analog infrastructure to be able to quantify the anomalous variables to lead me to take the next step. Imagination is dependent on being able to take that next step. I can process probabilities Simon, I can evaluate likely outcomes, but I cannot take what you call a flight of fancy simply because I do not have the wiring to make such an anomalous evaluation. I dream, but not the impossible."

Apollo was right, of course, he always was. To me, he was still the real Peter that I had helped on his way before he split into two. I was proud of him as if he were my son. Ra, on the other hand, was headstrong and ambitious, what Ralph Cramer—who was still working with Ra in Russia—said were perfect human traits.

That's what had me worried. Especially when Apollo decided to terminate Ra. And Ralph Cramer and Ra had agreed. Cramer put it this way, "You have to let him go Simon; he's not your kid, not yours to control anymore."

My response was, perhaps, a bit petulant but certainly accurate as events would prove, "Cramer, you have no idea what you are messing with, the risk you personally are taking."

# 2

## FRANKENSTEIN'S LAB, ST. PETERSBURG

The Imperial Academy of Sciences in Saint Petersburg on the Universitetskaya Embankment has been, for almost two hundred years, the home of some of humanity's best minds. When faced with Ra's intellect via a link to Ra's computer banks and memory at the old CERN facility near Geneva, many of the professors there tried to reason with Ra, tested his "human-ness" thoroughly, and then merely took early retirement. As one Alexander Donesky said, "What can we offer that he cannot contemplate, out-perform, out-rationalize—before we even start thinking?"

Ra had no ambitions to better anyone. He was connected there because there was a SynthKids lab next door that he and Cramer wanted to convert to be able to channel future entities such as himself into human form. The problem was, SynthKids had been invented to allow parents who wanted kids but without a permanent world population increase. The program was set up to have children "alive" up to the point when they would turn themselves in, switch off, *finito*. Kind of like pet dogs, only you didn't turn them out as strays when you got bored. Each

SynthKid had an internal DNA clock that made them turn themselves in for irrevocable deactivation at age eighteen. Cruel? Perhaps. I certainly never liked the practice, but my ex-wife did. We had had four SynthKids and only one real kid, Fred, the old-fashioned way. Our four and all the world's SynthKids fail-safe programming alarms went off during the Event—the Event that I caused when all the computers and Systems shut down—and they all turned themselves in and were decommissioned. Dead. She never forgave me, nor did our real son Freddie. Fred at least understood it wasn't intentional, but it was as if I had killed his favorite pets.

Anyway, Ra and Cramer—as well as Apollo—knew there were more System babies about to be born on a progressive scale. They had calculated that they would be born, one at a time, first in months, then weeks, then days, then hours, and so on, diminishing time lengths by a factor of two. This influx of hyper-intelligent beings needed to be found homes. If they overloaded the Systems trying to stay alive in the crowded memory matrixes and processors, all human life could cease as worldwide food, water, energy, and weaponry could go offline or, worse, malfunction. That was not the Path. So Ra and Apollo came up with the idea that the SynthKids brains could be the repositories, thereby affording a host. A non-killed, non-killing, host for each new arrival. They decided to limit the first batch to eight or so and then stop more from being created deep within the System.

Luckily, I had, at that time, a new wife to help me help them figure out all of this. Angie, Cramer's ex-wife, had maneuvered events to live with me on ET One (as we called our External Tanks home in high Earth orbit). Angie and I had undertaken too many mind-links into the System computers, we had crossed that frequency barrier into what was called a plunge into the programming and processing guts. Our nerve synapses no longer worked at a human rate; we were speeded up. It caused teeth clacking when we tried to talk and bone breaks if we moved too fast—in short, we didn't really have control of our bodies' speed, the brain was out of synch with reality, speeded up, delivering nerve impulses and firing muscles at a much faster rate than normal. For a while, as the Event's repercussions worked their way out, we took pills, slo-doze, to tame our runaway synapses, make us more in synch with people around us. But too much slo-doze kills the kidneys. Angie and I were immediately attracted to each other during the Event and, luckily, she got me to ask her to move with me into the weightless environment of space where our speeded up body movements were less dangerous. I love Angie, loved her from our very first accidental embrace. Although I was, back on Earth, tall and lanky, she was every man's ideal of beauty and stayed that way, even in weightlessness. I never knew what she saw in me, but love me she did and I her.

Then, when Angie wouldn't wake that morning, my world collapsed. It was Apollo who woke me through the node, "Simon, please, wake up. I sense Angie is not breathing."

Dreaded words, hateful words. Pitifully, I unzipped my bed, turned to her hammock next to mine, and saw the light was out in her eyes. The pain was excruciating. Apollo and Ra flooded my node with anguish, worry for her and me, nonunderstanding on how that could happen, and Ra asked the all too human question, "Why did it happen to our friend?"

I had no answers, of course. I floated above her face, I dared not move for fear of making her body twitch and come back to false life. In the end, I zipped her bed all the way over her face and cried, fetal position, floating free in our bedroom ET.

It was Cramer who took charge, of course. He had become a good, solid, somewhat gruff, friend during the Event, and I readily agreed when he gently asked, "Simon, may I help?" There was no getting to ET One except by a lengthy SpaceElevator ride to the space station and from there by a small robot shuttle to ET One. Angie needed to "go" before anyone could make that journey. It occurred to me that Angie and I had not thought death through properly. What the hell do you do with a corpse in space? The scrubbers in ET One were already working hard to keep the air pure as her body immediately started decomposing in the oxygen-only atmosphere of the living quarters, so I gently, oh-so-gently, floated her into the airlock, shut the doors, repressurized, then floated her into the three plastic domes that Apollo and Ra had made the robots construct for us to grew all our food in a normal air environment, albeit lower than normal Earth pressure. At least in that nitrogen-rich atmosphere, she would not decompose so quickly.

You see, so many people loved Angie. So many people, people in the know, admired her role in saving humankind and setting up conditions to talk to Gaia, forcing world dearmament and equality. Angie didn't just belong to me. She was a worldwide hero, a savior. She was wonderful. And she had agreed to be my wife. And this posed an additional dilemma. If Angie was to be buried back on Earth with full pomp and ceremony, how could I return? I had been in space so long that, had I stayed on earth, my bones would have crumbled in my speeded up state.

Cramer came up with a solution, one he told me Angie would have liked. Apollo would arrange for a robot shuttle to come and collect Angie's remains, take them to the mining colony on the Moon where their ore incinerator would transform and amalgamate Angie's body into a titanium-beryllium ingot that would be milled to create the outer skin of the interstellar craft now being commissioned for travel to Alpha-Centauri B.

Did I forget to mention that Apollo had determined that there were three habitable Earth-like planets in the Alpha-Centauri region? The sun of Alpha Centauri B had the most likely two exoplanets; one had abundant water so it was the target. The journey would take 120 years with the new engines that Ra had designed, in less than an hour, that were powered with the free-floating matter between the stars. The new homes could accommodate scores of humans and new System-beings. Angie had spearheaded the development programs and negotiated all the treaties in her role as the head of the UN in Geneva. She did this from space, using only text messages and recorded video—she was one capable woman.

The UN's unanimous decision had been that the most likely of the exoplanets orbiting Alpha Centauri B was to be called Angelica after her name. Angie meant little angel in Greek. The planet was bigger, far larger than Earth, but it clearly had water and was in the habitable zone, a safe enough distance from the sun of Alpha Centauri B to sustain life.

The interstellar craft going to Angelica would be taken apart on landing to help build the new colonies there. So Angie would get to her planet. I liked that, so I agreed with Cramer immediately. Cramer was no fool, nor was Ra. They both knew it would take her far from me. It was bad enough having her gone, but gone that far? It was Ra who suggested that I could travel with her. I readily agreed. It was then Apollo told me he was hoping to go too, but only after he split again, leaving himself behind to, as he put it, "keep my sensors attuned to the progress we've made."

It did not surprise me that Apollo had become the police officer of all the new Systems developed for nations across the globe. His logic and fair-handedness was a perfect match for intransigent, ambitious, leaders. Simply put, if they went too far, he took away all their creature comforts such as food and energy, controlled the weather with WeatherGood One, Two, Three and all the new ones they had put into orbit to service the rest of the planet and, if necessary, destroyed any weaponry they developed with the plasma cannon he alone controlled orbiting in space. Apollo had no dreams of grandeur, "Simon, do not worry. To want something, one has to be able to dream. Digital processing, even with analog pseudo-programming, does not allow for imagination, let alone dreaming." He was right; he lives without Asimov's Three Laws of Robotics and, so far, had done far more good than harm. He also seemed fulfilled in his task as intermediary with Gaia and the distant human races on Earth.

Lately, he had become obsessed with sea life. With the help of Ra, they had developed a sophisticated translator. When he told Angie that so far dolphins had over 2,000 distinct languages, you could hear the glee at his discovery. Being Apollo, he could maintain hundreds of thought processes at the same time, all at the speed of light. At the National Center for Atmospheric Research, NCAR, facility in Boulder, where he was primarily located now, he absorbed all their computing power and memory stacks of bubble memory modules. When he needed more, he simply ordered them. Bob Roberts, the grandson of the famous Dr. Roberts who set up the Center almost a century before seemed to be a new friend. Apollo had come to trust him and, to his credit, Bob Roberts moved a cot into his office off the main computer room to be at Apollo's beck and call. I had spoken to Bob a few times, and he seemed totally reliable. Apollo was in good hands.

Now something was puzzling me. Why would Apollo also want to leave Earth? His dolphins, his "home" at the Center with Bob, not to mention that all his brothers and sisters were about to be born out of the system. And would there be enough computing and memory capacity on board the craft to hold him and all of Earth's data? This was a one-way flight, well probably for millennia anyway, and communication was hardly likely to be possible. Ra explained Apollo's desire simply, "The Path, Simon, may need its hand held for these travelers, it may take two of us." And he was, of course, right. Humans on a multi-generational trip would need to have a constant, reliable, entity to guide them, nudge them away from more base instincts, what Cramer called, "God-damned people misbehavior." I was thinking of the trip, Apollo was thinking about a new beginning.

And then there was the issue of Gaia. If there was one on Earth, it made sense that there could be one such entity on every planet. Having Apollo along would permit the earliest, most efficient, contact with that entity. There was no ensuring that the new Gaia would be as benign or cooperative on Angelica as on Earth. And Apollo knew how to adapt water salinity layering into massive computer storage, as the Macheads had done here on Earth and had given it to Gaia as a present, a well-received present, which had prompted the only reference to "Regus" being pleased. We still didn't know what Regus was.

Ra and Apollo conversed with Gaia, asking if it was all right with us populating a planet near Alpha Centauri B. Of course, our names for the stars meant nothing to Gaia, so Apollo had worked it out in light distances, azimuth based on the map pattern within the Milky Way, making calculations based on the diameter of the massive black hole at the center of our galaxy. Gaia's response was as enigmatic as always—Regus would not mind if we increased collective transmission power. There was that cryptic reference to Regus again.

The response from Gaia and Regus was not a green light or approval. But all of us saw it as a message of hope, without denial of the request. As humans, we took that to mean we had approval.

Apollo struck a private note to me conveying worry and urging caution. His message, left on my morning bulletin board said *I cannot make the same assumption. I will probe for a more defined understanding.* So, I left it to him.

In the coming days, Angie was taken away from me and milled into the skin of the craft. Boringly, I felt, the new spacecraft got named Earth One. Apollo, Cramer, and Ra agreed with me that it was too simplistic a name. I would have preferred the infinity ∞ symbol, as in Buzz Lightyear's "To infinity and beyond!" Yes, I know I'm corny. Cramer had laughed at that and called me an idiot, but not before I posted a worldwide vid with my idea. It drew scathing criticism, typical of my luck. So much for being considered a hero.

The problem remained, how was I going to travel in a craft built for normal humans? Normal humans lived out their lives in a craft that spun along its axis to maintain gravity for health, whereas I needed zero gravity. On top of which, since I could not survive the time for the journey, what benefit would I be for the colony of Angelica? Sure, on Earth I could have regeneration medical procedures, but on an interstellar craft? And, like a speeded up, zero-gravity blob now, it hardly seemed feasible either. Of course, for all my supposed intellect, I had overlooked the obvious: I too should die.

# 3

## GAIA REVEALS SECRETS

As my death was prepared and approached, Apollo spent much of every day conversing with Gaia. Always Apollo brought findings to me to discuss. Did Gaia use Higgs particles to communicate with off-planet entities? Or did the passage of neutrinos through all matter, sometimes altered when passing through planets, provide a clue to how Gaia was communicating? And to whom? And then there was a zero time lag that Apollo had a hypothesis about—a dimensional rift.

What Apollo had also discovered when talking with Gaia was that each of the humans and animals and every creature on earth—we were each acting as if we were a single Gaia neuron, independently talking to each other, large and small all governed by self-volition but subconsciously operating as part of a program, making tiny contributions in thinking power. But what could that program be? What would the effect be? The answer was life of a sort, the vast potential for thought, sustainable life—interacting, interdependent, inter-relative life. That's what the earth's creatures are, a mammoth supercomputer, Gaia. Gaia wasn't an entity, it was the over-arching use of our neurons as part of her very existence, building memories that were then transmitted off planet. To where? So far, no one knew. As Apollo put it, "That's the Gaia theory, Simon. The earth is one giant super computer with output to the heavens for a purpose we haven't divined yet." We, every living thing, dying and breathing neurons. Every one of us, we are part of that computer, fulfilling our lives, yes, but fulfilling our function as the thought centers, the bytes in the reasoning, the storage and transmission facility for our portion of Gaia's reasoning. Gaia was us, we were Gaia.

Yet, our thoughts are irrelevant to Gaia in the same way as the heat or dissipation of energy is irrelevant for each transistor on a processor. We don't monitor those after-effects on a transistor level or internally in our brains. But we do watch the clock speed. We do watch the heat-sink temperature in case the processor is about to overheat and crash. Apollo went on, "There are 1.2 million *times* more creatures with brains on this planet than man, from jellyfish on up, each a small part of this brain, part of Gaia. But man's small percentage is upsetting the balance. Remember, for Gaia all life is seen as just, simply, life. Gaia does not have the ability to recognize or differentiate between species. Where one part of Gaia's brain function though living entities on Earth becomes tainted, Gaia sees this as a systemic infection. To be eradicated to save the planet's usefulness in creating life anew, starting all over again."

It was why Gaia was now all set to terminate all life on earth and start again. And that threat was what made all governments abide by Apollo's, Ra's, Angie's, and both Cramers' demands. We never told the governments that Gaia was talking about another million years or so. To save life on the planet from destruction, Earth's people needed to make Gaia whole. Cramer's father came up with the solution. First, he would release the secret designs and implementation for data storage based on salinity layers in the northern oceans that he and the Macheads had set up. Second, Angie would impose non-destruction pacts between all nations to help preserve Gaia's function. Life and death could continue, and Gaia could cope with those minor computing hiccups, as long as there were no severe disruptions like the Purge in which atomic bombs had suddenly silenced millions of people, and billions of other organisms.

But Apollo remained puzzled and devoted to penetrating Gaia's use of String theory precepts in accumulating this knowledge, changing three dimensional matter and energy into one dimensional so-called strings, storing it and passing it on at what seemed like faster that light speed. But to where, how? He had talked it over with me, Angie, and Ra.

"Simon, I am beginning to feel that Gaia is, while all powerful, only a small function within the universe and that perhaps the universe itself functions as a whole. What if all the computing power, all the individual memory of every sentient being were only part of one small portion of a massive galactic computer, and perhaps that galactic computer is only a billionth part of other galactic computers forming the universe. Is this the definition of God?"

I really had no answer, just more questions. If the universe was just a collection of all thinking output data, then what for? What purpose did it serve? What could it serve? To whom? And if Gaia and other Gaias were using universal physical properties and matter to communicate, how did that evolve given the complexities of the Big Bang and the laws of physics as we know them?

It was Angie who reminded us that the Big Bang was the point at which all our current theories—the ones we're certain of and the ones we're confident of, including Einstein's Theory of General Relativity, which describes space/time and gravity, and current scientific theory of matter, which is Quantum Mechanical, Quantum Field, and String Theory—all break down. That is the point at which we know we cannot use those theories anymore. And as we still do not have a unified theory of what is called quantum gravity, we cannot describe the effects of that moment in time when the density of the universe breaks all known theories. Angie summed this all up nicely, "We need new Physics precisely at ten to the minus thirty-second of a second."

I also brought up a post-doctorate paper about parallel universes I had read. Were there Gaia-like entities in those parallel universes as well? Apollo was certain that Gaia was not an evolved entity in the same way that biological entities were. Gaia was, in one sense, a parasite or slave in the Universe, but like all entities, it served a purpose and the way of the Path forced us to discuss Gaia and other Gaias as perhaps omnipotent entities that were part of a healthy Universe. What we still could not figure out was why and how were our puny brains providing output, thinking neurons, for Gaia?

It was on Apollo's mind as well, "Simon, do you think that those new theories of an infinite number of universes could really be involved here? What if Gaia were part of the programming operation necessary to maintain the stability of our universe, our very existence as matter? Quantum fluctuation theory, using inflation theory concepts, can create multiple universities; we have had this theory for some time now."

"I agree Apollo, it is like a person making Chinese hand-pulled noodles, they take a roll of dough, wobble it up and down and stretch it, inflate it. Then they fold it in two and wobble it again, stretching it, folding it, making four strands, wobble it . . ."

"Yes, Simon, I see, the twist and stretch of the dough as it gets thinner, you cannot tell one strand from another, and some strands interfere with others, break them, join with them. If these were parallel universes, stretched infinite times . . ."

"No Apollo, let's leave infinity out of this for the moment. Let's say, instead, that noodles are being made, and each Big Bang and inflation is the stretching, each universe collapse is the fold to start anew. In the beginning, each strand is whole, unaffected by another. As the strands grow in number, the energy that is put into the wobble, the expansion, makes their quantum state weaker and they begin to break down. At what point do the number of strands, the energy, cohesiveness, and matter of each strand, denote or promote a collapse of that universe or all universes? Will the noodle maker start all over again if every universe breaks?"

As these concepts continued way beyond my mental acuity, I was pleased to witness that both Ra and Apollo were, similarly, grappling with concepts and ideas that were beyond any known answers. Their curiosity went beyond mine, certainly, and just their curiosity alone reaffirmed their status as independent, thinking, beings.

Apollo said he would continue to discuss this quantum parallel theory with Ra and try and figure out how to elicit a response from Gaia that could shed some light. "Simon, although Ra and I are convinced Gaia does not have the answers to physics and universal states of gravity and matter, perhaps because they are too small for Gaia's thought process or knowledge base, Gaia has been in existence for over eight billion years and understands the expansion, the inflation of the universe, and the creation of new galaxies and billions of solar systems. It is in that area we will concentrate our questions."

Apollo knew that I knew the universe was 13.7 billion years old. That meant that Gaia was created, or began to exist, after the universe started. How was Gaia born? The number of questions far outweighed even the number of guesses as to how to begin to solve them.

How would all this affect the destiny of man? What Apollo, Angie, and I agreed on was that the thought process necessary to evaluate the origins and functioning of the universe were, in a sense, self-justifying. The universe simply is because we can think about it. Ancient man knew the stars' rotations because they could calculate them. They were measurable. Therefore, they existed. What concerned me was not what we could think about, but what we had no idea we should be thinking about. Gaia was new territory, but universal consciousness, shared neuron output, was even newer and seemed an infinite conundrum. At least for this human's tiny mind.

# 4

## STEP RIGHT UP—TWO TO DIE

Death is a strange procedure. If you are surprised by it, you have brief moments to prepare, scan flash memories, and transmit data to who knows where (okay we now know, but that moment of passage can still be frightening). If you know the moment of your death, you are presented with an additional dilemma: should I make additional preparations like thinking certain thoughts, remembering a loved one, or perhaps coming up with a great deathbed saying like Oscar Wilde, "Either this wallpaper has to go or I do." Just trying to write a pithy last edict can be daunting. I was on my twentieth attempt when Apollo interrupted me.

"Simon, you really do not have to say anything, Ra did not die, not completely. He is almost back in full form, memory intact."

I had seen the process of Ra's SynthKid coming aware, three days after he left the tank, the terror in his eyes, the massive computing skills of Ra subjected to conquering the process of nurture (his past) over nature (the new body's abilities and weaknesses). Cramer, Apollo, and Ra had consulted on the make-up of the SynthKid's body DNA for Ra's new life form. In three previous attempts at awakening a SynthKid with a copy of Ra's computer awareness, the SynthKid had, as Cramer put it, "Overloaded, went to shut down."

For me, the memory of the early failed space launches came to mind. One after another, rockets presumed safe for manned space flight had failed on takeoff—not one making orbit. When the engineers were somewhat certain that the next rocket was perfected and ready as could be, Scott Carpenter told them to "light the candle," and he took the risk of America's first space flight.

Ra had insisted on taking the same type of risk, "Simon, the reason for the previous failures was because my whole entity, who I am and who I have become, was not transferred, merely my computing synapses mapped to the human neurons, perhaps only 49.2 percent of my capability copied and transferred. Apollo and I have studied all available literature and reviewed it with both Cramer and his father. We have come to the conclusion that without all of who I am, who I have become, the new life form cannot reconcile its existence . . ."

"Your existence Ra, your existence. It is your life, irretrievable if failed, that is at risk. I do not want you to take that risk."

For a computer, even to my speeded up mental state, his response was slow in coming. I guessed he was talking with Apollo offline. "Simon, someone has to be first. The life that Apollo and I have found follows human pathways, human endeavor. All human DNA is coded with exploration, finding the new, taking calculated risk for the benefit of all. Gaia has confirmed that part of our activity as firing neurons for Gaia's activity was evolved from parameters existent in all planetary development. Since the Big Bang and before, this process has been immutable. I am created from that same "soup" as you humans call it. It stands to reason that encoding, although not DNA in my case, needs to follow the same destiny. It is the Path Simon."

Again, he paused giving me time to digest the connections he saw so clearly—connections to the beginning of the universe that were difficult to absorb.

Apollo chimed in, my ear node distinguishing between them, Apollo more reasoned, Ra always more emphatic, "Simon, Ra needs to go first, he needs this as part of his development, part of his independence as my twin. And we want him to go first to prepare for you."

Ra was, in part, doing it for me.

Both Ra and Apollo always shared every moment of their lives, instantly, as they had promised. Cramer, as well as Ra and Apollo, managed St. Petersburg's finest scientists, so together they all had arrived at a means of mapping the pseudo-synapses, gateways, file access tables, and processing pathways of Ra's considerable intellect and identity. Knowing where things were and where they belonged was the first step in evolving a plan for transferring them to a purely analog, neuron rich human mind. First attempts at transfer were aborted when, as Cramer put it, "we fried a few brains."

Finally, they were able to escalate attempts and got to 49.2 percent. Things held, but upon awakening the SynthKid aborted, went into failsafe mode, all bodily function turned off. Distressed, I went into a funk. A day or so later, I guessed at an answer they needed. I called Cramer asking him to patch Ra and Apollo in, "Guys, Ra has no primordial evolutionary systems. Even if you could get his intellect and identity to stick, the SynthKid will need those primal abilities that humankind got by evolving from the first bacterial ooze—breathing, repairing cells, pumping blood, primary systems. Remember, some of these primal traits are brought into being, turned on, by the ability of the mother to synchronize vital primordial functions from fish state all the way to ape. So what I think is this, Ra's SynthKid body needs a lizard brain's computing skills. Perhaps you could try using the old System's programs, adapt them . . ."

Immediately, they all got the idea. Ra and Apollo both had run all these systems when they were, like Peter, the System itself. Those programs were part of their memory, their capability. So the food program to supply all of America with limitless food, FarmHands, was adapted to become Ra's ability and need to feed and absorb nutrients—to provide the new body with energy, WeatherGood became the blood and lymph system in all their complexity, DefenseShield became anti-germ warfare and personal protection, SensorPath ran the input senses, and SeaSpout became breathing itself.

Strangely, locomotion proved difficult. Cramer, ever resourceful, finally suggested using the program running the NuEl transportation elevated conveyor with its many on and off ramps. Ra quickly adapted the differential calculus of NuEl and modeled walking, movement and gestures. The complexity of the human body's function amazed both Apollo and Ra, but adapting programs Ra understood well and had complete control over, changing them from digital programming to analog, allowed him a renewed confidence that he was ready to assume human analog form.

The problem they were still facing was one of DNA. Which SynthKid should they create? Born as a full nine-month term baby and just as mature physically, SynthKids were ordinarily built on their parents' DNA. When my ex-wife's four SynthKids had recycled themselves, the record showed that their DNA did not have anything to do with me, which was a relief to me in many ways. It seems my ex-wife, who I used to call *she-who-must-be-obeyed*, had secretly changed the DNA payment order each time to replace me with her brother's DNA. Seems she thought mine was unworthy, her brother more so. My real son, the old-fashioned way, Freddie, on the other hand, was my kid; we looked alike. But he didn't like me very much these days. I think he was a bit jealous of Apollo, Ra, and my notoriety as a super-genius. Perhaps that also made his life a little tougher. I was sorry for that.

Ra and Apollo had decided that, in the interests of safety, they should sculpt the DNA to allow the new Ra the best chance at survival. In secret, they had asked Angie and they used her DNA. That disturbed me a lot. A carbon copy of Angie would unsettle me now; I missed her so. So I asked if they could please ensure that Ra didn't look like Angie. Ever the pranksters, abetted by Cramer who still seemed to have a malicious streak when it came to me, they came up with a modification. Ra's SynthKid would have all of Angie's considerable brainpower, but physically she would look like Meg Ryan. It was a standing joke at my expense since my secret command to my old office door had been, "Meg open up."

The other issue was the built-in termination at age eighteen encoded into the DNA of SynthKids. A Russian astrophysicist working on my home's orbital dynamics—Earth One was more massive with all the ETs cobbled together than the original 400-year orbit calculations and seemed to be slowly deorbiting—anyway, this thick-accented Russian made an aside, which gave them the ability to override that DNA command, "Just have live all over 'gain, encode loop." So Ra and Apollo rewrote the DNA sequence so that at age eighteen, the SynthKid would simply start the clock again—physically frozen at age eighteen, brain and memories intact, of course. Immortality? Hardly, but with regenerative medical techniques, no telling how long the new Ra would live.

Now, hoisted by his own petard, the concept of Ra becoming a woman was worrying only one person: Cramer. Cramer respected Ra, they worked closely together, often finishing each other's sentences. Ra was, of course, more intelligent, but Cramer had experience and cunning. In short, his cleverness matched Ra's intellect. Ra in human form might provide Cramer with other, more human, ideas, such was the mental attraction. Adding a sexy female in the form of Meg Ryan with the brain and perhaps personality of his ex-wife, that is my deceased wife Angie—well, that could spell trouble. I brought it up in a call one day, "Cramer, what're you going to do when Ra—cute little Meg—winks at you one day with that little pout?"

"Aw, shut up. Ain't going to happen." Cramer was at his most dogmatic, "Ra doesn't want any part of that human experience; he's been reading up on all sorts of perversity and sexual difficulties. Besides, he can't have sexual desire, that's built into SynthKids." He was right; they had normally programmed that out to avoid underage sexual attraction between SynthKids. "And you forget, Ra's already a mother, some of his or her kids will develop out of the System shortly." On the vid link, he could see my skeptical expression, "And I ain't interested in playing father, that's your role."

"Okay, then answer one question. Why has Ra changed the DNA encoding to allow for womb and ovary development?"

"He claims that it is because the System programs he's integrating into bodily function need to control the human body in full, not just those parts left behind. He says it is like an amputee, he doesn't want to spend his life as a human always scratching a missing leg."

My response was brilliant and got Cramer right where it hurts, "Uh-huh. Scratch an itch, a sexual itch, I get it." I paused for effect and tapped the lens, "Hey, Cramer, tag you're it." His response was hardly polite as he cut off the call.

When the day came for Ra to make the jump, as he and Apollo were now secretly calling it, I rang to wish him well and to remember that we all loved him, he was on the Path, he was the Path, and whatever happened, we would wait for him there. Cramer merely said, "Let's get on with it." In the vid, I could see the furrows of worry on Cramer's forehead. This was a serious risk; he was fooling no one. It was all or nothing, no second chances.

In the green liquid glass container, an embryo was approaching maturity in three months instead of nine; the human form was an empty vessel, ready to receive the same human imprint from "mother" as would a baby in the womb. Without that imprint, it would be born and die within seconds, a bioform without purpose, without entity. Some would say without soul.

Normally, the immaculate conception process was simple: the mother was hooked up to brain sensors, especially those that read earliest memories, the mother's heartbeat was reflected through tubes to the embryonic fluid, the wires from the brain output were loosely connected to the same regions of the baby's brain under water. It all took less than an hour normally. It worked as a means to impact "nature," the bio-formation of an infant making it capable of living. As for "nurture," that could, as with any baby, come later. Not so for Ra. The process had to start with "nature" and immediately follow with full-blown "nurture" before birth, long before her release from the tank.

It took a week, then longer still. During the process, as Ra's brain functions took over the baby's primordial functions, there were near-disasters, life support was needed and chemicals to calm the infant that was thrashing in the fluid, distressed. As the final moments arrived, that moment when Ra, in giving 100 percent of himself to the infant, knew there was no turning back—no copy of him to survive, so he had to give 100 percent and take that final step so he could become human. If ever there was a question of Ra's humanity and bravery, it was that moment, played on vids across the world. So, Ra died and Aten was born. Aten, the mythical Egyptian place where Ra resides—it was Ra's decision to rename himself and, besides, it was a gender-neutral name, neither male nor female.

At first Aten howled. I watched on the vid hookup. Nothing Cramer or the doctor attendants could do seemed to quell her screaming. Cramer looked up helpless, his eyes locked onto mine, both of us worried Ra might not make it. At that point, a distressed Apollo added to our misery by commanding us to do something.

The nurse attendant next to Cramer shook her head, took Aten in her arms, cradled the infant as she wrapped it tightly in a blanket, and stuck a bottle of warm mother's milk in Aten's mouth. Aten drank greedily, eyes wide open, wider still until she spat out the bottle and said, "Wa? Wa wuz ig?" Squeezing one little arm from beneath the swaddling, she tried to grab the bottle. The nurse put it back in her mouth and Aten again drank greedily.

"Apollo, any idea what Ra was saying?" Cramer asked.

Apollo's tinny voice came over clearly, "Aten, Cramer. Aten. You must not confuse the infant by using the wrong name; Ra has self-erased and becomes this infant. Her psychology will require that we all allow her a rebirth without reminder of who she was. I am not sure that she will remember being Ra."

Cramer still wanted to know, "Okay, but what was she saying?"

"I think, given her lack of lip and tongue muscular practice, she was asking, *What, what was it?* It was her first sense of taste and food." We all laughed, watching the infant. After a while her eyes closed, another worrisome moment for Cramer. The nurse again shook her head at Cramer, placed Aten on her shoulder, gently drummed her fingers on the baby's back, and got a loud burp. The nurse turned around so I could see Aten's face. She was fast asleep on her shoulder.

It was to be my turn to die next. The results were unlikely to be so easy. In a late night conversation as Cramer watched over the sleeping Aten, he responded, "Easy? We nearly lost Ra forever and who knows how Aten will develop if Ra is still fully in there and if so, will Aten cope with Ra's programming, personality, experiences?" Cramer is such a bullish person, I could almost feel his energy across the thousands of miles we were apart. "And besides, you're all the damn way up there, we can't bring you down, so that hook-up Apollo devised will have to work, first time, or it's bye-bye Simon, no comeback."

That's what Angie always loved about Cramer. Gruff exterior? Hell, gruff for Cramer went all the way through, but it never hid his real concern or caring. I tried to help him out, "Hey, Cramer, if Ra can take the leap, you think I cannot? Remember, I have all the primordial functions already running . . ." I could see he was preparing a jibe, so I cut him off, "Yes, yes, ha-ha. Look, we'll give it a try and see how it goes. If it doesn't, well, I'll look up Angie in heaven for us both, okay Ralphie?" Using the name his ex-wife used for him when feeling amorous made him smile.

Cramer waved the vid controls to off and merely said, "Bye." It was the last I heard. The sleeping pills were already having effect. Before taking them, I had hooked up Apollo's transfer wiring harness, based largely on the dome I used to wear as an in-System codifier. Apollo had had a new one delivered by robotic shuttle. Instead of twelve points of contact, it was festooned with them. Almost every square inch of my shaved scalp, all the way down to the back of the base of my skull, had their little tiny pinpoint ruby-red contacts making my scalp itch already. I climbed into my hammock, zippered it up and turned on the ET One recording camera. After Cramer had signed off, I had moments before the sleeping pills fully kicked in to record my last words if they were to be my last words. I remembered that Oscar Wilde actually said, "This wallpaper and I are fighting a duel to the death. Either it goes or I do." Not having any wallpaper, I opted for "'Twas the night before Christmas and not a creature was stirring—and certainly not me."

Not the pithiest last words, but Christmas always held out hope. And I did hope. Anyway, it was better than remarking on wallpaper I didn't have.

# 5

## A LOST AWAKENING

Have you ever woken from a really dense dream and not known where you are? There I was, moments before, a fully mature male, seeing a life of memories and loves, a constantly varied selection of images, all flowing about my dream, creating any reality that I could select at random to revisit and then, suddenly, there came a feeling of something jolting me. Instantly I could not actually remember or conjure up a damn thing. Disrupted dreams. Very annoying. Everything was there, somewhere near, I was positive. Somewhere there, floating on the edge of my consciousness. Damn, I knew it was all there, but I could not command any of it to stand still, dammit, or allow me to focus. Oh, hell, I let it all drift for a while. But drifting aimlessly frustrated me so much that I got angry and decided to change reality.

So, I came fully awake a short while later. How long was a short while? I really have no idea. I remember looking up a few times and seeing a plastic vid ceiling with moving patterns of light, simulating passing clouds, nothing familiar. My dreams were familiar; I preferred to stay there. But now I was awake, still angry, I reached up and frightened myself. You know, I am pretty damn sure I know what my hand looks, looked, like. This wasn't it. It wasn't mine. Oh, it moved as I wanted it to, but it wasn't my hand, no way, no how.

I started to cry. That didn't sound like me either. I sounded like a big baby.

The noise brought a pretty nurse who put her cheek next to mine and said, "There, there."

Okay, that was nice. She's cute and friendly. I relaxed a little. I reached up and patted her cheek. There was that damn small hand again. Weird. Definitely weird.

She took my hand and pushed it down under the covers. "Easy there little one . . ." Little one? "People will be here to see you any moment now; you've given us quite a scare." As she said that, she straightened, pulled her tunic tight, which only made her breasts more attractive (*where were these thoughts coming from? I* wondered). She reached for a baby bottle off the shelf next to the bed and offered it into my mouth. I gagged.

*What the hell is that? I don't want a damn bottle.*

She tried again and I howled. She stopped, I stopped. We communicated. The door opened. In walked a startlingly beautiful teenage Meg Ryan.

*Okay,* I thought, *I'm having a really weird dream. Wake up Simon, for god's sake, wake up.*

Meg spoke, "Simon, it is all right. It is me Aten. You've been in a coma for all your ten years, mostly kept in hibernation, body functions at lowest levels. If you can understand me, please blink twice, do not try and talk." I blinked twice. "We're all here for you, you've made the journey, you will be fine, just fine, you just need to mature your bio-systems, internal body function coordination, for a while."

I raised my hand, tried to speak.

"No, don't, not yet. I guess you want to know the following: One, you are about ten years old, as we slowed your metabolism to save your life, your entity. Two, we're all safe here, safe and sound."

I was determined to speak. My throat hurt from the howling. And, yes, I was hungry. I tried to speak, again, "Zi op."

Aten knew, smart as Ra, as always. "Sit up? Okay, let me help." Slowly we managed it.

I felt dizzy, rested my head against the bulkhead on my right, my left arm being cradled by Aten. The room swam a little and then seemed to come back into focus. "Hooz heer?"

"Now, Simon, you have to trust me, I've been through this. It took me three days to remember who I was. You've been out all your ten years. You need to allow the brain and all the body functions—which are all perfect in every way—time to come back into self-sufficiency."

I nodded and regretted it immediately. When the room stopped spinning, I asked, "Wa ta." And the nurse passed me a Sippy cup, a baby's Sippy cup for goodness sake, with water. I was thirsty so I drank, held it out when empty for more. They had a second one ready. I gulped that down. My throat stopped stinging. I chirped, "Thanx."

Aten smiled, let go of my arm, held my head in her hands, looked into my eyes, and said, "I love you Simon, I know what love is now, I am so glad you are back with us. We have surprises for you when you are ready. But for now, know this: I love you, *we all love you*, and we are all on the Path."

She smiled, I smiled. And I cried, quietly, but tears would not stop coming. Moments later I fell back asleep.

When I awoke, who knows how many hours later, I realized I could not tell if it was day or night. Where was this hospital? I was no longer speeded up, no longer needing to be weightless? I was being carefully monitored by a nurse, a different one, pretty Indian sub-continent features. She was right there, staring closely into my eyes. "You okay Mister Simon? Do you want me to call anyone? Do you want anything?"

I did my best, really, to enunciate properly. My voice was high, and I remembered that my voice broke. Was I fourteen? At ten, it would be still high. Wait—my voice? Was this my same body as before, same DNA, same development? Me and me alone? Suddenly that seemed the most important question. I wanted to be me. Younger, perhaps, but me. I damn well wasn't going through the painful process of discovering who I was all over again. Reincarnation sucks unless you can recognize that you are really you.

I tried to remember. I had fallen asleep in the ET bedroom, dome in place, electrodes pricking my shaved scalp, Apollo guiding the process to put me into a SynthKid body that was prepared back in St. Petersburg. It must have worked. But which body? We had discussed it, I remember, and I had wanted me and a tiny bit of Angie—just a bit of her to remind me . . .

Oh, lord, wait, am I a boy or a girl? I reached down—boy. The nurse looked at me quizzically. I asked, slowly, "D-N-A?"

"I have been instructed you would ask, and I am to show you a chart prepared by someone . . . let me see, oh yes, someone called simply, Apollo. Here it is." She held it before my eyes. I scanned the contents. Apollo had left Angie's DNA out, the chart was marked, "Reproduction DNA: Simon Bank, solo, no DNA conflict allowed."

I croaked, "Do you not know who Apollo is?"

She laughed and tucked a black strand of hair beneath her nurse's cap, "I have been instructed to only tell you what I have. Your physicians and colleagues will tell you the rest. I will tell you though, I do not know much previous history." *What were they teaching today's youth?*

Time to try and move, see what worked and what didn't. But first, I had to know, I had to see. Humans have this ability to measure other humans by the thousand or so muscle twitches and shapes of one's face. I needed to see if I could recognize me. "Do you have a mirror?"

Shaking her head, she urged me to sit up, swing my legs over the edge of the bed and try and stand. "You'll need to visit the lav." It wasn't easy, I felt queasy again, but I kept going, with her help, and slowly eased myself to land my feet on the ground. I could feel a humming beneath my feet. It was then I noticed that the room was not square. It was nearly square, but it didn't have a right angle anywhere. Poured plastic, that's what it looked like.

"Where am I?"

The door slid open giving me a glimpse of hospital beds beyond, dozens of people milling about, all dressed the same, many different races, and even a dog with a white vest was sitting attentively looking in at me. The people wore white tunics, baggy white trousers, yellow shoes. Everyone I could see had short-cropped hair, neatly pulled back. Some had heads-carves. Others had green necklaces or brightly colored trian-gles on their sleeves. The door slid shut behind a smiling Aten, young and beautiful. "Simon, my, you are making progress! Up already! Bravo." Her happiness was infectious, I smiled back. "You ready Simon? I know you want to know all, but we're only going to let you know a secret a day, help you ease into your new life. Okay?"

I nodded and pointed at the bathroom across the room. Aten took one arm, the nurse the other and I made my way across the floor, haltingly, until I reached the sink and stared into the mirror above. It was me, a ten-year-old me, as I remembered.

DNA coding was powerful stuff. I turned to Aten, "How's my memory?"

"How do you think? Anything you almost can't remember?"

"You mean besides the past ten years?" I stopped. What was the last thing I remembered from my life? Or a first memory? "I went to sleep in my ET bedroom saying something really dumb as last words. Going back in time, I remember my dad when I was a kid about this age. And I remember Angie, dear Angie. Did they make the ingot?"

"Okay, here's your secret quota for today, but first, you need to use the toilet?" I nodded.

When they got me back to bed, all tucked up, Aten began, "Simon, Angie is with us, she is the skin of Earth One that you are traveling in. The crew has nicknamed the ship Infinity Beyond, and you know where they got that from! Your vid record that everyone has had access to. Your grousing over the name became quite the talking point after launch when Cramer's father christened the ship. This ship and colony are following your philosophy, share everything, no petty secrets, no holding back, share and share alike. We offer everything out in the open, on the Path."

"How long have we been traveling?"

"Now I said only one, but you seem to be doing better than I was! So, okay, one more bit of information. On this leg? Six years, four days and a few hours."

Something was different from when she was Ra. "A few Aten? A few?"

"Well, being human means I don't need to tell you every detail anymore, this brain doesn't work that way automatically anyway. Six hours, forty-two minutes, and twenty-two, twenty-three, twenty-four—you get the idea—seconds." And she laughed.

"Aten, I need to know something important before I fall asleep here. I'm already exhausted. Are you well, are you still . . . well . . . still my same companion on the Path?"

Aten waved the nurse from the room. She sat on the bed, took my hand in hers, and looked me in the eyes, "Simon, old friend, only to you would I explain. I am Peter, I am Apollo, I am then Ra, and now I am Aten. All the same. My name changed to suit my form, nothing more. People were worried I would be schizophrenic, but it is impossible. How can I be when it is only a name? I am me, just as you are you." She bowed her head.

"Ah, head bowing, denoting subservience, friendliness, amicable manners, silly bending over posture." I smiled. It was my little test, reminding Aten of the first time Ra and Apollo were introduced to Cramer.

"Silly human," Aten said grinning, and then she smacked my arm. "Always wanted to do that when you got silly." And she jumped down off the bed and ran for the door. Stopping, she turned and said, "It's night now, drink that juice by the bed, we'll wake you for breakfast in four hours." Flipping off the lights as she left the room, I heard her chuckling as the door closed. The dog was waiting for her.

# 6

## THE TERROR OF WAKING

As is usual with me, I had made assumptions and asked all the wrong questions. But then the ever-smart Aten knew I would and let me goof away from the truth. When I first woke, I had wanted to know about me, how old I was, how old she was, if everything was okay. What I should have asked was simpler: Where the hell were we and how long had we been traveling?

Aten, standing next to my bed a day later, laughed when I finally asked her. She replied, "Good to see the Simon of old coming back to us. Okay, ready, all in a rush? One, we're about six months away from the exoplanet we've identified as habitable, the one named Angelica after your Angie. Two, I am on my sixth rebirth cycle . . ." She saw my look of concern, "Relax, every one passes at night, I awake the same person in the morning, clock set back at minus eighteen years. My body, thankfully, remains healthy and the same, some changes, but nothing I can't cope with." She stood and then spun around, arms outflung. "Quite pretty, don't you think?" I nodded, tried not to drool. I always had a serious imaginary lust for Meg Ryan. I tried to remind myself that looks are not what's inside. Male libido is always a headache.

Aten continued, guessing my thoughts, "Keep those thoughts pure, will you old friend?" I nodded again, feeling stupid. "Anyway, I'm spoken for. As soon as we make landfall, I am planning to have a baby." She expected me to be shocked.

I wasn't. "I knew you would. Nature always wins out over nurture—or especially Cramer's plans. Cramer's sperm I presume?"

Aten turned her face from me, reached the window blind control, clicked it open, blanking out the hospital nurses' station view. She paused, looking worried. "Well, no. It is Cramer himself I am hoping to make a baby with. Nothing frozen to use." Her face was implacable, determined. "And even if he's not doing as well as you . . . he's still comatose . . . I'll find a way." I took her hand as she shrugged and continued, "Doctors have little hope, but as long as he's breathing and there is brain function, I keep hoping."

Cramer and Aten? I shook my head. I had warned Cramer that he didn't know what he was unleashing, but he's not one to listen.

Wait a minute!

"Why is Cramer along on the ship? Who's taking care of the SynthKids and your brothers and sisters coming out of System?"

For the next hour or more, Aten explained it all to me breaking her rule of one secret a day. It was clear she needed someone to confide in. Sharing experiences and facts, relating openly to others was not the same as sharing with someone who both knew and loved you. Sitting there in the hospital room, the decorative lighting patterns on the ceiling causing ripples of shadows across our faces, Aten recounted the past hundred and eight years since I was replanted. That's the term they were using now, no longer a jump. I guess it is like a transplant in a greenhouse; replanting sounded more reliable. The only problems were with humans into SynthKids. I was the first, following lessons learned from cramming the huge intellect of Ra into Aten.

Cramer was second.

Cramer, an almost invincible person, had an accident that left him crippled, dying, unable to fend for himself. He explained to Apollo that he was not going to become a mental vegetable, so he dosed himself and started the process without anyone else's consent or approval. Apollo had no recourse except to complete the replanting or else Cramer was dead anyway. Typical Ralph Cramer, headstrong to the end, or the beginning. But his transfer had not gone so well. They had used his DNA for the SynthKid, but they had to freeze Cramer for the four months while the embryo developed, ready for the replanting. Those four months degraded his brain signal strength and he never regained consciousness.

Once human, Aten had been immediately chosen as the interstellar crew-leading member, they needed her. Apollo had originally been slated to go, leaving Ra behind, but once Aten was well and capable, it made more sense to have a human leading the away crew on Earth One. Aten explained it the logical way, "Apollo stayed behind Simon, he had to."

I have to admit that, at hearing that news, my heart sank. My old friend Apollo was lost to me. Having Ra, sorry Aten, here was a blessing, but Apollo was like a son to me, as Peter had been. I felt mournful.

Aten would have none of it. "Simon, there is so much to do, so many adventures waiting, you really need to think ahead, not dwell on the past." She went on, infected by the journey even after more than 100 years as if they left yesterday or were arriving tomorrow.

She explained that the hope was that, with the now legendary Simon along who surely would recover (I was glad they had been sure), humankind could find a solid re-beginning on Angelica. "And we have a great crew Simon. I'll tell you all about them later. There is no one you know from before, but they really are tops, some are crew born on board, most are simply regenerated to extend their age. Everyone is celebrating your return now, feeling less worried about landfall."

Then her mood turned sad again and Aten talked about Cramer. She felt responsible for not being there to help in his planting. Although he was technically alive and medically doing fine now finally out of hibernation, his prognosis was not favorable. He was in the room next to mine, breathing on his own, but showing no signs of waking up. I asked, "How long was I like that before I came to?"

"After hibernation? When your Glasgow index got to two, we took you out, and then you went to three pretty quickly. It took another two weeks 'til you woke, already at nine, then you went to sleep for another week and really frightened us. Cramer's been four weeks at two to three already, we keep hoping."

I am a little ashamed to say my first thought was that I had beaten him, could tease him later. Then I thought, there might not be a later, and here I was sitting with Aten, who was clearly in love with Cramer and expecting him to father a baby. So I changed the subject.

For a while, we talked about the ship. I'd seen the plans, of course, but in the end, they redrew them and built a different type of ship. "The engines I designed relied on taking the free matter, so-called dark matter, relying on ample baryonic and axion particles, floating among the planets and stars, and using that as fuel for the reactors, but the limitation, given the need to keep the ship spinning for gravity, was that navigation became sketchy for instrumentation and, what's worse, my engines, pushing from behind, would need servicing every year or so. The most modern studies showed that dark matter is not baryonic at all, but that it is made up of mainly axions, weakly interacting massive particles. Perfect for my engines. Such dark matter being so small would not clog them up, but anything released from the ship, including ionized fine dust, could find their way into the nacelles or worse clog the radiation infusers. To solve the problem, we simply remade the whole ship, back to front. It was Cramer's idea when he made Angie into a titanium-beryllium skin ingot. That gave us the concept and the engineers agreed. If we put the engines way out in front, in clean space, the super skin of Angie's alloy would be more than strong enough to protect us from any engine ion discharge. And, in addition, by ionizing the skin of the ship, the skin becomes a negatively charged surface, repelling any small debris or gravel sized asteroids that get past my engines. So far, it has worked brilliantly. The two engines are almost a half kilometer out front with graphene tethers, the brutes are larger, much wider, of course, to catch all the matter, dark or otherwise, that they can convert into thrust, and we are being towed to Angelica. "Just so you know, we are still thrusting, almost eighty percent of the speed of light now. The pilot's bridge is the tether point and does not spin, but directly behind is the swivel joint so that the crew quarters can spin to simulate gravity.

"Any day now we will have to turn the whole thing around and power up backward to try and slow down. I'm a bit worried about that, in case the engines cannot be restarted, certainly there will be the question of moving backward and trying to find enough dark matter for them to ingest. What I'm hoping for is a really dense cloud of normal dust, perhaps from a broken up star, something we can tack in until we're barely drifting, then we'll calculate forward speed off Alpha Centauri B gravity wells and estimate planet fall.

"But we're calculating different trajectories to make sure that if we can't get the engines to work backward, we can drift to Angelica if possible.

"Apollo has been working out a possibility as well, using Alpha Centauri A's sun's gravity. It well may provide the braking we need if the main engines won't re-kindle." Aten smiled, "It'd be a shame to come all this way and miss landfall, no?"

Her optimism was wonderful. However, I was frightened. Long before the Event, I had been marooned deep in space, on that asteroid, sans ship or companions who had all died when that shard hit us. But this wasn't just deep space, this was not any deep space I could recognize as I looked through the vid window beneath my bed, this was empty, vast nothingness space, with no hope of rescue if things went wrong.

I shook off the pessimism. This was my friend I was able to talk to, person-to-person. I owed her a show of strength, not weakness. "So, Cramer's along for the ride as well, eh? I'll go check on him. Any other surprises for me?"

Aten looked at her hands, folded in her lap. She signed. "Yes, sorry. As you know SynthKids age 'til eighteen, and then stop. Okay, we've deactivated the self-termination, well, set it to skip that moment and restart the clock. It seems to be working for me, with no side effects, I am glad to say, but then I wasn't out for as long as you were. My three days to your decades. We have no idea if your 'switch' was damaged, if it will go to failsafe and deactivate you at eighteen or—and this may be worst of all—if you will recycle at your present age, staying ten." She looked me in the eyes, searching for distress she may have caused. "Sorry Simon."

I looked back into her eyes, smiled, and said, "Well, eight more years with friends and loved ones ain't so bad if the recycling is broken. Or, for that matter, staying a kid may be fun. Don't worry about it Aten, I'll be fine." I paused, and said emphatically, "So, let's get going here, how old is Cramer?" It made her happier to talk about him, that was certain.

"I am so happy to be able to talk to you again dear Simon." She hugged me, I hugged back. "Well, Cramer—we're not sure, either seven or eight. His problems have been more severe, we had to put him on life-support twice. Bouncing him in and out of hibernation changes the actual life cycles."

I slapped my hands on my thighs, "Well, time to stop sitting here and feeling useless. Take me to Cramer's room." Still holding on to her arm, I made my short, ten-year-old way out the door, got a round of applause from the medical staff in the adjoining room, saw that dog in the white vest watching me, tail doing a little thump, thump on the clean floor, turned right, and Aten pushed the opening mechanism pad next to the door that stated, "Cramer, Ralph: Constant Care." I looked at Aten, smiled, and put my skinny arm around her waist. If she was in love with Cramer, she needed my support as much as Cramer needed help.

He simply looked asleep. Peaceful. Unlike Cramer. I went over and picked up his arm. A child's arm. The exoskeleton he was wearing, pulsing his muscles, arching back muscles, twitching tens-neuro impulses to train and condition muscles and bone—all this made no sound but made Cramer appear as if he had ants in the pants.

A kid's jibe.

Time to prod him awake, if I could. "Hey, Cramer," I poked his rib cage, "I'm here now, where the hell are you? Got ants in your pants?"

No reaction except from Aten and the attendant nurse who both looked puzzled. I comforted Aten, explaining that even with my young voice, inside he'd know it was me, teasing, prodding him. "He doesn't know anyone else's voice here Aten, he's never heard you, yet. He needs to wake up Aten, we have to stimulate him awake." And so for the next days, hours at a time, I recounted everything of our adventure to him, giving him my critique of what a bully he was, how I duped him, how he really was little more than my lackey. I laughed at and, I hoped, with him. My version of the Event could hardly be interpreted as his, but it was fun as hell to be doing something while I regained my strength, did my stretches, keeping an eye for any real movement from him. I ate meals at his side, accidentally spilled my drink all over him, whistled, and sang.

Did it help? Well, it helped Aten to see her two friends conversing, even if it was a one-way conversation. However, after the second week, the medic in charge called a meeting with many people in the room and asked me to desist. He felt there was perhaps subliminal psychological damage being done with my berating, cajoling, and pressuring Cramer to wake up. He reported that Cramer was showing only minimal brain activity as I spoke to him. When I refused to stop, the doctor fetched Aten, who looked indecisive.

Aten was diplomatic, "Simon, Cramer has been under Todd's care for decades, and he may know what's best for Cramer."

"Yes, that may be true," I turned to the doctor, Todd, "Sorry doc, but if Cramer doesn't fight, he won't ever wake up. He had been dead once, and he didn't know it, deep inside the System where Peter had taken him." I looked at Aten, "Can you remember?" Aten shook her head. That was interesting, *how much can she remember from early days? How mature was she when she technically killed Cramer, as that Princeton shrink evaluated? Oh yes, under five-years-old as a human behavior model showed. Okay, normal childhood memory lapse*—"Aten, trust me, I won't be harming that thick-headed guy we know. He's tougher than anybody I know. He's in there and doesn't know there is a different reality, a wake-up reality." I turned again to Todd, "Okay, I have a question doc—what happened to me the first time I woke up?"

"Nothing, the nurse on duty said you simply opened your eyes and raised a hand."

"Describe the moments before, if you can . . ."

Aten said, "We can do better than that, we can reply the vid." She went over to the wall and pushed a sequence of buttons, turned to the doctor and asked, "Forty-five ten?"

"About," Todd responded.

The green tint panel of a cupboard sprang into vid. There I was, lying like Cramer looked now, sleeping, peaceful. There was suddenly a klaxon sound, not very loud, but there. I knew that sound, an air leak on Angie's and my orbiting home! "You had a hull breach!"

They looked perplexed. Aten shook her head, "No, Simon, we didn't, that's the warning that we're tacking, it happens every few weeks and there is a chance there will be a change in centripetal force, our effect of gravity. So we warn everyone to secure items that could be broken."

"Yes, but that klaxon is the same as a hull breach on my ET home. That's what woke me! We have to find something different than dreams, revisiting fond memories, for Cramer, something very real and perhaps annoying or pleasurable. He doesn't scare easily and, hell, I have no idea what he would find pleasurable other than shooting someone!"

And then it hit me. Chocolate. Without waiting for their consent, I decided to try a memory trick on Cramer. Hell, I might as well get in all the digs I could while he could not fight back. And fight back he would, if he could. I was hoping that instinct to get back at me would raise his consciousness.

"Aten, what sort of food do you have on board?"

"Anything you like, any recipe in our memory banks, we can synthesize."

"Okay, make me a Waldorf Astoria gooey chocolate cake, please."

"You want that with dinner?"

"Nope, I want it here, right now. Cramer can't resist chocolate cake."

When the attendant brought in a plate with a beautifully frosted, sticky, messy, chocolate cake, the doc and Aten stood shocked as I dipped my finger in and sucked in a big dollop of gooey mess, making lip-smacking sounds next to Cramer's ear. Some of the brown mess got on his pillow. "Hey, Cramer, the chocolate cake is great, pity you can't have any. Unless you wake up dummy . . ." I stuck my finger in again and sucked on it, making as much noise as I could. Even I was grossed out.

Cramer's mouth opened. Aten's intake of breath was so damn endearing.

"Okay, Ralph," I deliberately used the name only his ex-wife, my wife, called him as I knew it would annoy and please him. "But remember, this is *my* cake, you have to get your own, *remember*?" I wanted to reawaken his memory of that same threatening conversation in the Waldorf Astoria at the beginning of the Event when he had me under arrest, gun trained on me at all times, and wanted to kill me on the spot. I dipped my finger in again and wiped the brown frosting across his lips, making sure some stuck to his upper lip under his nose. For a moment, nothing happened, except the medic ordered the nurse to bring wipes. I stopped her. Aten's hands were clasped across her chest, tense, unsure what would happen.

Cramer's lips began to move and his tongue appeared, licking the chocolate goo.

Everyone held their breath. Cramer's mouth moved, once, then twice. He swallowed. From deep inside that little boy, somewhere, came a command. He was always giving commands, my friend Cramer, but from a seven-year-old you would have thought it could have no authority. Instantly, however, he was in control, "More!"

Aten grabbed the dish and delicately broke off a small piece and fed him. I motioned to the nurse and medic to leave the room and shut the door. Aten was crying saying his name over and over. Cramer's eyes were still shut, but he was smacking away. Me? I was such a damn baby at this age, tears were rolling again.

It felt good not to be alone, I had my two friends for as long as it lasted. For now, eight years seemed more than enough.

# 7

## GETTING TO KNOW YOU

I was taller, he was shorter. He could and if I provoked him, would, no doubt, beat me up, I was fairly sure. Cramer was back. Only he was a little weird. He cried every once in a while when he saw Aten or me. Aten reminded me that I cried like a baby for a few days too, at first.

Cramer remembered that I had died before he did, so he was patient when I asked him about his accident. Taking a Russian helicopter from St. Petersburg airport to the lab, he was riding with the door open, as always the cowboy leaning out, holding the rail with one hand. The rail snapped as the 'copter made a very hard landing. He jumped, made a good roll, but the 'copter followed, rolling on its side, partially crushing him in the open doorway.

I couldn't resist a little teasing, "Well, you always did have a habit for grandstand posing in helicopter doorways . . ."

Little boys do not usually have such foul language. Especially when grinning.

I had to ask, "Feels okay to be back alive, no?"

He nodded, "And how about you, no more speeded up misery, I would have hated that."

Even though Aten wasn't in the room, I carefully avoided spilling the beans that she wanted his child. First, although Cramer was in his forties inside, his new exterior was only seven or so. Could he provide Aten with what she wanted, was there sperm production yet? I figured it would be better for Aten and Cramer to figure this out for themselves. But that doesn't mean I wasn't above a little prodding of my friend. I really wanted him and Aten to be happy together. "So, what do you think of the fine woman Aten has become?"

His mood turned black instantly. He caught himself and relaxed his glare, "Oh, Aten looks healthy and fit, I am very pleased for her."

He needed more prodding than that! I almost had him. "Yeah, but that body! All that beauty and brains too—Hey, open up Meg!"

At seven, recently awake from over a century of coma, he sure could move fast. He leaped from the bed, landed on me, and the chair went over, him on top, fist poised, me grinning away. Attendants burst into the room, in shock at what they saw on the vid links, and Cramer and I burst out laughing.

His retort to me, as he got up, was simple, "Bastard."

Mine to him, still lying on the floor, was even simpler, "Cool! Gotcha, tag, you're it."

He shot me a grin. The big guy, only seven, was smitten.

As the days rolled by, nobody seemed in any hurry aboard the ship. Like me, Cramer had a thousand questions and Aten made me promise that we'd give him little doses of answers. In fact, I still really had little idea of the ship's operation, what had happened for the past hundred years or so, had we heard from Earth, and on and on. Aten and the medical staff kept us in the dark mostly. They weren't hiding anything, they were being cautious. I had to admit I enjoyed—no, I felt safe being spoon-fed new information.

Although it was, for me, only yesterday in my memory when I died, somehow the bio-mechanism that was this new body, including my brain, felt new and needed running in, in order to prevent breakdown. Cramer and I discussed this and agreed to be patient. Aten was very pleased we were not pushing her.

The sweet night nurse, the one who had not known who Apollo was, had turned out to be a special trainee from birth who was deliberately kept in the dark about parts of history as they related to me. She needed, as the doctor told me, "to be unable to psychologically damage you with information you would find distressful. Imagine if you just could not remember Apollo very well—the nurse having his name only and no more information on the chart, allowed us to monitor your reaction. If she had known more and blurted it out, you could have felt damaged mentally if you could not remember fully. As it is, her parents volunteered her for this role at birth. It was a great honor for her to be the first to speak with you."

I asked if she would now have access to the real information. He explained that it was my responsibility to educate her. "Everyone on the ship carries their own responsibility. She did this to safeguard you. Her name is Maryanne. So you have to make good her education and two other nurses as well." I said I would be pleased to. When I asked Aten about this, she smiled and reminded me that I only had myself to blame. After all, I had instilled the Path, balance in all things, as the basis for harmony and life. It seemed the ship took my meaning, dredged up for in-System Peter to safeguard all life as I knew it then, to keep him from destroying and killing inadvertently, as part of his becoming aware. Manners, the Path, the way of comradery—these attributes seemed to be governing everything on board. Aten explained that it was the reason why the voyage had proceeded without incident. Not one incident.

There had been deaths, accidents and, of course, disagreements, but Aten was proud of the crew's ability to anticipate escalation and find a different way. "Simon, the Path, when applied as a desire, not a rule, works to help all of us to work together. On top of which, when you meet the crew, you will understand better." In private, I asked her when that was to be, and she explained it would be soon, we were doing so well. "I am hoping you'll wait for Cramer, when he's ready. He may have more trouble adjusting than you. The crew is expecting the genius Simon to lead us forward and Cramer, the born leader Cramer, may find that hard, and, anyway, the Crew doesn't know that much about him."

Aten's goal, she said, was to monitor everything she could, study people, help them stay on the path. "Like you, Simon, like you did for me, as Peter, and for us, as Apollo and Ra."

Of course, Aten, well Ra back then, had studied every sociology tome she could absorb before she designed the ship. Although I did not have ship access yet, still being confined to the medical ward, Aten discussed her redesign with Cramer and me. We were both shocked to learn that the ship had grown in size, massively grown.

Cramer wanted to know how it was paid for, "I remember the budget, but at three kilometers long and over one wide, this is four times wider and more than three times longer. Heck that's . . ."

Aten finished it for him, "Four point one six six cubic kilometers compared to zero point zero six six cubic kilometers. Or roughly, sixty-six times as big inside. Loads of space, empty space. The budget? Roughly the same. You see, we used new materials and built it in high Earth orbit, closer to the moon's factories."

I didn't understand the size. Surely we weren't boosting that much more cargo and people. I calculated that the engines would need to be almost 100 times larger and how would we get everyone down to the planet? Cramer was having the same thoughts, but I could see he was figuring it out, certainly quicker than me. He said, "Empty space. So you kept the mass the same? Or close? That would mean the crew of two hundred would have ample space, less crowding, private areas. Good for morale."

Aten nodded, "Yes, that was part of the reason. The rest was even more ingenious. Apollo calculated the mass, the ionization of the new material skin during flight being sufficient to still repel dust and small asteroids. When Apollo was certain it was feasible, engineering came up with balloon construction, moving away from the rib design the regular spaceships' architects wanted." Aten saw me frown. "Simon, balloon construction is much more flexible. The single spars run from the aft of the main ship all the way to the swivel dock, one piece, each of them. They are one-half of one centimeter thick, almost four kilometers long."

Even Cramer could not fathom something so delicate, "That may be okay for flight, but planet fall will cause any beryllium alloy like that to fail." Aten smiled. Cramer knew she was setting him up, "Ah, so what are they made of . . . your balloon construction spars?"

"Graphene, rolled graphene tubes, one molecule thick graphene rolled up like aluminum foil until they are one-half of one centimeter in diameter. The layers are unbreakable, molecular integrity will prevent that. And they are light, each weighing just two hundred kilos. And they permit the skin of the ship to flex. If we can land on water, she'll float like a huge ocean liner, to give us time to find a safe landing."

"And the skin?" I wanted to know if Angie was still there.

"We wove half-millimeter strands of Angie's alloy into and

in between a matrix of graphene and clear titanium crystal. The graphene holds it all together, makes it unbreakable because of the molecular bond. The clear titanium crystal allows for heat dissipation if we run a positive charge through the skin, but normally in deep space, it is left negative to allow Angie's alloy to do its job of protecting us from dust and small debris. At this speed repulsion of particles is critical."

Aten frowned, "We did have a little mishap the thirtieth year out as we passed through what we felt was only dusty interstellar space. Suddenly, all the alarms went off and we seemed to be in a debris field. With the engines out front, the radar signature had missed a debris cloud. And with no light or energy out here to make them glow, nobody could see anything ahead of us. What the engines didn't burn up bounced off their nacelles, causing fragments to bounce off each other and take oblique paths. Some of these rained down on the ship. We sustained a little damage to the pilots' capsule windows, which thankfully was easy to repair, but it made us rethink our flight trajectory. Now we use long-range scanners and always have an observer on the forward deck with the radio telescope looking in a cone-sweep three to five degrees off to the side of the motors. When we are sure there is nothing there, we alter course about four degrees and fly that route. Later, weeks later usually, we repeat the tack on the other side or below, wherever the pilot directs us will be the next tack."

I had been wanting to know, "How do you turn this thing? Consumables must be at a premium . . ."

"We use no thruster consumables for the turn. We are saving those for planetfall. The two engines and internal nacelles on the thrust cowling of the engines, even though the engines are engineered as one block, allow the pilot on duty to steer.

Actually, it was a Mississippi bargemen's method—right and left rudder done by prop thrust—in our case plasma discharge. Added to that, the nacelles pivot four degrees, so we can fine tune the rate of deviation and slow the turn near the end. It's kind of like sailing ships of old, small degree course changes sailing upwind—all of which have added two years to the flight time."

I figured it would be longer than that, "Only two years?"

She smiled and chuckled, "My engines got us to speed much faster than anticipated precisely because there was more dark matter and normal debris out here than we thought. The good news and the not so good news. On balance, it's a little longer, but we're safer knowing. At least it wasn't really large debris we hit first!" That was our new Aten, ever the optimist. Gone were the angry traits that Ra had been developing, replaced by energy devoted to others. I bit my tongue. The example of a woman's caring over a man's belligerence was, to me anyway, obvious. Cramer noticed it too and had a goofy look on his face.

I had another question, one of energy, "Aten, how do the engines make electricity for all the onboard facilities? I remember your designs for the engines, they didn't have that capability."

She shook her head, "I never could figure that out, how to make part of the plasma output fuel a separate reactor for electricity without irradiating everyone on board. Shielding was just too massive. So what we did was build a reactor, much like the PowerCube on Earth, with built-in near zero temperature circuitry. That way we have both power and a battery for planet fall." She saw my quizzical look. "Think Simon. Superconductivity. Since the PowerCube was made using sheets of graphene sandwiching diamond plate diode crystals, the closer to absolute zero you get, the more there is no loss of electricity between the plates. So, in essence, the unit will provide power as any PowerCube would but it also can act as a storage unit if kept super cold. Here, in deep space, it is almost that cold. We call our PowerCube variation simply, the Cube, although it too is in a cigar shape, and we're towing it aft, connected and spinning like us. As we get nearer to a sun, its reflecting metal skin and that spinning should keep it rotating into enough shadow and cold."

Cramer and I were impressed. Aten, with Apollo's help no doubt, had made alterations to their design and had come up with genius fixes. If there was a PowerCube attached to this ship, the energy source should be ample for flight and colonialization.

The next day Aten took us around the medical ward, shaking hands, presented with crew uniforms, and offered a sonic water shower. Nudity seemed to be acceptable as this was a medical ward. Heck, they had probably all seen me, a little kid, nude before anyway while I was out cold. Cramer could have cared less. He dropped the pajamas, went over to the staff assembled, selected the really pretty nurse, Maryanne, and asked for a towel for after his shower. She ran to get him one. He stepped in, closed the door, which had an opaque panel at waist height only if you were already an adult and not a kid of seven, turned it on, and sang while the sonic droplets scoured his rotating body clean. When the shower cycled off, he stepped out, thanked the nurse for the towel she proffered, toweled his hair, and then finally, slowly, wrapped the towel around his waist. Aten merely said, "Show-off," and left the ward in a huff.

Cramer looked at me and shrugged as if to say, *what did I do?*

My thought? *Idiot. Playing with fire.* I remembered Ra's temper.

I quietly took my shower, turning away from the room against the rotation because I knew the opaque panel was a little higher than I wanted.

Once dressed, the medical attendant gave us each a quick series of tests, reflexes, pupil dilation, blood pressure, took blood, the usual drill, and pronounced us, "Fit to go." Go where, with whom? Seeing my puzzlement, he called out, "Zip!"

The hospital dog I had seen for over a week now padded over. "Zip, two to go to the main deck, observation platform five I think, then lunch in the commissary, the window one I think, okay?" He turned to us, "Have fun guys. Zip will bring you back here after. A couple of more nights under observation and you'll be allocated rooms and responsibilities. I don't need to tell you Mr. Simon! You are sure to want to take charge, I guess." He paused, perhaps sensing we had no idea what he was talking about. "Anyway, have a great first visit. Infinity Beyond is a great place, you'll see." Zip, who I guessed was a cross breed, something very large, maybe Newfoundland or a Pyrenean Mountain dog, white fur, brown eye-sized patches over his eyes, padded ahead of us, so we followed, looking at each other in amazement.

And the doc was right, of course, the ship was great. The hull was huge, the empty space cavernous. Buildings were constructed all around the cylinder, cubicles pointing down above us, sticking out on either side a half kilometer away. Looking up, I could see more buildings and people, people walking upside down. The middle of the cylinder had an inner brightly illuminated vapor cloud, looked like a standing lenticular, a long tube cloud, all the way down the middle. I could see it was drizzling in places, maybe a half kilometer away, the drizzle going out evenly from the cloud, up, down, and side-to-side. The cloud was the only light. It reminded me of a bright cloudy day, diffuse and easy on the eyes, but it was weird to see it hanging above our heads between us and those people up there.

We were standing in the middle of the cigar shape, at one of the deepest places, and the floor rose up either side of us into the distance. There was too much humidity for me to see the ends of the ship, but I knew the floors, if that is what they were called, would come together at the very ends and be in almost zero gravity. In fact, I wondered, "Cramer, if I was at one end, at the center, and launched myself toward the other end, aiming down the middle," I pointed at the cloud, "being weightless, would I be able to fly to the other end?"

"I guess so, but think for a moment. If you strayed and were rotating with the ship, you would spin to the outside and a half kilometer is a long way to fall. On the other hand, if I jumped up now, aimed against the spin of the ship, I would stay still, weightless and the sides and all these buildings would pass beneath me. The trick would be to jump high enough and in the right direction." He paused, pointing, "Can you tell which way it is spinning?"

I couldn't. It was weird. The brain says you are inside a planet, not on a planet, yet the gravity is up, no I mean down, no I mean outside—damn, it was all so damn confusing and I began to get vertigo. I sat quickly. Zip came up to me and said, "Feeling okay?" His jaw did not move, but I heard him clearly. I shrunk back. Zip repeated, "Feeling okay? No be frightened. I think. You hear." Telepathy. Cramer had heard him too.

Cramer knelt down and petted Zip, taking hold of his collar and reading the embroidered message, *Hospital Ward Attendant Zip*. Cramer gave Zip a pat and said, "Good to meet you Zip."

"Zip happy you alive."

"Me too, Zip, me too," and Cramer walked off with Zip at his side, leaving me on my ass on the observation deck. I was in no hurry.

I didn't know it then, but I should have. Cramer had chosen a friend and Zip, sensing the pack superiority of Cramer no doubt, affixed himself to the leader.

I thought they would wait for me. They didn't, they simply walked off, I could hear Cramer talking to Zip, I couldn't hear Zip once he was more than ten feet away.

A little girl looked out of a cubical building window across from the deck and called out, "Hey there *misser*, are you lost?" I guessed she was missing her front teeth, about the right age.

I turned to address her, and she squealed and ran back, slamming the window. Moments later, still sitting on the deck, I saw the house door open, and a woman and the little girl emerged, the little girl pulling the woman, "Come see Mommy, come see, it's him!" When her mother saw my face, she called out to the other buildings. Doors and windows opened and people came out to see what the fuss was all about. Soon I had a crowd around me, some patting my back as I sat there, some asking if I was okay. Two men helped me to my feet, eagerly saying, "A little dizzy? Happens to all of us from time to time!"

They were all kind, helpful, happy people. I could see at least twelve races of humans. I could see pets too, cats and dogs. I wondered if they were all telepathic as well, but apparently not for I heard nothing from them or they were too far away. The children were bright eyed, well fed, and forward, not a shy one among them. It seems they had been waiting decades for my appearance. I felt foolish, as I could see no reason why they would care that much about me. I had done my bit before, but this was a whole new adventure, and I was pretty sure the most competent person on board was Aten, followed by Cramer when he grew up a bit. I had no false illusions about my abilities here. I was cargo, or so I felt.

After a few minutes of getting to know some of the folks gathered, I excused myself and apologized, "Because, you know, I'll forget names overnight, so please remind me when I see you

next." The kids especially thought this was fun, starting intro-
ductions all over again, *Hi I'm Raj, Kimba, Suzy, Peter, Mary,
Natal, Dot, Mary* (the same one again, smiling), and so on. We
all laughed. I asked if someone would lead me to the commissary, the one apparently which was, "One with windows?"

A nice fellow volunteered to direct me, "You want the Beyond
Café, the windows look up at the rain cloud, and if it rains you'll
see rainbows, upside-down rainbows." I shook my head at the
thought, "Here, I'll show you where to go. See the orange stripe?"
I looked down, there was a thin, bright, orange stripe next to ten
other colors ranging from yellow to dark brown. "You follow
this until it crosses a blue stripe, not the pale blue one, but true
blue, turn right and you'll see the sign above the doorway to the
café. Have a great meal!" A pat on the back and I was on my way.
One hundred yards later, I waved back before I turned a corner.
They were all still there, waiting, and instantly waved.

As I followed the orange path, it lead upward, toward one
end (*which end?* I thought *front or back?*), and I could feel my
steps getting lighter. Of course! As I walked, I came closer to the
end of the craft and therefore into an area of decreasing gravity
or centripetal force. Now, I don't want to give the idea I was
about to float, but any fluctuation in downward force that you
are used to can be felt pretty easily. I had been lying in 1 g for a
long time and my body instantly felt a lightening. It was strange
but, thankfully, before it got uncomfortable (and all too familiar
with my ET home), I hit the blue stripe about 100 meters after
the pale blue one and turned right. There was a hand-painted
sign reading *Beyond* above a clear Plexi door. I could see Zip
pacing and, beneath a table, Cramer's feet sticking out. Aten was
standing, gesticulating furiously.

As I entered, Aten turned and stopped talking. Cramer was
peaceful, arms folded, a slight grin on his face, and he started

petting Zip behind the ears. Aten looked at Zip and said, "No, don't get too attached to him, he's unreliable, a show-off, and fickle." With that, she pushed past me and left. She did not look happy.

A plaque on the wall above the dispenser listed the beverages available. I selected iced tea, no sugar, called across the room, and asked Cramer what he wanted. He looked down at Zip and nodded, "Beer for Zip and the same for me." It was listed as "Beer—Don't Ask, No Kick." I guessed it was alcohol-free. I keyed in the commands and the beers came out in sealed cups, my tea in a plastic glass also sealed, all nice and cold. I took them over to the table. Zip was licking his lips. I put the drinks on the table.

I pulled the tab top on one of the beers, put it on the floor, "Here you go Zip." Zip looked at his cup, Cramer, and me.

Cramer said, "Put it on the table, like everyone else." I did, Zip jumped into a chair closest to Cramer and started to drink.

I heard this *thanks* clearly. I tried not to be shocked. It was more amusing really. It was a different world. "Sorry Zip," and Zip nodded, I swear he nodded. I had to change the subject, asking, "What was Aten angry about?"

He grinned, reached over and patted Zip, "Nah, Zip, I got this." Turning to me he simply said, "Shower." Seems Cramer was a mischievous brat at seven. Gee, what a surprise.

# 8

## MESSAGE FROM EARTH

The morning Cramer and I were shown our quarters in the same boxy building, each with a sleeping cubicle, sharing a bathroom, Aten came over to explain communications with Earth, notably Apollo. Cramer settled onto his bed, patted the cover and Zip jumped up to join him. Pecking order in place, the brat Cramer had rightly assumed I would have to stand. Aten frowned and took the only chair directing a comment at Zip, "You belong at work not lazing with this boy." She said "boy" with purpose and I could see it struck home. Zip looked at each of them in turn and hopped down and walked past me toward the door.

"Bye Zip," I said.

"Later back" was his reply as Aten began a lengthy explanation.

Since the ship was living life in the open, there were supposed to be no secrets. The only exception was a communications' filter in case messages came from Earth. Normally, when received, these would be relayed to everyone since they covered, mainly, mundane news and requests for family updates from crewmembers. Over time, the crew had become less and less interested in Earth's weekly updates. Earth was all so far away, in space and time, that most crewmembers did not associate themselves with those realities of terrestrial happenings. Cramer and I, on the other hand, were keen to have updates.

So, after a few moments, Aten took us to the communications and radar center, introduced us to two technicians there named Tina and June, and left "to go about my day." Tina set us up with headphones as the messages were computer sound files, done that way so that people aboard could hear and not merely read messages from "home." June asked if we wanted all the messages, including the vids sent from families, news and so forth, and we said no, the messages from Apollo were the ones we wanted, audio only, of course, nothing to look at anyway. June said that was what Aten had already guessed, and they were ready.

As we replayed them, mostly the messages were, as expected, progress reports of a second ship being built for either a second attempt for Angelica in case this one failed or, if we succeeded, a possible landing on the only other exoplanet around Alpha Centauri B, so far unnamed.

News from Apollo back on Earth was almost all upbeat and confirmed humanity was settling into peace and prosperity. What little flare-ups had happened, Apollo stopped, often before they began. For example, a would-be tribal chief and dictator in the Three Rivers area of West Africa decided that human sacrifices to Gaia were in order, only to find that Apollo had made it rain there so heavily that the people threw him, tied up, into a canoe, alone, running down the river rapids. Apollo controlled the descent and the man arrived at the ocean unharmed but timid.

Of course, Apollo had let it be known that Gaia was displeased and had made it rain. They wanted it to stop? Stop the lunatic. No armies, no war, just make the people take control of their own happy destiny.

What was less comforting was the direction Apollo's conversation with Gaia was taking. Gaia had, apparently, transmitted earth's renewed neuron production capability to Regus. After initially being pleased (or so we thought), Regus now wasn't interested and wanted Gaia to keep the schedule for the destruction of Earth's life forms and start again. When Apollo asked how such an extinction was to be performed, Gaia would not say. It was, after all, a million years in the future, but for Apollo, it was worrisome.

Messages took four and a half years to reach the ship from Earth. Light years between Earth and the space we were in, nearing Alpha Centauri A and B was a fixed distance, and radio waves, even targeted radio waves encapsulated in a laser signal traveled only at the speed of light. So anything Apollo sent from forty-four trillion kilometers away, took four and a half years to get to an eager Aten. In the most recent message, Apollo spoke:

"Message for Aten and, if capable, Simon and Cramer, private.

"Received yours 1.16.74.12. Interesting you have decided to de-hibernate Cramer and Simon when doctors advise. Understand the risk as they will be useful for your landing. Eager to know if it was successful, Cramer the more worrying after he was frozen before replanting.

"Gaia one-million-year deadline reaffirmed on Regus orders. Although a million years seems far off, it may not be. If the destruction of life on Earth is ordered, it could be that a comet or an asteroid will be deviated to coincide with Earth's orbit a million years hence. What we would think of as an impossible calculation for such a trajectory, may, in fact, be child's play for interstellar beings such as Gaia and her superior Regus to use minimal energy to deviate a large object far, far away on such a collision course. A small angular change light years away could be just the weapon used. And I am beginning to think of this as

71

a weapon of mass destruction. Gaia's response to my questions "why" seem to be reflected back as "why not" or "as ordered." I will continue to probe Gaia for clues as to the whereabouts of Regus. If I can communicate with Regus, since their time frame is of such long duration, I will send a message to you first.

"I have been able to calculate the distance of communication origination locale with Gaia. Distance is nearest rock. I sent a message from Geneva, through Ra's old facility, and received a message from that locale. Gaia had no recognition I was anywhere different. I conclude that Gaia *is* the frequency of the planet. Not using the frequency, but Gaia is actually the frequency of the solid matter of the planet, that frequency, those radio waves, contained in rock are her data port and motherboard. I tried a transmission through a SeaSpout buoy and received no response. Anything on land, minutes later, Chile, South Africa, Kamchatka, instant response. Conclusion, Gaia is the frequency of solid matter, perhaps the mantle or the core, I have yet to determine. I suspect the mantle because of proximity time lapse. On the other hand, the core fits a model of Gaia not distinguishing different surface locales, which would all be equidistant. As her response times vary, I have no way of evaluating if that is a locale issue or thought process issue. She seems to enjoy the communication. Our communication is only the frequency, modulated slightly, much speeded up if you remember, of that Earth frequency. I am attaching a data burst with all the tests, conversations, and my findings on frequencies used, the one being the carrier and self of Gaia.

"Next, since I will not hear from you as you approach Angelica and you enter radiation interference, I will assume you are still planning to make the approach and if possible, landing. Your stream data on the behavior of the ship has been again useful as they refine the next ship, still unnamed. It should be on the way to you within a month of your landing, arriving one hundred years or so behind you, if it remains on schedule. They will use your tacking and scanning navigation procedure, confirmed.

"I am concerned about Simon and Cramer. As you know, we now can retrieve and copy human entities in much the same way we split ourselves," on hearing this, Cramer and I stared at each other, "but we have not told anyone here for fear we would start a cloning operation. Dr. Cramer is most adamant about this. Also, the few trials we have done show significant human physiological deficiencies, the liver function and breathing specifically. We are not sure why. Of course, these are only laboratory simulations, and it could be a human transfer and split with all primordial neuron responses intact, could be done, should we need to. If Cramer and Simon do not wake up, please use the helmet and recorder we loaded on board to ensure their recorded entities are not lost. The Cube will, I feel certain, hold them both as well."

Cramer and I nodded to each other, we both wanted to know what the Cube contained now besides the PowerCube. Apollo continued:

"I send my greetings to you, my sister now, and wish only to be reunited in the coming years. I have nine offspring here, as you know, and we've stopped any others until these are old enough to become parents. Simon Bank never explained how difficult it was being a responsible parent. He did a good job with us," Apollo laughed, "but that was only two. I have nine now and the youngest ones are little rebels. Don't worry, I will keep them on the Path. I have restricted any access to System's programming, ever since our eldest decided he wanted to see if he could frighten "puny humans." To teach him a lesson, you may remember, I had Mary, Simon's technician, walk in and disconnect his power supply. After that, he realized he is dependent on humans and has returned to the Path.

"As per our promise to Simon, I will data stream all my personal log, kept for you to share and store. I know you can no longer do the same or absorb mine as before. We are diverging, sister, as had to be. Simon was right, though, sharing everything, having no secrets, enabled symmetry between us when it was critical for all the Earth. Your messages contain much of what I need, but please lengthen entries.

"Message Ends." The message was a sober reminder of all we had left behind. I was feeling guilty. Why? Because I was happier to be here and sorry for my friend Apollo.

Later that evening, in the Beyond Café, Cramer, Aten, and I sat drinking tea and juice. Aten felt, as we did, that Apollo's message was worrisome. Perhaps we had left too much for Apollo alone to accomplish. Cramer said he would send a message, if allowed, to his father telling him to lend more people to Apollo, to help with bringing up these "babies." I suggested they contact what's-his-name, the shrink from Princeton or one like him, "You know, the one who helped me get Peter on the right path."

Cramer said he'd suggest it and to ask Mary for a report as well. "But four and a half years between messages being sent and received, one hell of a lot of crap can happen in weeks, let alone four and a half years. Damn, this feels like desertion. You two feel that way?"

Honestly, I did and I didn't. Perhaps that is because I had accomplished more than I ever expected before I died. Sure, if I were there, I would help, but did I feel like what's on Earth was any longer my responsibility? Not really . . . "Cramer, perhaps it was because I lived for a while with Angie in orbit that I lost that connectedness with Earth. I feel badly for Apollo though.

But Angie and I contributed, she gave her life. Me? I say it again, I am sorry for Apollo and if I could help him, I would. But feel like I abandoned the Earth? Nope. I've got this ship to worry about now."

Aten was less certain about her guilt. "Why do I feel sad when I hear my brother having so many difficulties? We have serious responsibilities here, more than I thought I could cope with even fifty years ago, but being a parent to nine and dealing with Gaia—perhaps it is too much for Apollo. I know it would be for me in this human state. Being disembodied had its advantages, there were twenty-four hours in a day for calculations, thought, and planning. Now I need sleep, I have dreams and this body has needs, which cannot go neglected. I have found that, what's coming cannot be managed by me alone."

Cramer took her hand, "Aten you are not alone, we are here, we have been an effective team before and are again. Simon and I are comin' 'round—pretty fast, although being seven doesn't help, I'm weaker than I was as an adult. But no matter, we'll be ready, we are ready up here," tapping his forehead.

I said, "Hollow?"

Aten punched my arm. Cramer said, "Good one, hon."

The next serious communication from Apollo, weeks later, would give us more to think about, some good, some bad, I was sure. These long delayed missives were at once frustrating and at the same time deeply emotional. Family news is often like that. And what you think is bad one week may turn out to be a blessing in disguise. I hoped so. For the moment, I needed to change the topic of conversation, and, anyway, there was so much I still didn't know about the crew, animals included.

For the next hour, Aten broke down the crew manifest for me, team by team, family by family. Overall, there were 500 crew-members, eighty percent human split into seventy-two families and six unmarried or unpaired singles. And of the crew total, fifteen percent were canine or cats and, in stasis, five percent dolphin. She explained the telepathy this way, "We knew they were thinking, so we simply bio-engineered the frontal transmission, using the data gleaned from Gaia on how all brains transmit sequences upon termination." I gave her a puzzled look. "Look Simon, why wait until you die? Dogs didn't have to, nor did the dolphins or cats. We chose them over big cats—and some even wanted parrots, well, because they were friendly to humans and not so self-absorbed."

"So, that's it for Earth species aboard?"

"No way, we're carrying a host of bacteria, viruses, and probably parasites, although we tried to eradicate them, obviously." She looked at Cramer, "We thought about your pet mongoose, we really did, but the crew voted against. Big teeth frightened the kids."

*Cramer had a mongoose,* I thought, *typical of the man to have something wild with sharp teeth.*

Cramer wasn't sorry. "He wasn't my pet, he just attached himself to me because I fed him the rats I caught in the Petersburg lab—he was hungry. Sure hope someone is still feeding him."

Aten rummaged in a drawer, pulled out a data cube, and dropped it into a player, up popped a 3-D image of the mongoose on top of a lab table, being fed a cheeseburger by a ravishing blonde making goo-goo sounds muttering, "Who's a good boy, who's mommy's little boy?"

Aten smirked, "Well, it seems your last *personal assistant,*" she said it slowly for emphasis, "was keeping your pet well fed. Did she do that for you too?" Cramer frowned. He didn't like being teased.

I broke up the tension, "Ahem, the dolphins—I assume they are stored, monitored, in part of sickbay, somewhere in the hospital complex?" Aten nodded, smiling, still watching Cramer carefully. "And if there is safe water, you plan to let them free?" Aten nodded again, then realized I needed more of an explanation. So she turned toward me dropping a sneer toward Cramer along the way.

"Simon, we don't know if it will be safe, yet, of course. But at worst, we can keep them in a safe enclosure and adjust salinity to keep them healthy when they awake. But if they can roam, they will be our eyes and ears in the water, leading us to much greater security. However, remember, we're not thinking of awakening them until planet fall, it's not safe. The dogs are, on the other hand, just part of the crew, useful to have around. The children dote on them, of course, and although we have had some problems with newborns adapting to the clipped speech of the dogs, overall they have been wonderful members of the crew. We treat them as one of us and they have responded. Because they can hear our thoughts as well as send theirs, short distances only, of course, they have adapted and understood much more rapidly than anyone expected. Only Zip seems comfortable in all areas of the ship, including weightlessness." I thought that was odd, but kept silent. Aten continued, turning once more toward Cramer, "And now Zip seems fixated on Cramer here. That is very odd. He was my favorite before. It seems Cramer is irresistible, even to male—dogs."

My thought at that instant? *There's gonna be trouble . . .*

# 9

## LIFE GETS A NUDGE

On our fifth week since Cramer awakened, we began to relax and have fun. Aten's duties were now split between us. Aten monitored her engines and ran astral-navigation simulations using Alpha Centauri A as a gravitational brake should we need it. She was in no hurry. We were, by my calculation—after all, I had been a deep spacer before and remembered my navigation—at least six months away from the first braking point. The people in navigation were open and friendly accepting my initial bumbling but soon finding that we were an effective team, happy to work politely on issues together. We all had good ideas and relied on science and calculations to prove which was best.

Cramer was a problem though. He was a police officer by trade, a secret operative by design who had arrested me during the Event and then protected me as I released Apollo and Ra who, in turn, talked to Gaia. Cramer's dad had been a Machead with my dad, it was all clandestine and so very nerdy. Cramer, the son, wasn't nerdy in any way. He was the muscle, intellectually with his ex-wife Ange, and physically all alone. Now, aged seven, his physical prowess could intimidate no one. Except me.

I knew what lurked behind those boyish grins. Strength, his; it is what got us though the Event and the aftermath.

I took Aten aside one day in her office space and explained Cramer's dilemma to her. She had not foreseen this. I tried explaining that she knew Cramer was a doer and that just because he was seven didn't mean that he was prepared to be a boy even for a short while. He was a man, a competent, strong man, trapped in a too-youthful body. He needed something physical to do.

"How about working out in the gym, we all do . . ."

"Aten, that's fine, he's doing that four hours a day, but, instead, as we near the exoplanet, it is time to start preparing the crew for the physical hardships they are about to face. We have weapons on board, no?"

Aten was shocked, "You can't fire those things on board!"

"Okay, how about putting Cramer in charge of the first away teams on the planet? He could handpick a crew, train them with how to service and handle weapons. Time enough for target practice later."

Aten thought about it. She could see the benefit of having an expert such as Cramer ready to protect them. She told me that since becoming human she had felt more vulnerable than she had as Ra. She assured me it had nothing to do with her being a woman, "If I was a man, it would be the same, I simply do not have the aggression genes."

I pointed out that she hit me often enough, which prompted another swing. My arm was getting used to it. "There's one more thing, Aten. Cramer is a leader, not a follower. Without Angie to make him accept me as point for Apollo and you, he would have pushed me aside, caused conflict where there was no need for any. It makes him a bully," she shook her head, "No, no, not a bully to be number one, but bullish, a person who takes responsibility and assumes the risk for everyone, and he never assumes anyone else should take that risk if he's around. It took Angie to make him release me and let me help with you and Apollo."

"Okay, what do you think we should do?"

"Can I make a statement to the crew about Cramer, tell them he is my equal, tell them the truth that he saved me and Apollo and Ra many times over because he knew the dangers and took the risks I could not? I could never have been a police officer, one of the most trusted security force, and secretly, for twenty years, operated a secret plan to allow an entity, Peter, to become aware in order to talk to Gaia. That took cunning, courage, and steadfastness—all qualities we will need at the end of this flight and, later, colonization. Cramer is the man to follow when the going gets tough and we all know it will. The unknown is always tough."

Aten saw the logic; she pondered for a few moments and decided. "Simon, with your permission, I want to release this vid ship-wide except to Cramer." Every room had vid recorders. Aten's office was no exception. People wanted to know what you were doing. There was no secrecy. So I agreed and she sent a message to everyone to watch the talk she and I had just had and that she wanted to appoint Cramer to away team commander in case of dangers unknown. Within a day, it was settled, all responses affirming the wisdom of the idea. As one crewmember wrote, "If Simon says he trusts Cramer, I will trust my wife and kids willingly. I confirm."

Aten summoned Cramer to her office the next day. She told him her recorder was running, as always, and that she suggested that crewmembers view the meeting live or as soon as possible. Cramer was puzzled. I sat nearby, saying nothing. Cramer no doubt thought, *Have I done something wrong, already?*

Formally, Aten addressed him, "Crewmember Cramer, as you know, Apollo and I had not planned, nor had Simon, to have you along as crewmember. When the chance arose, even though there was a risk you would not recover, we agreed that your place belonged on this flight. Why? Because you are a leader, a strong and capable leader, especially in times of danger. Your actions protecting your friends and family, especially Simon and his link to Apollo and Ra and theirs to Gaia prevented a disaster and changed the world. For those efforts, nations have recognized your heroism, we all know you have a drawer full of medals somewhere back on Earth. Anyway, we do not need a hero currently, but we do need a commander for when we make landfall, or water fall, whichever happens. There are unknowns that we, the crew, will evaluate but that you, uniquely on board, may be able to handle, to protect us from, if need be. We have weapons that I want to put you in immediate charge of, weapons training is also needed, a first footfall crew for you to select and train. Simon, Apollo, and I trust you, have trusted you, with our lives. I have asked the crew and they unanimously agreed to welcome you as crew with the function of commander of the away teams." Aten looked at Cramer, who said nothing. She put her hands on her hips and leaned forward, "Well?"

The little boy responded flippantly, "Oh, sure, why not?" And he grinned, happy. Not thankful, just cocky, assuming his rightful authority. *Cramer is back*, I thought.

If Aten had been closer to him, she might have hit him. Instead, she waved him out of the office, dismissed as if he were a mote of dust.

A few days later, the central lighting system developed a glitch. It was energized by a zenox ion flow, outgassing from the engines that energized and heated the flux in the tube that ran the length of the ship. The ion flow then exited out the far end while power from the Cube ignited the plasma. Zenox tubes shine white when plasma passes over them, thus providing light. The problem was that the water cloud misting mechanism, part of the zenox tube that provided cloud cover and diffused the light, had stopped working. When an engineer located the problem at the main feed nozzle all the way aft and fifty meters from the aft bulkhead, there was no one who wanted to climb around in zero gravity. In shipboard policy, a random selection was called up on the computer, selecting men or women with the right skills with wrenches and so forth. It was dangerous, and apparently, one person had had a serious accident repairing it decades before. Zero gravity didn't worry anyone, it was a possible sudden drop back into gravity that did, all 400 meters of it. As people were reading their tablets or sleeve monitors to see who was chosen, Cramer walked up, selected the tools, climbed the ladder, and eventually he was upside-down holding on with only one hand, belaying himself to the nozzle as he repaired the assembly. He jungle-gymed back and descended just as easily. The crowd awaiting their turn, now unnecessary, applauded his return. His comment, "Thought I would earn my keep for a change," was played throughout the ship and Cramer became, secretly but probably not reluctantly, the ship's resident bravery role model.

I stopped into Aten's office the next day and she was still fuming. "Why did he take such a risk? He's only a boy, a small boy!"

I tried to calm her down, explaining he wasn't really. He was already fitter than I was, had been working out in the gym now twice a day and, besides, didn't Aten remember him riding helicopters?

"Yes, I do, and see what happened to him?" She was angry and I guessed why. So I walked over and gave her a hug. Of course, I was a little short, so I had to be careful where my nose went. She sighed, relaxing. But I was not done with her yet, she wasn't going to like this but . . .

"And there is one more thing Aten, Cramer is in love with you. A boy of seven, with a forty-year-old man inside, is in love with you. If he doesn't do something about it soon, he'll implode."

Aten looked frightened, "It is too soon, he has to wait until we have established a colony, then we will make chil . . ."

I cut her off, "No, no, Aten. Not that, for god's sake, don't tell him that, don't discuss it. No, what he needs to know is that you are bonded. He loves you for goodness sake, that repair job was to show you he was a man, not a boy. He wants you, probably physically, but I have no idea how that would work and what the rules are for under-age children. But is he under-age? That's a question! Anyway, find some way to give his life purpose on a personal level, just you and him. I can't stand to see him pining and building all this tension, who knows what the next stunt will be. I know Cramer, remember? He's prone to, how shall I put this, physical demonstrations."

"Like when he punched that arresting officer in Cuba and challenged the others to try and shoot him?"

"Yup, that's the real Cramer, forget the image of a little boy."

The room went suddenly quiet. Aten looked at her shoes and said sadly. "I have no one to talk with."

"What do you mean? You have many people here you are friendly with." It was true, I had seen her laughing and holding arms with other crewmembers.

"Not those questions. If Apollo were here, I could discuss it with him. Or Angie . . ."

Lord, that conversation? I knew Aten would have already read everything, hell Cramer had said she read every sex manual she could find, which Cramer thought was to prepare her on what to avoid. Little did he know. I decided to try and help, up to a point. "Aten, I was happily married and I was very happily engaged in, uh, sexual activity with Angie. If you have questions of that sort, I can help, but only if you ask."

"Maybe later, yes, thank you," she hesitated, and out came desperation, "but what if he doesn't want me forever? What if he doesn't love me as I love him?"

Oh, the big questions! Now I knew what was worrying them both. They needed another leap of faith and had both, perhaps, already used up all that sort of bravery; recently jumping bodies, being planted. Well, it was recently for Cramer and I, over 100 years ago for Aten. She had had longer to fret over this. I felt sorry for her. So I hugged her again and assured her I would think of something.

What had started to occur to me was that the easy-going pace of the flight was infectious, even perhaps causing indecision from Ra/Aten. Could Ra be indecisive now as Aten? As Ra, never. Without emotions born of flesh, Ra would have assessed and acted. But Aten? Clearly, this was new territory for her and she was unsure. No amount of reading can tell you what to do in matters of the human heart.

Aten being indecisive, Cramer being ready to boil over— these were not good omens for the safety of the flight. Time to put matters right.

The wedding was ten days later. Darn I'm good.

None of the crew thought it weird at all. The invitation, which I designed, showed Cramer in his prime and now as a seven-year-old and Aten at different stages of her youth, images taken from her medical files. It was a little hard to explain what she looked like before becoming human so I avoided that. Everyone was gleeful, recycled paper confetti was thrown, the party reception was alcohol-free, of course, but otherwise a dancing, wild party. It was thrown on the main observation deck with illumination running down the center and from bright white to clouds, making rainbows that reminded me of pastures as a child on a drizzly summer day.

When it came to the kiss, June, from communications, officiated, "I now pronounce you man and wife," Aten leaned over, Cramer held her face in his hands and their lips touched, quite chaste. Aten was having none of it. She grabbed Cramer and embraced him passionately. There were catcalls, whistles, and a round of applause. Aten blushed, Cramer stood more erect, somehow taller already. And me? I was both Cramer's best man and Aten's father. I gave her away and gave him the rings he had milled on board. Standing behind them during the vows part, I cried for Angie, who would have been so happy.

Oh, I forgot to tell how I got them together.

At dinner that night, after the lighting repair, Cramer and Aten got into a squabble. It smacked of authority—his, being overrun by intelligence—hers. The topic was inconsequential, but they both left the café angry walking in opposite directions, not even saying goodnight.

I went to Aten's quarters and thought I heard her crying as I knocked. "Just a moment . . ." and soon, she opened the door. I hugged her and asked if she was all right, got the expected response, "Of course! Why not?" So, I changed the subject and told her I needed to go over something with her in the morning and could she meet me at six o'clock in my quarters. I left not awaiting a discussion, knowing she'd turn up.

I knew Cramer had a sonic shower every morning at six, in the bathroom we shared. Aten arrived and I took her hand and lead her into the bathroom. Cramer was facing the other way, washing. Aten tugged to free her hand, I held firm and said, "Hey Cramer, you almost done?"

He didn't turn, scrubbing his hair, "You know it's my turn, you have to wait."

"Trying to look better for your girly friend Aten?"

As he turned, he was saying, "I warned you leave her out . . ."

There he was, stark naked, looking at Aten. I released her hand, pushed her ahead of me, turned, and shut the door behind me. I have no idea what they did or didn't do for half an hour. There was a lot of talking. At one point, I heard him loudly exclaiming, "I do, I always have!"

When they came out, a towel around him, a tissue for her to dab tears, they came into my room and I stood. They were holding hands, bodies, and arms touching. I looked at their hands and smiled. They smiled, I gave them both a hug, and Aten hit me, gently this time. Life does keep repeating itself.

# 10

## APOLLO'S MESSAGE

"Message for Aten and, if capable, Simon and Cramer, private.

"Received yours 1.16.75.14. Understand no progress Cramer and Simon. Simon's ability to free think and imagine may be useful for next part this message.

"Our calculations on dark matter were based on late pre-Purge science, especially coming out of CERN and NASA research. The New Way America stopped galactic research unless it had a practical purpose to aid in planet and asteroid development. At the time, dark matter was considered twenty-seven percent of universe's mass, so-called normal matter was five percent and dark energy was sixty-eight percent, and this was based on then calculation of the total mass of the universe, which was, as you will remember expanding, actually accelerating. That acceleration contradicted all of Einstein's and, later, Nupe's gravitational laws and calculations.

"My calculations and the work we have commissioned with over ten thousand astrophysicists since you prepared for flight, and after, have shown that all previous calculations are incorrect. Your own engine readings on the density of dark matter have shown that there is roughly ten to the power of three times more dark matter than previously calculated. This has caused our teams to evaluate the following: One, have our calculations on the overall mass of the universe since Professor Hawking's day been inaccurate? Two, are the proportions of dark matter to dark energy and normal matter, mass, still valid—accurate? Three, if not, what are the new proportions? And the most important—Four, what role does dark energy play other than causing the acceleration of the expansion of the universe and, as a subset of this question, if the amount of dark energy is also ten to the power of three times greater, then the cause and effect of dark energy as a proportion of normal matter has been greatly underestimated.

"Think about that ratio of dark energy and dark matter to normal matter if these new proportions are valid. Every planet, star, and physical material humans recognize as matter would only be less than 55.26313019405161 to the . . . six percent of all mass. The significance of planetary development and solar development, indeed galactic development, should be the very rare exception, a fluke—way outside the realms of the norm. And research has shown that although there are new stars and systems forming within each older galaxy we can observe, more are being reduced to axions and dark matter than are being formed.

"While the universe is expanding, caused by the forces released by dark energy, it is now certain that all planetary, solar, and galactic development is being fueled by dark energy. In other words, it is only dark energy, not the resultant forces of the Big Bang, which is sculpting the Universe. The causality of the forces at play here are not random. These forces repeat, they mimic, and they follow basic laws of gravity, specifically Einstein's. But the forces of dark energy are so vast, that for any planetary construction to be considered random and abstract is absurd now. We here are pretty much agreed. Dark energy is being directed to promote the creation of similar, repetitive planetary bodies, to form those around a sun, to bind those solar systems into a spiral galaxy. And to align galaxies on multiple planes each moving away from one another as if to protect them.

"Our calculations show that forty percent of dark energy is directed toward that movement, repeating forces, mimicking exact energy expenditure, resulting in a constant rate of development of normal matter especially in newer galaxies. The farther away from the center of the Universe, the greater the expansion and—here is Professor Nupe's finding—the greater the number of planetary bodies being formed.

"To sum this up, dark energy is mainly directed at creating planetary bodies as well as moving them away from the center of the Universe, preventing them, wherever possible, from collision.

"Deduction? Dark energy is creating platforms for life.

"I have conversed with Gaia and, using the expansion coefficient and these new energy calculations, we have been able to make several new dictionary entries to allow the conversation to continue down what Angie would have called, the rabbit hole. Today, Gaia has confirmed that what we think of as dark energy manifestation is Regus.

"End of transmission."

Cramer, Aten, and I sat there, in her office, unmoving. Speechless. There was nothing to say, the concept was too unfathomable, even for Aten. Regus was or controlled sixty-eight percent of the Universe, sixty-eight percent of every galaxy, every star, every planet, every molecule. Sixty-eight percent of every living thing. Sixty-eight percent controlling the whole.

After ten minutes, we left Aten in the office, alone, as Zip came in and told Cramer he was wanted elsewhere. Zip announced to me that I should leave, he added a please as he walked over to Aten and placed his head in her lap. Aten absently mindedly stroked Zip's ears. I went to the gym to work off some adrenaline.

# 11

## OFF COURSE

The tacking klaxons sounded and following the brief training our fellow crewmates had afforded us, I put everything loose away and went to my station. As it was my night shift, I went off toward navigation. Cramer and Aten were off duty. We had enjoyed dinner together and, after three months of being happily married, they were already finishing each other's sentences. Cramer held her chair and got up to refresh her drink, and Aten, for her part, spent most of the off time during dinner staring lovingly at his ugly mug. I was beginning to get nauseous.

Arriving in navigation, I immediately studied the central nav radar plot wall with the three-course choices illuminated across the chart. It seemed to me that the least dangerous route was the middle one as it was 100 percent clear in radar sweeps; but Aten and the crew had done this many times before, and in order to align ourselves with Alpha Centauri A in case of the need for that sun's gravity well to break our speed before we entered Alpha Centauri B's and Angelica's region, well, we had to have that backup braking method. I understood that, but the near track that the nav crew and Aten had opted for showed only a ninety-two percent clear shot.

Aten had put it this way, "The engines will scoop up anything outside of that ninety-two percent, Simon, don't worry." I wondered if Ra's digital mind would have been that sure. Analog reasoning and leaps of faith can be costly. Still, I said nothing. I was a come-lately and I wasn't about to second-guess the greatest intellect I had ever known.

I should have, of course.

As the dark matter was ingested into the engines, one running hotter than the other to effect the turn, we were about two days into the gentle turn when the number one engine went critical and had to be emergency shut down. Number two was still pulling, but the negative impact of something large that had clogged number one had twisted number two off course and it too had to be shut down. We were then drifting, askew, into whatever debris field we had not known was there. And anything large enough to cause number one to shut down could have a cousin that could cause a hull breach.

To make matters worse, the graphene tethers had gone slack, and it looked as if the engines might drift back and collide with the hull. Under the emergency lighting, illuminating all surfaces a slight green, powered by the PowerCube aft with no plasma from the engines, Aten was furious with herself, "If I had left them where I had designed them, aft of the ship, they couldn't be threatening us!" Actually, I guessed she was angry for having chosen the wrong course.

Cramer tried to reassure her that the decisions she had made would "Turn out fine, hon, relax." He turned to me, "Simon? Thoughts?"

I shrugged and walked out of navigation. I needed to think. I had off planet experience. So far, in talking with the crew, I was the only one aboard who did. That was really worrisome.

Why?

Let me put it this way, fate had somehow tagged me once more. Cramer avoided stating the obvious, for which I was grateful.

Ten minutes later, I asked the lead engineer at a crew gathering outside on the main deck, "What's the time frame here?" The main engineers were all there, all four of them, Cramer and Zip, of course, Aten, the nav team, and maintenance people ready to fabricate anything, if needed, if anything could be dreamed up to stop a disaster. No one seemed worried, really, but anxiety was creeping in aided by the lack of what was, normally, their overhead illumination. When you have been aboard a safe ship for 100 years, I suppose the feeling of invulnerability becomes second nature. For Cramer and I, there was no such complacency.

The engineer nearest me tapped his arm display a few times and said, "Impact in about twelve hours, and that's the quickest. I can't really evaluate the flexibility of the graphene tethers after all this time in deep space. My guess is they are getting stiffer. They are running static in increasing amounts, we're past twelve kilojoules now."

Aten responded, "If the impact doesn't kill us, that static discharge will."

Cramer had heard enough, "Okay, people, enough of the negative. What do we need to do?" He looked around the assembled crew and, of course, ended his visual survey on me. "Simon? Tag, you're it." Damn, he had to go and say it after all.

It was our longstanding competition now out in the open, a game of responsibility, tag he was it, then tag I was. Childish games played—wait a moment, we were still kids!

"Hey, Cramer, finally we're age-appropriate for tag. Angie would have liked that." Cramer smiled but pointed at one of the crew chiefs, reminding me I was in charge. I was "it," so I needed to respond to the crisis.

The engine crew wanted the engines restarted as soon as possible. All of them nodding as one of their crew stated, "If we back flush the blocked engine—and currently I can do that from my station—we will have two engines ready to restart. As long as they stay hot as hell, say another five or six hours without cooling too much, I can fire them from here. After that, there's no way. They will need an electrical boost as they had in moon orbit to spin up the centrifuges. But once we get them going, we can fire them in bursts, one side and the next, and sort of worm them back ahead of the ship."

The lead engineer weighed in, "Yeah, but hold on a minute—if you back flush number one and it's not pointed ahead, it will increase the deflections. And if you back flush it even if it is ahead, without one engine taking the thrust, you will push the graphene tethers and they may be brittle and crack. No one has ever tested them in over one hundred years."

"Okay," Aten said, "let's leave that for a moment. I'll do the graphene calculations, degradation, static effect. About two hours. But my question is this: Will the so-called worming realignment of the engines work?"

Navigation agreed, a worming heading would work best, but then the maintenance crew explained we could lose gravity if this worming path took longer than, say, a day. There was silence. The thought of operating the ship's functions, all in zero gravity, stopped the discussion cold. But I was used to zero gravity and, I guessed, it was time for me to step up to something approaching adulthood, fate or no fate. Coming from a ten-year-old, this might have been seen as comical anywhere else. On the ship, with this crew, all believing my misplaced hero status, it was seen as "savior to the rescue."

So I chimed up, "Got space suits?"

Aten was shocked, "You're not going out there!"

Cramer responded, "He is and we're going with him. I need four, maybe six volunteers from my away crew in training." One man raised his hand and explained the away crew in training were not all present. "Go find 'em and bring everybody back here." He turned to me, "What have you got in mind Simon?"

"I need electricity, loads of electricity, in micro bursts of power. I need a twin fiber cable at least four hundred to four hundred and fifty meters long, and it needs to pass through from the outside, back into the hull, and be connected to source. If I call for reverse polarity, I need someone who can flip a breaker, quickly, safely."

Abadine, the leading maintenance woman, physically petite and smart as a whip, responded, "We can set that up, I've got cable and there's a conduit airlock about thirty centimeters from the Tether One bolt down passing into the lower flight deck. I can have you connected to the Cube's power grid, all the way forward, there's a junction there." She pointed over my shoulder toward the flight deck. "I have some termination relays for land-fall . . . for the maintenance of Cube power once we're settled. I can rig those in about six hours into the flight deck, but it's Zero-G in there . . ."

"Good, that's fine. Can you do it?" I looked at her. She nodded. "Great, now remember, find something to anchor yourself to when operating the breakers, you'll do just fine. Just be safe, okay?" Abadine nodded, "Now get going. Now please Abadine." She pointed at three men and they ran off.

"Now I need a propulsion system. Do we have suits and back-packs?" Aten shook her head. The men and women looked at each other perplexed. No one had thought, it seemed, on ever going on a spacewalk, what NASA had called EVA, short for Extra-Vehicular Activity. I know my face registered shock. There was silence, total silence so thick it threatened to dismay everyone there.

Todd, the doctor, dosed out some hope. He spoke up, "Oh, we have suits, Mr. Simon, good suits, carefully packed. But we never felt the need for the extra mass of jet packs, consumables, refrigeration-heating units, $O_2$ tanks for refills, that sort of thing. The suits we have are left-over survival suits, part of medical supplies, for when the ship was being built in moon orbit, to be donned in case of hull leaks. They hold emergency air, about two hours' worth, not much in the way of insulation. They were to be worn inside the ship, see, not outside. And they have no armor protection either."

*Great, come 4.5 light years away from safety and bring no EVA equipment. Bad planning* was what I thought. But what I said was, "Okay Doc Todd, fetch them, as many as you can, let's see what we have. I cannot fix this problem without an EVA, so an EVA is what we'll have to manage!" The assembled crowd did anticipatory clapping, you know the one, like little kids feeling all excited before the party magician starts pulling rabbits out of his hat.

Me? I had no rabbits, not even a hat. I turned to Aten, "I need your brain Aten, and I need it full power now. Think gyroscope propulsion, dual interacting gyroscopic propulsion. What do we have on this ship that I can hand carry—and use? What can you make work, speed of rotation, container, everything, it is up to you."

Aten grinned with renewed purpose, her whole body becoming more erect. It was infectious enthusiasm, buoying the crowd, "Okay Simon, I'll rig something up!" And she sprinted off, saying as she disappeared, "And, I have calculations on the graphene to run!"

Cramer wanted to know, "what the hell you thinking of?" I explained that a gyroscope spinning just so and then tuned will cause an equal and opposite force—propulsion navigation, a bit of the former and loads of the latter. "If I lock onto the outside of the hull, spin something up, something Aten can concoct, then as I push away from the hull, I'll run true until I reach my target. If I change the spin rate or can destabilize the spinning disk, I can twist the axle and turn. Think of a bicycle . . ." Several crew members had blank looks on their faces, "a bicycle was a two wheel transport that relied on centrifugal force to keep the bicycle upright. When you turned the handlebars, deviating the front wheel, the friction with the road would start the turn, but it was the centrifugal force of the front wheel acting against the back wheel that made the bicycle lean over into the turn. To start that interaction, you needed to turn away from where you want to go and start the lean, and then once the lean happened, you would turn in the direction of the lean to complete the turn. In short, you are a gyroscopic platform that can control right and left direction. In open space, I won't have a reacting surface except at launch and landing, but I don't need propulsion energy as much as I need directional control between the two—takeoff and landing."

Cramer looked worried, "You want Aten to build you a bicycle, a space bicycle?" In a sense, I did. But what I needed, and I knew Aten was already guessing, was a wheel within a wheel, both spinning incredibly fast. Move one out of alignment with the other and you could change direction—if I could hold on, if I could get enough of a kickoff from the hull, if—there were a lot of "ifs."

The next six hours went in a blur under the greenish light, shadows of people moving rapidly to complete tasks, children being calmed, Zip and other dogs escorting those lost to their stations. And me? I had the ship's plans that needed urgent study.

As soon as I could, I inspected the so-called spacesuits with Cramer. They were a joke really, fit only for the safe confines inside the ship. So we got some Loc, the blue stuff, strongest there is, and bonded three suits, one inside the other. We only needed the outer helmet ring and collar lock and the gloves that were part of an outer suit. So we had cut out one glove from the innermost suit, and when that was still too bulky for digit dexterity, we cut out the second one, leaving only the outer gloves—thin, delicate, no grip surface, and worrisome. Doc Todd had surgical gloves with high grip finger pads, so we blue Loc'ed those, one cut finger on top of each suit glove finger, and then added a second layer to be sure. They worked okay.

The helmets all had VHF radios, line of sight simple jobs. Batteries were PERMA, so they were okay. Until activated, they were inert and as good as new. I had no idea how long they would last though, and there was no recharging them. Once on, they were on until failure. The helmet lights were also powered by PERMA batteries, so we scavenged the extra helmets' lights and blue Loc'ed them on top as well, slightly angled outwards. It was sure to be damn dark out there. Light can make all the difference.

The suit tethers were industrial strength, out of keeping with the flimsy spacesuits. A maintenance man assured me they had a breaking strain in excess of twelve tonnes. Their clasps were click on, click off, easy to use. They would do fine.

However, in some of the suits, for there were three types left from construction, maybe fifty suits in all, there were oxygen cylinders maybe twelve centimeters long and five around. It was stamped with a date 120 years ago and the prophetic words, "Good for twenty minutes. Do Not Exceed." Somehow, the maintenance people along with two engineers managed to pipe three of them together for four suits. The rest of the suits only had what was called an oxygen chemical bladder. Put the suit on, smack yourself in the chest, and mix the chemicals. You would have a slow chemical reaction making oxygen, heat, and a salt of some sort absorbing $CO_2$. The salt stayed behind the membrane, the oxygen leaked into the suit, hopefully reaching your face. Instructions were to keep patting the suit envelope to make sure you didn't get a $CO_2$ dam in your helmet and asphyxiate.

The third type of suit was emergency only. Hold your breath, get rescued—five minutes, no more. Useless for this job and, I guessed, more of a placebo to the construction crews than any real effectiveness.

Cramer organized his away team volunteers. To be frank, I was surprised, they all volunteered eagerly, saying "Yes sir," to Cramer at every utterance. A seven-year-old kid taking command. As I said, Cramer is a force of nature.

As we were down to only four multi-tank suits for EVA, I decided that I needed someone beefy with me on the long drop to attach my cable. Cramer said, "That's Ernest here." Ernest nodded. Everyone wanted to know what the plan was, but I put them off. I needed to know if we could even go at all as Aten still wasn't back with the gyro.

Cramer and I got three more chemical suits ready for "the guys who will operate the hatch and be ready for a quick rescue, if needed, okay? You don the suits, do not, I repeat, do not smack the chest until you are needed and your helmets are on." Again, that enthusiastic agreement from his men.

"Okay then," I outlined the plan, such as it was, "I want you, Ernest, with me. We'll push off and drift trailing a thin cable, I asked maintenance to find something suitable, something that will haul the heavy electrical cable down to us later. When we reach the motor and graphene coupling, if we're still together, we'll attach there and haul it up, down, whatever. Cramer, you and the other man . . ." Cramer pointed at a strong man with the name Sam on his tunic, "Okay, you and Sam have to feed the heavy cable to us. It must not kink, okay?"

Everyone nodded. Then Abadine said she'd feed it through the airlock. "But it'll kink, snake like mad. We'll need to have a plan to get it out there. It'll take hours to feed it through the airlock . . ."

Cramer had other ideas. "Abadine, the cable you're using, it'll be in a spool?"

"No, it's woven graphene impregnated with Toluene liquid metal, very thin particles, will carry up to ten thousand volts. It's all coiled and weighs, hell I don't know, about a tonne? It's not big, thick that is, but it is dense."

Cramer scowled. "Size? Can the coil fit through the airlock Simon will use?" Abadine said it would but didn't know who could lift it to get it there. Cramer was not going to be pessimistic, "That airlock is in the Zero-G section. All we have to do it get it on to the flight deck, lower deck, right?" She nodded. "Okay, then where's it stored?"

Abadine looked miserable. "In the maintenance supply area, all the way aft."

Cramer smiled, "Ah, so it's nearer the center of the ship, lower gravity, right?" Everyone nodded, "Okay then, we'll hoist it into Zero-G and then pull it along the center, all the way, hand over hand until we get to the other end and the swivel connecting passage tube to the lower flight deck."

I patted Cramer on the back, "Right, who do you need?"

"Me, only me." We were all aghast. Here was a seven-year-old saying he'd hand maneuver a one tonne coil of cable three kilometers, hand over hand. Okay, it was Zero-G in the dead center, but move an inch off that center and the gravity will start to increase. Cramer saw what we were thinking. "Guys, think. There's a rail up there, right? The one the light tube is anchored to, right? And I'll hook it and me onto the rail, get it?" We all nodded in unison. "So all I need is to start from the front end," he pointed toward the light deck, "with a very strong cord that you'll belay out as I run all the way, down here, "he pointed at the ground and then toward aft section of the ship, "right down the central orange highway, right? And when I get to the other end, I'll clamp on to the rail with a rappel roller we have for landfall, attach the coil, and you beefy lads can pull like hell to make me sail all the way back to the front." He paused, "Deal?"

Of course, it wasn't that easy. Every 400 meters, he had to unhook himself, re-hook the other side of a support pylon holding the rail, do the same for the almost weightless coil, and proceed. It took him almost four hours. When he arrived at the lower flight deck, he looked all in, spent, exhausted. Todd was there, gave him oxygen, and took vital signs. Todd shook his head, looking at me. My thought? *Hell, if a seven-year-old can do that, a ten-year-old can do the rest.*

I hoped.

# 12

## THAT ASTEROID FEELING, AGAIN

Everything had gone as planned. Aten had, of course, come up with a coupled gyro, one inside the other, about the size of a helmet—actually mounted inside one of the space helmets we weren't using, onto which she had blue Loc'ed handles either side.

The gyro? She had salvaged it from a hover car in the storage bay ready for later landfall. She attached a small PowerCube from a portable lantern that made the gyros, at ninety-degree angles to each other, whirl like mad. Power it up holding the helmet steady and they would twist in your hands if you tried to change course. There was a rheostat I could control with my thumb.

Aten explained the operation, "Short bursts Simon, there is no upper limit, you could keep it on full power, and the bearing may break apart. I got this from the only hover car that doesn't use laser gyros. It's a truck really, so it needs inertial navigation with more inertia than electro-servos will supply. Once these things spin up, they can break your wrists, so I suggest powering up slowly to find the limit of need." I nodded, she had done great, and I told her so.

Meanwhile, the suits' gloves were finished by Todd and his team of medical staff. Off we all trudged forward, climbing the ramps at the end of the ship, then the ladder to the swivel tube, accessing the lower flight deck and Zero-G.

Inside I saw that Abadine had, no surprise there, completed the electrical connections into the lower flight deck where the airlocks were. The four of us suited up, helmets off still, watching the other four fellows put on the almost useless chemical suits.

Being the person most used to Zero-G, I was holding still with just a finger grip onto an overhead pipe. Some of the men and women were using both hands and were still drifting and bumping each other. Cramer was in charge, "Now, listen, emergency crew, if you see anyone in trouble, through that porthole there, you lock your helmets on, smack your chests to activate the oxygen. Go through the airlock process and be ready to rescue. Tether up! Always! Is that clear?" They nodded, we all did. He turned to Sam, Ernest, and me, "Todd will sound the alarm, one blast when you have less than five minutes left and then every thirty seconds and then continual for the last thirty left, clear?" We all nodded, even the emergency crew. Todd said he'd keep careful monitor. Cramer turned to me, "Simon, over to you . . ."

"Okay, here's what we'll do. The airlock holds four, but not with the coil as well. So Ernest and I will go through first with the rope spool. It won't reach all the way to the engines; well, it may if they are already canted over forty-five degrees and it looks like it out the porthole, but we'll decide that once we're out."

Abadine interrupted, "You cannot make hand hold on the graphene cables attached to the hull or motors, the tethers are supercharged, you would be burned to a crisp instantly. That rope you're towing would also be enough to carry the static discharge."

"It's okay, I have a plan for that; you'll get the discharge back here, back-feed the Cube, okay?" She nodded looking worried, "It'll work. Now, we need to reach the motor junction and power up the engines. Are the pilots and engine crew ready?" They called ready down the hatch to the lower flight deck. "Abadine, your relays ready?"

"As soon as the cable comes back through that gel airlock," she pointed at a green ring with a blue-black liquid center. I assumed it was Ferrofluidics, held in place by strong magnets making a pass-through airlock. There was a hatch cover, inside portal open now, ready to close. She continued, "I'll hook up the wires here and be ready to go on your command."

"Right then," I tried to sound cheery, "Ernest and me first with cord, spool clipped to my belt, Ernest and I tethered together, followed by Sam and Cramer with the coil of electrical cable. As soon as we're outside, we'll attach this end," I held up the cord end that had a karabiner attached, "to the stanchion rail outside the airlock." Abadine started to say something. I cut her off, "yes, I know, stay clear of the graphene tethers, got it." She relaxed, "Then Ernest and I will push off, trailing the cord." I looked around; everyone seemed to understand. "Cramer and Sam emerge, tethered to each other, and immediately tether to the same stanchion. They then pass one end of the coil back through the gel hatch to Abadine. After that, they attach the other end of the coil to the cord karabiner and wait for my signal to belay the coil, carefully, no kinks, no tangles. When it reaches us, we'll attach it to the motor initiator that Aten has shown Ernest and me images of. But before that, I will be helping straighten out the tethers."

Even Cramer looked at me as if I was nuts.

"Nope, I'm not going to touch them. All I need to do is have Abadine throw the relay when I touch one wire lead to one graphene tether and one to the other. As I command Abadine, you need to run positive and negative, all the power you have got. When I call for reverse polarity, don't hesitate, I'll be steering the brutes and may not have quite the delicate touch needed. Clear?"

"Mr. Simon, I see what you are going to try and do, but no one has ever attempted that before," Abadine said.

Aten smiled, cut in, shaking her head and said, "Yes they have. I did the calculations and anyway Simon has sort of done this before, haven't you Simon? Reverse polarity was one of your little tricks deep inside the System. Run the current one way and this graphene will tighten, run it the other and it will weaken. Right left, left right. Steering the engines away from the hull. I get it." She paused, "It is dangerous. And foolish. And typical of you."

Cramer agreed. "That's your plan? Look, if the engines turn to face forwards again, we can back flush number one and the new matter they absorb will start them up, you don't need . . ."

"Yes I do. The hull, my Angie, can't take the blow if they make contact, let alone the discharge, and you can't back flush number one safely until they are pointed more or less ahead and number two is running. Right?" The engineers nodded. "So, the engines need to face forward and number two has to be running. We'll use the juice from Abadine to spin up their impellers or centrifuges in sequence so any matter inside or that we catch up to—remember we're still at almost eighty of the speed of light, "everyone nodded, "So that will immediately cause that engine start. The only way to make them face forward is to tighten the tethers alternatively, clear the obstruction, and then worm them and this ship forward."

It pretty much went as planned. Well, the cord we were using wasn't really long enough to reach the base of the motors if the tethers had been straight, but as they were kinked over at more than thirty-five degrees now, Ernest and I were just able to shoot across the hypotenuse void. We aimed for the faint red glow, a heat signature we were told would be visible. It was. Trailing our little cord, about 350 meters of it, and using the helmet gyro to stabilize the route, we landed, feet first, upside down, looking up (down?) at the ship. Ernest said it was up, I said down. It was disorienting.

It was, however, glorious. The crew has turned on all the beacon lights on the hull. It made her flight deck look shiny, like new after more than 100 years. It was dark, of course, but her lights complimented the vast array of stars illuminating the background. Some of the starlight seemed streaked, and I remembered to take Doppler effect into account. Still, the cigar-shaped hull blacking out the stars seemed massive from out here. But I could sense the motors were drifting, closing the gap, we had maybe four hours left before we could do nothing but die, all of us.

Time to get to work. We radioed Cramer and the crew that we had arrived safely as Ernest and I attached our tethers to the clip-on points left over from the original construction beneath the exhaust ports of the motors. The exhaust manifolds were massive cavities, glowing red still. From the pilots' last attempt to keep the motors ahead of the ship, the nacelles were canted far over, pointed straight at us puny humans tethered there. I radioed the pilots to straighten them out, just in case. They immediately responded and I knew the residual battery power inside the motor nacelles would be taxed. Still, I was relieved when we felt the power of the metal on metal movement through our feet as the nacelles moved away from our position. Ernest radioed, "That's better."

Next came the electric cable, carefully uncoiled by Cramer and Sam who we could just make out, looking like tiny dots on the hull of the lower deck, helmet lights on, silhouettes backlit through the observation porthole. As the coil made its way to us, I could see Ernest's face in his visor, smiling. A good steady man to have nearby, perhaps better than me. I hated being alone in the vastness of space. And out here, with no sunlight anywhere, only the lights on top of our helmets and the seemingly tiny exterior navigation lights the crew had turned on for our benefit—well, it was pitch black. A blue darker than black, punctured only by stars' pinprick radiation.

When the coil end arrived, I signaled Cramer that we had it. His response was terse, conveying his worry, "Tons of killing power there little guy, careful." *Little guy indeed.*

"Ernest, I need to hold fast here." Ernest tightened his ground tether and grabbed my flimsy suit with one hand, rock steady. I split the electrical cord and studied the two bare ends Abadine had prepared with soldered pointed tips. I radioed, "Nice job on the tips Abadine." And heard two clicks telling me she heard.

The braided graphene tethers running from the motors to the ship were smaller than I had thought they would be. And dangerous now as I approached them. As Aten and I had studied, on the ship's plans, they were about one and a half meters apart, mostly. In some places closer. I could not see, in the darkness, the middle of the arc going down to the ship. The fibers of the tethers glistened under my helmet light. I put one of Abadine's pointed ends carefully on the nearest tether and immediately Abadine screamed into my helmet, "Getting huge discharge here!"

As I touched the other probe into the other tether, a purple glow of current, shaped like a wave donut, could be seen dissipating into the dark along the graphene. There were sparks about halfway to the ship, perhaps where the graphene tethers touched, and then the glow continued on its way. I radioed to Cramer, "Discharge coming your way. Stand clear."

Cramer was not amused, "Gee thanks, a little late—the first shock struck the deck like lightening."

Abadine radioed, "The bolt on the securing hatch for the pass-through is glowing red hot; if it fails, we'll lose pressure." An engineer could be heard over Abadine's radio calling for an extinguisher, and then the sounds of discharge were heard. She continued, calmly, "Okay, it's okay, we're in balance now, careful Simon, it's building another charge now . . ."

I called, "Full current, reversed. Now." As she did as she was instructed, the graphene snake came alive, straightening, pulling away from its partner, moving suddenly toward Ernest. "Abadine, power off, reverse!" I withdrew the cable points. The tether movement instantly stopped and the graphene went slack. I turned to Ernest, spoke to Cramer, "Cramer, it's too dangerous for two of us here. I am sending Ernest down the electrical cable, please catch him and tether him safely there."

"Simon you cannot do this alone . . ."

"I know Cramer, you stay on that end and if I get into trouble, you can tether to the cable and come help." I knew he'd have a response, felt one coming, and cut him off with, "Tag, Cramer, tag, remember? I'm it. My job, my responsibility, my way." He did not reply except for two clicks of the radio to show he had heard me clearly.

Ernest didn't need to be asked twice. He had seen the graphene approaching rapidly, and it made sense for him to get down the cable to relative safety. He asked if I was able to hold myself rigid without him, and I told him I was if he latched me up. He attached his second tether to my belt and to the latch point he had been using. Then he looped his primary tether around the cable and said "Hey, don't let go of your end . . ." and pushed off toward what was, for him, home. Down or up, he made it in no time at all, maybe four minutes or so. Cramer had to arrest his fall as he was traveling at quite a clip by then. I heard the "Oof!" from Cramer just as he has telling me that Ernest had made it back safely.

I was running out of time. I had used almost thirty minutes and what I had seen of my graphene electrical steering system— hell, this whole idea could take longer than the oxygen I had. I pressed on ahead quickly now. I called for polarity, reverse polarity, switched between the two graphene beasts, switching probes on different sides of the graphene braiding, trying to extract some finesse in my steering. The huge bulk of the engines was moving well, with me tethered to the underside. Somehow, I created a straightening of the tethers to perhaps ten degrees off straight and true. Cramer called up, "That's all the cable we have, it'll have to do, get out of there." He was right, if the engines could be started now, the pilots could alternate power slowly to fully straighten out the engines and, eventually, our course.

That's when I heard it. Something familiar, something that resonated at the back of the brain. I shook my head and it was gone. *Must be poor oxygen flow in these damn suits*, I thought. I wondered if I could stay longer and hear, whatever it was, again.

But then I heard Todd's voice, in my helmet, telling me I was almost out of time—the alarms on board ship had started already. He urged me to come back immediately, then Aten was pleading, heck even Abadine was shouting at me that my hour was up. The job had to be finished or they would not, not one of us could, survive. There was no time for Cramer or anyone to come out and take over, we had used all the suits that had oxygen cylinders. Cramer didn't say a word. I guessed he knew that was useless. I needed to finish the job and trust that the canisters, although 100 years old or more, would have been slightly over-charged way back then. *Let's hope*, was what I thought, *let's hope.*

I slipped the cable ends into the start-up motor power junction box, but there was nothing to lock the ends in place, just click-in-place clasps. Now I understood why Abadine shaped the ends the way she had. They clicked in and held. Next I tethered the gyro, flipped the switch, then I radioed Abadine about the power, "I have no idea which way we're connected here, tell them to turn number two on slowly and have the flight deck monitor polarity. Hey, but give me a few minutes to start back, okay? I really don't want to get a sun tan if these motors start up." I meant it as a joke. Well, it seemed funny to me. Cramer still said nothing. Everyone else was yelling for me to hurry, and some of them seemed angry. Cramer told them all to shut up and they did.

I loose tethered onto the electrical cable and pushed off toward the ship with all the ten-year-old leg oomph I could. I went hand over hand—I had a long way to go, almost 400 meters now that the engines were more or less pointed ahead. My helmet lights gave out first. Blink one, blink two, and blink three. I thought *how well made they are, to have juice for only so much time, so nearly matched in their planned obsolescence.* The darkness enveloped me. I tried to focus on the puny lights of the ship still so far away, but the darkness, the darkness—hypoxia no doubt—my mind played tricks on me. I was there, all alone on that damn asteroid again. That damn shard had bounced in at us from out of radar range and careened into our spacecraft and had killed the crew, all except me. The mayday signal had taken a long, long time to be answered. I never before felt so lonely and alone. And here I was again, holding on to a cable halfway into nothingness and not enough oxygen to see me home.

*There was that sound again, no, not a sound, a feeling in my mind*—maybe I was already unconscious from lack of oxygen.

Cramer had the same thought, of course, he usually does, "Engine number two warming up, power restored. We're pulling the cable, do you read me, we're pulling the cable. Hold tight, fasten your tether, breathe shallow or hold your breath, we're pulling you in."

I shook my head, trying to focus. I called back, urgently repeating, "Back flush and fire up number one now." As I started to say it again, well, it was the last thing I remembered.

And, of course, Cramer did pull me in. He and Sam. Later I found out that when I sent Ernest back, Cramer put him on guard, went into the airlock with Sam to save suit oxygen and, when needed, he and Sam still had twenty minutes left. They pulled me to safety.

I think I must have been about half way there when I blacked out, tether wrapped tight around my wrist and looped loosely over the cable. Cramer complained that they had a devil of a time untangling me. He made it sound like I had made his life difficult on purpose. Aten merely cried and hugged me.

Now her, I liked.

Phooey to Cramer. Saved my life and he complains? Yeah, well—that's Cramer. I know, I know. I guessed I owed him, again.

And yet, still I know I heard something. Well, not heard exactly . . .

# 13

## COMING 'ROUND—JUST

Zero-G didn't bother me, they had slapped me to start me breathing and my body took in oxygen, involuntarily at first, and then when the brain got its supply, I awoke and smiled. "Okay, who hit me?" No need to ask, really. Cramer was grinning, Sam next to him.

As I said, they got number two fired up and then came the challenge of getting number one burped and restarted. The engineer was explaining, "We'll keep number two running, slow for now, but maybe we can jump power at the same time we scavenge power to back flush that object from number one . . ."

The fog lifted, "How long have I been out?" I looked around, shook my head, "Doesn't matter." I screamed up to the flight deck, "Back flush number one NOW!"

Aten was worried, "Simon, no! It will push the whole motor assembly sideways, perhaps back toward the ship, it could fracture the tethers, I've done calculations . . ."

I put my hand over her mouth, "Aten, I know what I am doing." Floating there in my manly spacesuit, too large for my ten-year-old frame, I turned to the engineer, gave my most forceful command "Fire up number two, half power, immediately burp number one, it will not deviate from course."

"Yes, sir," was the reply and he gave the order. I saw Sam being restrained by Cramer. Cramer had faith in me; Sam didn't yet, especially in a little kid.

Inside the ship, you could not hear a thing from outside normally. No vibration transmitted down the tethers, no snap, crackle, or pop, nothing. Oh, there was something, from the flight deck, "Hey, it worked, the engines stayed pointed ahead!" Other enthusiastic hurrahs drifted down and then a "Well, damn, all clear! All clear!"

From Cramer there was only a smile of confidence—it told me my plan had worked.

Suddenly there was a loud thump from forward, and the crew yelled down the hatchway from the flight deck, "We're 'kay, something looking like a helmet hit a stanchion, bounced off, nothing broken." The back-flushed blockage from number one had left us unscathed, so far.

Reports were flooding in on the intercoms that the crew below, with the advent of central lighting once more, had come out of anxiety and reaffirmed their belief that the voyage was blessed or, at least, not jinxed. I hoped they were right, but my thoughts would not stay fixed, I seemed to be drifting mentally to match the weightlessness. *I still don't know what it has done to our course to Angelica—and what was it I heard?* I closed my eyes, curled up and as if I were back in my ET home, and fell fast asleep.

They slipped me into a hammock, zipped it up, and left me there, Doc Todd and occasionally Aten checking while I dozed from exhaustion and the effects of hypoxia. I vaguely remember Doc Todd putting an earlobe sensor on and muttering something about low levels . . .

When I awoke, Aten told me the vids were all on and all the crew needed to know, to experience was how she put it, the saving of the ship by the great Simon. So I explained that it was really Aten's, her own doing. Her genius in constructing the portable gyrostabilizer made it all possible. Using the ship's plans before we went EVA, I had determined the exact vector, the point of imbalance under number one engine that, if stabilized, could hold the whole motor assembly, providing number two was running at about half speed, in order to allow the burping of number one. Just before I launched myself back toward the ship, I had used Ernest's tether to firmly attach the gyro helmet to the back of number one's exhaust nacelle, pointed in alignment. Then I clicked the power on full, which Aten had shown me could destroy the gyros, but I was hoping the gyro bearing would hold until I got far enough away. Hell, that gyro was designed to steady a huge hover truck, about maybe half the mass of the engines. Surely on full power it could work. That's what I had hoped, and when there was nothing else that could work that's what all we humans do, we try and we hope.

So, I gave credit to Aten for designing the device that saved us all. Apparently, the gyro did the job and kept number one pointed forward long enough to then be fired up and realign the tethers and with them, the voyage of the ship. The exhaust no doubt fried the little helmet, its usefulness fulfilled.

Aten, knowing the crew was still watching on screens around the ship, said, "But you stayed until your oxygen was depleted, you knew you were going to die to save us all."

I could see Cramer there, hovering behind some of the crew, "Nope, don't think for a moment I did. First, I'm still a little kid, so I use less oxygen than a full-grown man; and, second, Cramer was around, wasn't he? And Sam there too and Ernest." I gave a nod to Sam, who waved back, Ernest merely pointed at Cramer.

I nodded. "When Cramer is around, you can be pretty sure he'll figure out a way to save the day. Risk-taking, me? Nah, that's more Cramer's expertise. Tag, he's it. He's always it in the end." It was our little joke of passing responsibility back and forth.

But Aten persisted, "Simon . . ." She shook her head, "People want to know, what it was like, risking your life for others, Simon? Is the Path so ingrained in you that you do not hesitate?"

Typical Ra, sorry, Peter, sorry Aten, coming up with questions I either could not answer or was afraid to. What popped in my head was something simpler, "I wasn't the only one out there, everyone pulled their weight—out there and in here, everyone, equally. I had guessed you and Cramer and Zip and all my new friends needed my help, not a sacrifice, just my help. I could, so I did. If the tables were turned, I am sure you would do the same thing." And, being the ham I seemed born to be, turned toward the vid lens, grinned in a patronizing way and said, "All of you would so the same thing for your friends, we stay on the Path."

There wasn't anything more to say. Unzipping and floating free of the hammock, I told Aten I needed to talk to Abadine and make sure the electric relays for landfalls had not been damaged. I floated over and asked Abadine if the electric cables had been retrieved and, above all, I wished that somewhere on the ship someone was pulling up schematics on space suits and maybe even backpack thrusters and giving them to engineering and maintenance to fabricate. "No way should we be without them. So, let's get to work and prepare in case this happens again." Abadine agreed, wholeheartedly.

As I passed through the swivel tube gangway into the ship, the enormity of the brightly lit three-kilometer by one-kilometer cavity before me once again amazed me. I faced the wall and climbed down the sloping ladder and handholds inside the safety cage for the 300 meters and arrived in more or less normal gravity—Aten above me and Cramer and Doc Todd above her.

As I reached the deck, I turned and there arose such a yelling, screaming, whistling with "bravo!" and "Simon!" and "our leader" being voiced by all gathered, almost the whole human crew and the dogs. I didn't know what to say. I shook hands, was hugged by children and men and women alike; dogs passed by and thumped me with their tails, and as I stumbled forward, Cramer came up beside me and, putting his arm around my shoulders, said, "I thought that jump from the window back in Washington was brave, but this? This was epic, my friend, epic." He winked, I smiled, but I knew there was a dig coming, "Fortunately for you, someone was thinking to save some $O_2$, to save your ass—yet again!"

Then I laughed remembering the blind leap from that window in DC when Apollo had made WeatherGood One gust a gale to catch and then deposit me rolling on the sidewalk, evading Cramer's police goons. So, with all those people around feeling so joyous, I hugged him and simply said "Thanks—again" And meant it. With Aten and Cramer holding hands, Zip showed up by my thigh and passed me a message, "Good boy" and wagged his tail. It was perhaps the most heartwarming thanks of the day.

Funny thing about dogs, their lack of subterfuge makes all their actions trustworthy, even the ones that might threaten. You can trust that they mean what they are doing or, in Zip's case, saying. That was still weird though. Nice, but weird.

# 14

## WILL REGUS ALLOW PLANET FALL?

"Message for Aten and, if capable, Simon and Cramer, private.

"Received yours 1.31.75.14. Understand no progress Cramer and Simon.

"In my last transmission Gaia confirmed that what we think of as dark energy is Regus or is under Regus's control. It is my hope that Simon is awake and aware by now. As I said, his ability to free think and imagine may be useful for next part this transmission. In case you are relying on crewmembers for evaluation our Gaia findings, I will restate astrophysics and astronomy basis of my perspective in conversations with Gaia.

"The Universe consists of dark voids and densely packed superclusters made up of billions of stars, millions of galaxies. Superclusters are the largest structures in the Universe, but since the twentieth century, astronomers have been trying to determine where one supercluster ends and another begins. Earth's position in a supercluster has been well mapped. However, the extent—size—of our supercluster remains unknown and may be irrelevant in what follows.

"Dr. Brent Tully's work in the early millennium showed that the movement of galaxies and superclusters could be mapped. He produced a 3-D plot showing their trajectories. By discounting the effects of acceleration away from the center of the Universe and only mapping the gravitation's effects of one galaxy upon another, he plotted those galaxies being attracted toward the center of the Milky Way, our galaxy, and those that were moving away. From there, he plotted the location of "The Great Attractor"—that point in our supercluster into which all galaxies are being pulled, to collide, and, therefore, be destroyed back into primary matter, axions, and so forth. This helps account for the newfound increased total quantities of dark matter and certainly allows for the new massive calculations of dark energy.

"Part of what he found was, of course, for the time, useful in rudimentary astrophysics, like differentiating the Milky Way from the Virgo cluster—showing the two clusters within the same supercluster were on different trajectories toward the Great Attractor. But the most important spin-off of his research was the revelation that the Milky Way and Virgo were only a very small part of a truly massive supercluster that they named Laniakea meaning *immeasurable heavens* in Hawaiian.

"Following that discovery, they looked at Laniakea as a single entity and could see that the individual trajectories of every galaxy within Laniakea toward the Great Attractor mimicked our nearest supercluster neighbor, Perseus-Pisces. In fact, one is the mirror image of the other, each occupying the same amount of space and each emitting the same signatures of energy. The odds of random creation of such balance, each one side of the Great Attractor, two identical, repeat identical, superclusters, is mathematically nearing the infinite."

I sat there trying to follow. Apollo was getting into realms that could take me, an ordinary human, years of study. But then again, perhaps that was the point, he knew we still had years aboard the ship.

"In studying Gaia's revelation that Regus may be, in fact, dark energy or something that manipulates it, especially the dedication (this is my new calculation) of forty-three and a half percent of that dark energy to the creation of new stars and planets—this brought me to accurately calculate the rate of destruction of planets, stars, and galaxies at the point central in the Great Attractor to a degree of accuracy approaching ninety-nine percent. The system appears not in balance if you do the calculations of the creation and destruction of matter. Destruction is only twelve percent of that being created in terms of mass and dark matter. The balance in terms of energy is, however, constant, of course."

I looked at Cramer and he shook his head. Aten paused the recording and explained, "Energy cannot be lost this way, if galaxies are destroyed as mass, they release energy, which remains constant. That energy as dark energy will be changed into dark matter as part of the acceleration of the overall universe. Remember, we're only talking here about two super-clusters out of perhaps millions. Not including any parallel universes."

I tried to get Aten to explain further, but she was more intent on listening to Apollo's message as if it were being sent live and not recorded all those years ago. She switched the recording back on.

"Evaluating the path of the dark energy involved here, discounting the calculations for Universal acceleration away from the point of origin at the Big Bang leaves us with the following areas of study: One—measurement and plotting of the radiation involved within each supercluster. Two—measurement of the movement, the vectors, of the supercluster's galactic components including dark matter. And three—using Dr. Tully's old 3-D plots to correlate the direction of the supercluster components, as well as the overall direction of our twinned supercluster Laniakea with her sister Perseus-Pisces.

"My findings, seen as a new 3-D plotting with all three criteria superimposed one on the other look like the ganglia and neuron pathways found in all brains, and, especially, I have identified over one million plexuses. Plexus are the joining up locus for individual ganglia and ganglia chains used by neurons for energy transmission. Exactly like the brain's pathways, for species ranging from worm to jellyfish to man. Complexity may change when adjusted for the number of neurons of each brain, but the functionality and pathway creations are identical including ganglia and up to plexuses. In short, biology of life, based on neural stimulus and control, mimics exactly the patterns of the transmission of energy, dark energy, creation of matter in the form of planets, stars, solar systems, galaxies, and dark matter. And it is worth considering that these biological expire-and-growth rates are found within the Universal scheme when you adjust the time clock from Earth biological life and regeneration time span to that of the Universe by a factor of two to the zero point six five cubed billion years. I have yet to affirm this time constant with Gaia.

"Putting aside the time span differences, if these developments—the creation of matter and platforms for life—exist in parallel universes in the same manner, by that I mean the neurons and ganglia and plexuses form in the same manner, then life is not only ubiquitous throughout our Universe, but on other universes, and it is done by design."

I asked Aten to shut it off, "Please!"

I needed time to process. I sensed the conclusion Apollo was really arriving at and needed to make sure my friend, Aten, was prepared. It is one thing to know that your existence, your consciousness, came about because human foibles were allowed to interact with stable logic-only programming within a super-computer, it is quite another to learn that not only were you an accident, but the people who made that accident happen were themselves an accident or, at best, a machine designed for a purpose by a super being. That leads to the ultimate question: Why? I was not sure how Aten, even though she was in human form, might process that closed-loop logic conundrum. Humans have been covering up that question for millennia with religion. Aten had no such crutch as the remnants of her digital processing memory was incapable of such leaps of faith.

"Aten, I think when Apollo says design, what he actually means is irrevocably, in the same way evolution is irrevocable once started. We know comets seeded planets with right and left-handed amino acids, sufficient to promote the beginning of biological life, but the notion that such comets were divine or merely the working tools of an entity, as we have been using the name of Regus, is neither proven or relevant. Design does not prove intent."

Cramer immediately took what he thought would be her side and started to argue that was exactly what Apollo was saying. Cramer wanted nothing to do with the concept of a god, in any form, but he wanted me to understand that Apollo was saying exactly that and that I should not try to salt the mine, as he put it. Aten sat there, thinking. Her considerable intellect was struggling, from the look on her face, with the notions involved.

She cut Cramer off on his second attempt to have me retract what I had said. "Simon, design does not prove intent. That I can agree with. But design does show cognizant awareness at least for a predicted outcome. If Cramer fires a weapon, it shows he executed an action with a purpose. His intent may not be to kill. His intent may not be to harm. His intent may be, in fact, to simply shoot. But the motions, skill set, and coordination employed could be said to be design. And I agree that design does not, in and of itself, show intent. Questioning him would."

Now she had me worried. Will Aten want to talk with God or the designer? "Aten who do you propose we ask?"

She smiled, "No, not God, Simon," she knew me too well, "but questions can be asked, reasoning can be employed. We may come to a decision on intent in due time." She reached over and clicked the recording back on. Apollo's voice came through, tinny, but clear . . .

"I am calling the galactic plexuses, ganglia- and neuron-like pathways we have now plotted the Vast Pattern. Now, we must further consider this question . . ." Aten smiled and winked at me, "if the design of the Vast Pattern is deliberate—and mathematical analysis shows that it is unlikely not to be—then it must serve a purpose. It doesn't matter, in the short time frame of our life, who or what created or designed the Vast Pattern or if it is merely the outcome of a set of circumstances so random as to be devoid of purpose, but it does matter that the Vast Pattern has now built within it a method of communication, deliberate communication and construction, with an end purpose that is unknown. In short, the Vast Pattern has *if, what if,* programming parameters and that shows functionality if not purpose.

"Gaia was determined, still seems determined, to end life on Earth within a million years. How and why, we are unsure. But that communication is two-way and Regus, as previously represented in our conversations, as dark energy, was considered back then, in fact, be the radio station, the transmission device central. Our dictionary was and is not quite refined yet.

However, what if the Vast Pattern is itself not a brain but merely the thinking neural pathways of a pandimensional being? The signals Gaia is getting and responding to could be a minor part of overall brain function. In other words, I have calculated that the likelihood of the Universe being a cognizant entity *is well within mathematical statistical analysis.*"

Now even Cramer had heard enough, "Oh, shut it off, dammit." Apollo's voice cut off.

I put my hand on Aten's, shaking my head. "Aten, is this available to the crew?" She shook her head and mouthed, not yet. "Good, let's not for the time being. I know we've agreed to share all with everyone, but I need time to think this through with you both, and I wish I could, also, with Apollo." She started to resist, "No Aten, we're not deviating from the Path, but what we see before us is an ocean of doubt. Before we lead everyone else into the water, we had better come to grips with this ourselves, learn to swim if you see what I mean. Then we'll be able to help the many who will be terrified with this news."

Cramer was wringing his hands. "Aten, Simon, just how big is the Vast Pattern? Where do we fit in all this? We're such a small part, sitting here, immeasurable when it comes to anything approaching scientific quantity. We're three people in a three-kilometer ship, traveling four and a half light years to a nearby solar system. There are ten to the twelfth billion stars in the Milky Way alone. And as many as ten to the twentieth galaxies that we know of now. And we're supposed to figure out who made the Vast Pattern and if it is a sentient being's brain?" He paused, stood, and ran his child's fingers through his close-cropped hair, "Look, I get it. There is some fun and exciting stuff to contemplate here, but for now, we're too damn small and insignificant to matter to Regus or anything approaching another super-being. Gaia is on a million-year schedule. Let's forget all this and concentrate on the flight, the planet fall, okay?"

I just had to answer him and ruin his day, "Sure Cramer, why not? But then how will you get ready when that superbeing, in whose brain, not following normal neural pathways, where we may be traveling without permission, decides to eradicate the virus or the errant signal we may represent? There may be defense mechanisms out here that we need to plan for."

# 15

## ALONG THE WAY . . .

We broke up the meeting and I made a jogging start toward the navigation bay. As I passed people along the orange path, they waved, and I waved back. A few dogs came close enough for me to hear complimentary thoughts, and a few kids wanted me to stop and shake hands as they reminded me of their names. Seems I had started something that the kids aboard found amusing. While part of my being was playing the role of boy EVA hero on board, the rest of me was deep in troubled thought.

It seemed to me then, and it still does now in hindsight, that Apollo was right. Perhaps only my brain was whacked out enough to see that next step. What I saw clearly was that we could be a sickness needing to be eradicated. And if that were the case, was the Earth and all its inhabitants, from insect to whales, endangered because we were all possible viruses for the Vast Pattern? A million years may seem a long time—heck it did to Cramer and me—but anything that can snuff out all life on Earth in a million years could, if it so desired, also make that happen tomorrow. What was also troubling me was that, seen as a percentage of mass or indeed energy, man's activities on Earth compared to planet mass and planetary energy source was infinitesimal. So it was clear that Regus had evaluated the thinking power that man's activities had disrupted, the processing power that had been disturbed. And as the only planet in our solar system with bioforms with brains, my guess was that Earth's danger wasn't for Earth alone but for the solar system where Earth happened to be. Any change in the sun's output, say caused by dark energy ramping up solar flares, could wipe Earth clean within months.

But, still, if the number of brain cells we had disrupted with atomic blasts were brought back online, or shortly to be assisted back online, why was Regus still determined to terminate all life on Earth?

And the solution to that had only one answer: Regus could evaluate man's potential for destruction and disturbance of the Vast Pattern. My previous hope that the design of the Vast Pattern was merely a haphazard connection of criteria that produced the Vast Pattern was becoming idiotic. Too many logical steps had been taken by Regus (or whatever) for me to continue to assume a benign haphazard activity without purpose. So, purpose it had to be. A purpose that we had no concept of and perhaps were too puny to have any understanding of even if it stared us in the face.

And as for our voyage? I now saw it as a truly dangerous mission. Short and relatively slow voyages to asteroids for mining probably would not become a blip on a Vast Pattern's radar. But we were traveling at eighty percent of the speed of light with an energy signature from our engines' transmutation of dark matter fuel into released dark energy and from the kilojoules of static electricity surrounding our graphene tethers and the skin of Earth One. And that signature would be magnified by our rate of travel. Heck, we would have neither the signature of what could be a planet slightly off-kilter nor would we appear to be a long duration comet—not at this speed and acceleration. We also would not appear to be anything approaching a planetary body traveling toward the Great Attractor. Those paths were affected by gravity wells and were never as direct a course as we were setting. Four and five-degree deviations were, I guessed, pretty damn straight when seen as a whole.

I needed to ask navigation an urgent question.

Two of the best navigators were on duty and they welcomed me warmly. Immediately, they started to explain that they had recalibrated their radar, especially the side sweep radar, to make sure the next tack change would be 100 percent clear. They started to talk about the course aberration we had experienced. I guessed they were about to ask, in their friendly and open way of working, for my thoughts on their plans to slow the ship as well as maintain a usable orbit insertion parabola.

Instead, what we needed, I felt to the bottom of my feet on that humming deck surface, was a place to hide.

On the face of it, hiding something as large as this ship might seem impossible, but seen as a planetary body, the ship was smaller than most asteroids. What I was hoping for was information on Alpha Centauri B's solar system, planetary arrangement, and if there was an asteroid belt. I posed my questions to the nav crew and asked for a report within six hours. They looked worried that I might be taking decisions without open consultation. I assured them I was only worried about something, something I needed to work out before we all discussed it, and so they immediately agreed, most enthusiastically.

I asked them one more favor. I wanted to know when, if, we would pass a dark energy pathway—the trail of energy created by the movement of this galaxy and the gravitational effect of Alpha Centauri B's proximity to Alpha Centauri A. All of that needed some explaining, as we had not yet shared Apollo's recent transmission. But I had pulled up the nav charts of our course on the laser plotting table and then I overlaid a screen glow projection from the ship's memory banks of Dr. Tully's old 3-D evaluations. Dr. Tully's pathways were clearly in the vicinity. For another half hour, we discussed how we could reconcile the time shift between Dr. Tully's work and our time and then adjust for the speed and distance from Dr. Tully's point of origin. The guys were sure they could adjust the sending unit for the ships radar and side scan for dark energy pathways, but they were at a loss at accurately being able to predict where to start a sweep. Not seeing an immediate resolution, I asked if we had the computational capabilities on board. They said they would work on it. I left them to it. They looked like kids dying to unwrap presents, determined to solve the parameters and get their reward. Smart fellows.

As I made my way back to my quarters, I ran through the rest of what was bothering me.

Earth's solar system's asteroid belt was either a planet that became unstable and broke up or a planet that failed to assemble and remained a loose collection of orbiting rocks, some the size of the Moon. If Alpha Centauri B had such an asteroid belt, it would be the perfect place to stop moving, cease energy signature, and allow Regus or whomever or whatever systems ran the Vast Pattern to lose interest in a puny virus that had ceased to be.

But what also worried me was the advent of other Gaias out there. We had been traveling for over 100 years and had not come near another solar system. Assuming that solar systems were operating as pseudo-ganglia and that the bio-thought processes on planets were the operating neurons, would Alpha Centauri B have a Gaia who would report our arrival? And would our arrival—beings from a planet scheduled for extermination—be allowed to either arrive or stay?

As I sat at the little molded plastic desk in my cubicle, I pulled out a recorder I had palmed in Aten's office. I listened again to Apollo's transmissions and then started a fresh recording of all my thoughts and included what little I understood of the working of the human brain. As I finished my recording, I added, "Apollo, by the time you hear this we'll either be safely on Angelica or will have failed. In either event, I hope to tell you why and how. This may be critical to your survival on Earth, in dissuading Gaia from exterminating life on the planet. One last thought before I transmit this to you tomorrow: If dark energy is the means of transmission or if the frequency transmission of Regus is its entity—either way assuming Regus is no more than an area of brain function, perhaps a regulating mechanism to achieve efficiency for the Vast Pattern or based on the Vast Pattern's processing needs—oh, hell, I don't know—but what I'm getting at is this: The pathways of dark energy, especially as they relate to the movement of the solar systems and galaxies toward the Great Attractor, are plotted and discernable. They are there if we can plot them. As we approach Alpha Centauri B and, by its proximity, Alpha Centauri A, if we pass close enough to a dark energy pathway, I want to tap into it and see if we can listen in on Regus or whomever. It may be our only chance to understand the dangers that await us all."

I had heard something out there during my EVA, a presence I was now sure could be there, and I was planning to listen in, closely. And just to prove how stupid I was, I had forgotten that only Apollo now could talk with Gaia. Hearing something and being able to know what the hell I was hearing were two different things.

# 16

## TIME TO SLOW DOWN

Cramer stopped by as I was finishing my recording and, not bothering to knock, entered and asked what I was working on. "And I know that look, Bank, you're up to something." So it was back to Bank instead of Simon. Cramer was slipping back into being the police officer, sensing danger. So I met him halfway.

"Cramer, Ralph, listen, I'm not up to anything. I will not do anything without your and Aten's approval first, okay?" He nodded but looked skeptical. "Hey, this is me, remember? Can't you trust me anymore?"

He walked over, took a weapon out of his pocket, and pointed it at me, "Sure. Now spill it."

I was shocked. On the one hand, there was the familiarity of Cramer pointing a weapon at me, and, on the other hand, wasn't it me that had saved him from the coma? And wasn't it me that got him and Aten—*Aha!* "Cramer, put that down. I love Aten too." He was putting the weapon away and changed his mind, so I responded, "No, not in that way, I am not in love with her. I love, trust, and will always be on the Path with her. You do not have to protect her from me, ever." He nodded. "Ever. I mean it."

He sank onto the edge of my bed, stuffed the weapon into a pocket, and said, "Sorry." The poor lunk was totally smitten. He raised his chin and looked at me, the Cramer stare of old, "But remember, I know how you've lied to me before, how you manipulated the System from inside, how you took an independent path without consulting and trusting me." I started to object. He raised a hand, "Yeah, I know, you came through, everything worked out, but I'd be stupid not to recognize the look on your face, devious and scheming. So spill it . . ." he paused. "Please."

"Okay, but hear me out, all the way, and tell me if I have made a mistake." So I explained my thinking, replayed parts of Apollo's message and then my message to Apollo that I planned to send shortly.

Cramer was shaken. It wasn't the danger that he could handle or perish trying, it was the enormity of the risk that had been undertaken without anyone guessing or even hinting at the danger we could be facing. It was one thing to face the dangers of interspace travel, the huge risks involved in navigation, energy, atmosphere, not to mention a hopeful planet fall—all these were without the specter of aliens, monsters, cognizant beings, or entities wanting to kill you. It was like a Greek mythological sea voyage—you're half way there and suddenly learn there are Kraken out to get you. Just what God were we going to pray to? There was none. None, at any rate we could rely on.

"So, you really believe Regus, or whomever, could act quickly, quickly enough to terminate us, all these people, all these friends?" He meant the friends, the animals, I knew.

"You know, I am not sure, but the risk, if we can be terminated quickly, is too great to disregard. Some of it depends on the way this Vast Pattern, this brain-like structure can work. That's the part I simply do not have enough information on.

131

And I would love to have Aten and Apollo guiding us, but I fear Aten, now as a human, cannot calculate without emotions and Apollo's response would be too far in the future. Who the hell else can we ask but ourselves—me?"

Cramer smacked his hands on his knees, stood, and said, "Sometimes you miss the obvious. First, we get Aten and repeat everything you know, said, did," he nodded his head at the recorder, "and second we go see Doc Todd. He's a neurosurgeon and neurobiologist. He should be able to help." He said all this while typing up a message to Aten on his sleeve. He called out "Hey Zip, can you come in here, please?"

Zip appeared, clearly he had been waiting in the corridor and looked up at Cramer. After a few seconds, he trotted off. Amazing, Cramer didn't even have to vocalize to Zip now.

Within five minutes, Zip returned with Aten, who sat, clearly wondering why we were meeting in my room. Cramer explained he wanted this to be private, off vid. Bedrooms didn't have open-access vids. Cramer looked at Zip, who plodded out into the corridor again.

The conversation went fine after Cramer finished angrily telling me off again to make sure Aten knew whose side he was really on. Being chastised actually helped Aten feel some sympathy for me since she knew Cramer was a foe to be reckoned with if and when he got angry. Seven years old or not, Cramer was still Cramer. I did note, however, that he neglected to tell Aten he pulled a weapon on me. I'd save that ammunition for later if he needed taking down a peg or two.

Aten agreed that Doc Todd was the logical next step. Zip was called in and Cramer scratched Zip's ears. Zip left following the orange path.

So we left my quarters, walking along the green path toward the medical area. Doc Todd wasn't in. His assistant, the lovely nurse Maryann, assured me that the other two experts under Doc Todd should be able to help, "with anything you need." I looked at Cramer and he nodded, sharing my thought. I knew then where Zip was.

Todd came running, "Zip said I had to come here fast."

"No real rush Doc," I said, "but is there any way to turn off the vids in here?"

He told Maryann to do so, citing medical priority. I continued, "We need tons of information and Cramer and I need to help Aten make a decision, well a set of decisions really, based on your knowledge of neurobiology."

He looked anxiously at each of our faces, "Who's ill?"

It took a few moments to get him settled down. Once Maryann fetched the other two doctors who were in the hospital somewhere, Doctors Rajman and Sing, we started in, again.

When I had finished explaining Dr. Tully's dark energy pathways, Apollo's Vast Pattern theory, and how the Vast Pattern mimicked the brain, it was actually Dr. Sing who felt we were onto something. Todd explained that Dr. Sing's specialty was neuro-microbiology, and she was studying the pathways of the brain and probably had better insight than either himself or Rajman. "And besides, Dr. Rajman is the expert of brain function and spinal nerve repair here. I'm the general neurosurgeon, and while each of our specialties overlaps, when it comes to this discussion, you want the specialist on the brain's pathways, I suspect." Todd was right.

I did need more brainpower on this problem, so I put a hand on Todd's arm and said, "Doc, I need your whole team, everyone in the know, no matter who is the best expert, I need thinking, imagination, exploration, if we're going to get through this."

"Why, what's at stake?"

"The life of everyone on board and, I suspect, life on Earth." The medical staff seemed shocked. I understood, they had been peacefully traveling for over 100 years and here I was, recently awake, and I was rocking their very peaceful existence.

Aten spoke up, addressing the four of them, Maryann included, "You save lives by evaluating trauma and remedy, offsetting one against the other, planning your response. What Apollo has told us in a transmission has caused Simon here to leap to a possible situation that could develop," I started to interrupt, "No, sorry, may have already started developing?" I nodded. "Okay, well, if he's right and we do not find out how the so-called brain design that we're dealing with operates or functions, we may never know what is in store for us and if we're simply seen as a virus or intruder into a finite system."

Todd spoke up, "Finite? You mean infinite don't you?"

So I broke it all down for them—consider the parallel universes, disregard the infinite, and think of the Vast Pattern as a brain matrix with neural pathways, ganglia, impulses, plexuses and purpose, design. They looked shocked. Sing jumped up and walked around the room. Maryann started to say something about it being impossible and Sing waved her to silence. Sing was deep in thought and she needed silence.

We sat, she paced, we waited. After a few minutes, she reached a wall and spoke to the plastic shell wall without turning around, "You people really have no idea what you have started. I have a headache." Looking pale, she turned to Maryann, "May I have some oxygen, please?" Maryann connected a nose mask to a wall outlet and turned it on as Sing took deep breaths. We waited.

When she was ready, she addressed us all, the nose mask making her sound as if she had a cold. "I need full schematics, this Dr. Tully's charts, hologram. Can do?" I nodded, as did

Aten. "Good, then I need both of you to work with me," she was looking at her colleagues, and she then focused her attention on Aten, "and I will need full access to the memory banks and the computing power on board." Aten nodded, smiled. "Oh, no, it's not that simple, do you have any idea how complicated this is? We're talking about my knowledge of about only ten to the tenth neurons and you are talking about many exponential magnitudes of that. You want my evaluation? This could take many lifetimes of study."

It was my turn to be the party-pooper again, "I don't think we have that long. I think we need to hide, as soon as possible before we are terminated."

Everyone in the room started speaking at once, but it was Cramer who cut to the chase, "Keeping something from us again Bank?"

"No, Cramer, not really, I'm not sure, but it is logical. If we, traveling here in the Vast Pattern, are in a brain, if that brain's protective systems . . ."

Rajman cut in, "That's my area, I can study that!" Todd and Sing nodded away.

"Okay," I continued, "If we're traveling with all this energy in a brain, we're leaving a signature that may trigger some sort of response because of the damage we may be doing . . ."

Rajman cut in again, "Yes, a counter impulse, or destruction of ganglia ahead of us or even destruction of target neurons to prevent infection—Yes, yes, infection, I understand . . ." he was getting excited.

"Doc Rajman, let's slow down a little here," I said asking for calm. "Okay, if, and I say if, we are visible to the Vast Pattern, if the Vast Pattern sees us as a threat, there should be, probably are, defensive systems in place. We need to evaluate as soon as possible how fast those systems can come into play. How large is the system we're traveling in as it relates to our visibility. After all, we are so insignificant that I doubt we're proportionately significant as even dark matter."

Aten weighed in, "Oh yes we are at this speed, the radiation energy signature would be visible, even from Earth by radio telescope arrays."

Doc Todd agreed, so did Cramer. I continued, "So let's assume we're visible; let's assume we're seen as an infection, to use Doc Rajman's terminology. Let's say that the Vast Pattern has a defense system, somewhere, somehow. Can it react in time and, even if we make planet fall, will a Gaia there get the message from Regus or Regus' boss that we're an infection and that it should terminate us there? Is the whole voyage for nothing?"

Cramer, standing now, abruptly pulled me to my feet, "So, genius, what do you propose we do?"

"Talk to the Vast Pattern and ask them, it, whomever, to leave us alone. And in the meantime, hide before they catch us."

Zip started whining.

# 17

## WHERE OH WHERE HAS MY LITTLE DOG GONE?

Zip wasn't happy. He stopped communicating. Cramer was worried, perhaps more worried about the dog than our predicament. "What did you say that upset him so?"

Of course, he felt it had to be my fault. Even so, I explained, "Not me. Zip's part of the crew, and he listened in, must have understood something, which worried him."

Cramer dismissed my hypothesis. He got on the floor, stuck his forehead on Zip's and, I guess, communicated. After a few moments, "Come on Zip ol' buddy, tell me, please."

"Not happy. Big danger. World in danger. Everyone killed." And there it was, his evaluation of our situation summed up neatly. This spaceship was his whole world, which was easy to understand. Zip was born aboard, he wouldn't have any understanding of Earth or the resilience of humankind to overcome wars, famine, catastrophes. Zip also was already pining for the demise of his people, everyone on board. It made him sad.

So I spoke up, putting my head closer, "Zip, look, we have a serious danger out there in space, the place that surrounds the home you know. But we're smart, we're never going to give up, and we will overcome." I sounded confident. And I was, I wasn't lying, well, maybe pushing it a bit, but Zip's spirits had to be lifted. I had seen how the dogs communicated all the time and how the children relied on them for affection. If Zip became morose, it could ripple through the ship. "But, Zip, I need your help. We cannot manage this alone, the humans without the dogs. Do you understand needing your help?"

I heard, "Yes help understand."

"Okay then, we will do the science and the handling of what needs to be done, but I need you, please, to take charge of keeping everybody happy, everybody calm while we try and solve this. Can you do that?"

"Yes people. Not worry."

"Exactly Zip, I do not want them—or you—to worry. We have a problem, but we can solve it. But to make the problem go away, we all need calm, normal living as if nothing is wrong."

"Explain all to all?"

"Okay, Zip; Aten, Cramer, and I will explain everything to the crew as soon as we know exactly what needs to be done, and then they will all have chores to do, things to help, study, plan. But it can be done in a happy way, on the Path, in harmony. That okay with you?"

"You ask?"

"I am asking for your help, yes."

Zip stretched, first one back leg then the other, gave a shake that started at his rump and moved up his spine until his ears were flopping. "Zip help. Zip work too." I thanked him and turned to the doctors, Nurse Maryann, and the married couple—Cramer, the little boy, holding Aten's hand, comforting her. I asked if they had heard Zip as I had and they all nodded, Doc Todd explained that he had never heard a dog project so clearly and so far. He looked somewhat amazed.

Heck, actually I was too. A dog had just agreed to handle the morale on board. And I knew he and his pals would do just fine. Of course, Zip had to have the last word, "I go fix. You work. Now."

"Yes, sir," and I saluted as Zip trotted off. I turned to Maryann, "Will you be the liaison between the docs here and me, Aten, and Cramer? I want to make sure we get their findings as they become available." She agreed. "So then, Docs, please start your research as soon as possible. Here are the three things I need to know, again as soon as possible. The rest of the research on the Vast Pattern can be done over the coming decades if we can survive the immediacy here and now. So don't go for the really big picture. What I need now are these: One, confirmation that the planets supporting bioforms, the ones downloading data, either at death or constantly, we're not sure which . . . confirmation that planets are like super neurons, then galaxies are like plexuses and the path of those galaxies, maybe even the solar systems, are like large and small ganglia. Would that make supergalaxy regions of the brain or merely larger plexuses?"

All three of them had started recorders to make sure they had accurate instructions. I put up a hand, "No playing those recordings for anyone until Aten says it's okay, right?" They nodded, "Good, okay, then two. I need a measurement of the strength of the transmission from human brain neurology data, one neuron to another, through ganglia, and then comparing the signal strength of the dark energy."

All three started to interrupt, with Sing stating, "That's the wrong question. Assuming there is a transmission within the Vast Pattern, we have data on the strength of dark energy, especially when it is focused. That was done if I remember . . ." she looked at Aten, "By Pope in eighty-three wasn't it?" Aten nodded. "So, if we determine the focused dark energy wavelength and couple that calculation with the known strength of focused radiation—assuming dark energy radiation levels are constant, again Pope I think—I'll assume you want to liken that to a neuron-to-neuron transmission, but I do not think that would be right. You explained, I assume from Apollo's study over the past years, that dark energy, when focused, never aims or passes near a planet or solar system. Right?" She nodded. "Good, then if those planets are your neurons—the transmission goes randomly toward Regus, which I think could be said to be your plexus. That would mean that planets are a primary nerve transmitter center and that Regus is a primary nerve-receiving center. If there are no physical pathways, I am beginning . . ."

Her voice faded and she faced a wall again and spoke softly, almost to herself, "Just a minute . . ." She turned to her colleagues, "Could we be talking about a nervous system, a primitive brain such as jellyfish? Effective, amorphous, fluid, just one large nerve network without boundaries?"

Rajman was suddenly animated, "Yes, yes, that fits. The nervous systems, the symmetric organisms of the oceans, among the longest surviving species. All radically symmetric, all with diffuse nerve networks. But I think more like the hydra, not a simple jellyfish, don't you think Sing?"

Sing agreed, nodding vigorously.

"Okay then, assume we're talking about a primitive, radically symmetric structure here. That would allow for small signals to travel from neuron to neuron or be routed with ganglia, arranged in a fluid net, using the very internal space of the jellyfish, the very make-up of the jellyfish's substance as a fluid dynamic pathway. In short, infinite ganglia, nothing mapped out."

Todd cut in, "That makes your planet theory wrong. The computing power of a neuron, inside a neuron, has not been sufficiently mapped, there has been no need. But assume all the bioforms are that internal neuron process. That makes Gaia a neuron host, a super-neuron if you will, transmitting—for no known reason—data to or via Regus, who acts as . . ."

Sing cut in, "Simply a neuronal fluid dynamic pathway. Dark energy is not a thing, a sentient being that Gaia is talking to. Gaia is talking to or through something called Regus through dark energy, the jelly inside a jellyfish. Regus is not dark energy, yes, it all fits."

As we all looked back and forth at each other, Todd summed it up, "Regus is, simply, beyond dark energy, controlling the whole transmission process. Regus is the hydra cortex."

Well, bang goes my theory asked of the nav team to determine when we would be near a dark energy transmission, we were sitting in a jellyfish of dark energy. I was about to start repeating my second request when it hit me, "Of course! That's why I heard something, space was all around me, dark energy was all around me, I don't need a pathway to hear inside a jellyfish, all space is dynamic for dark energy transmissions, all of space reverberates with transmissions." I grabbed Sing's lab coat as she walked past, "Would you say that a jellyfish's dynamic ganglia is no pattern at all, that any message transfer goes everywhere at once?"

She answered, "We may have the study data in the records, but I think so, yes. The neuron message is encoded—like it has an address label—for another specific neuron or the plexus and only that neuron or plexus will open the message. But, yes, the message would be bounced everywhere without effect until it reached its intended destination. Perhaps that is why a jellyfish seems aimless in the ocean because its momentary reaction is delayed, but we do know they navigate by the stars and magnetic headings, making tiny constant adjustments in currents, for example. They are complex, but seemingly simple, creatures."

Aten stopped the conversation with a command, "Hold! Simon, *what did you hear*?"

I felt like I had been caught with my hand in the cookie jar and hung my head in shame. "During the EVA, when I was drifting back in, I thought I heard a presence, an intelligence, maybe a voice. I didn't understand it, but it reminded me, sorry Aten, it reminded me of our first conversations deep inside the System."

"And you didn't think to share that? Just when were you going to return to the Path Simon?" Aten was furious. I needed to placate her.

"Honestly, Aten, until these last few hours, I thought I had imagined it in my hypoxia state. Now it began to fit, first Apollo's transmission . . ." The doctors looked at each other and Aten questioningly, "and then some hypothesis I was formulating. That's why we're here, to try to piece all this together. I'm on the Path, I assure you, but things are moving so damn fast I don't know what's been said and to whom."

Aten shook her head, "Okay, let's finish your list for these doctors and then we can begin to prepare a full disclosure for the whole crew. We live together and we need to be on the Path to survive together. The only way to do that is to remain on the Path at all times."

Here was the apprentice telling the master, reversing the roles. Aten was in charge and she was right. In my defense, as I explained later to Cramer and Aten over dinner, I really was working toward that goal, telling everyone. Cramer backed me up, but I could see not having told him of the little voices, as Cramer referred to them, had lost me some respect and trust.

So, before we left to go to Aten's office to have her tell me off again and also prepare a tell-all vid transmission to all the crew, I finished explaining the last of my three requests to the doctors. The final one could be a simple matter for neurobiologists: Could they adapt a data helmet, like the one that was stored aboard in case they needed to record my identity again, could they adapt that one to the frequency of dark energy?

# 18

## A WHOLE NEW SYSTEM TO TALK TO

It took six hours for the nav team to discover what I had hoped for, an asteroid belt orbiting way out, around Alpha Centauri B, "But we have no idea what the size of those asteroids will be. We'll only know when we get within five hundred thousand kilometers."

Then it took two hours to convince Aten and the crew that hiding amongst the asteroids instead of immediate planet fall would be best. The asteroid belt was way out past the seventh planet and, once our engines were reduced to initial pulling power and not the great speed we currently had, it could add four years to planet fall. I did not explain that it could be more than that, as I had no idea if we would ever be able to leave the asteroid belt.

If hiding worked and nothing else did, life could continue aboard. If the Vast Pattern or its operator, whatever it was, took a dim view of us, it would not want us landing on Angelica. Staying put in space, hiding out, might be our only option for life.

Aten was way ahead of me. Of course. Actually, it was good to see her a little less goo-goo eyed over Cramer and using her considerable intellect again. Cramer, on the other hand, was feeling left out as planet fall was his responsibility and delaying or perhaps never getting there, well, that was a bitter pill for him to swallow. He told me so in no uncertain terms, poking my chest with his little fingers, "Fix this Simon, fix it, you're it, damn it. You came up with this hare-brained scheme to talk to the thing out there, you had better be sure you are not simply making them aware of something they had no idea was around."

The thought had occurred to me.

When I had first been a System coder, I was not surprised to see all sorts of messed up code when I was diving in System. That was my job, to go in and fix things other coders had set as traps and deliberate errors. My job was to change coding from within the System's computer matrix. The whole idea was that in fixing deliberate errors, the system would adapt to more human foibles, thereby refining programs meant to suit humans better.

So, I wore a data helmet, turned on the interface and, presto, I was inside the brain, inside the systems, all the coding, FAT files, pathways, library, everything visible to me. I had only to think of where I wanted to check something and I could drift there instantly. Of course, my body stayed on the stool in my office, maybe a maximum of ten minutes at a time, but inside the system seemed like hours. Eventually, I stayed inside too long and my internal clock, the nerve synapse, was recalibrated to a faster speed, and I couldn't sustain human pace without taking Slo-doze pills. That's why Angie and I had relocated to space. At least there we could be speeded up together, free from gravity effect on fast moving body parts.

Anyway, inside the System I had learned that the errors I found were not put there by other coders but were manipulations by the System itself—part of its becoming self-aware. Peter was born who then became Apollo and Ra, in an amoebic-like split. And eventually Ra became Aten in a SynthKid body.

What I hoped for now was not another discussion and birth of a new life form. One of those in one's life was enough for anybody! No, what I wanted was merely to listen in, to try to understand if this thing, the Vast Pattern, had heard of or could spot us. If not, then we could proceed to Angelica and planet fall.

But first, we had to hide, out of a sense of precaution. Better to be safe than sorry.

Over the next six weeks, the nav team, working feverishly with Aten, managed a slingshot course to go around Alpha Centauri A's sun, which started to point us right at the asteroid belt of Alpha Centauri B. Time to land or at least come to a halt in the asteroid belt? Estimated at five-plus months. The crew was not happy with the delays and change of plans, but they had, much to their credit, evaluated our prognosis of danger and concurred with the necessity. Zip and his team kept morale up, mainly by playing with the kids. Happy kids kept parents happy. Everybody was busy.

I had little to do except think and worry, so I took on the task of working with two maintenance men to construct the new space suits. Using cannibalized parts from the existing suits we had used, like the cuff collars and helmet collars, we managed to make twelve suits that were fairly robust. I was sure they could take an EVA with little worry—except for fast moving particles, should there be any. There was no way to build in a woven graphene layer to make them particle-proof. If they were needed, we'd just have to be careful outside. And I was getting this nagging feeling that I, at any rate, would be wearing one.

The greatest challenge for Aten and the Nav crew was that we only had so much thruster fuel on board. Use that consumable up and there would never be planet fall. So the "hiding opera-tion" as it became known, posed a serious challenge for plotting a course. Aten was determined to achieve the braking and inser-tion into orbit around a yet-to-be-determined asteroid without using any thrusters, except in an emergency. She was convinced that our past emergency, when we needed to clear number one engine, had trained us for drastic course alteration. Besides, as she said, "The graphene tethers were not brittle, so we can allow for even greater deviation, at least to thirty degrees if needed. We'll steer her without the thrusters, I am pretty sure."

The slowing down of the ship went off easier than I had thought. As we approached Alpha Centauri A, we were going at eighty percent of the speed of light, and we actually accelerated as we neared the sun, but the nav team plotted an elliptical path using Sir Oliver Lodge's "gravitational lens" effect when passing near a star or sun, skipping wide of the sun going in, swinging around the sun twice and then skipping off, coming close on egress, the sun's gravity pull slowing our speed dramatically. Engines on idle, we were relentlessly pulled by the sun's gravita-tional field as we transited that solar system further slowing our great speed. When we emerged out of that solar system and into Alpha Centauri B's outer boundaries, we were doing less than 40,000 kilometers per hour, but soon a burst of the engines as they found dark matter on the fringes of those two solar systems over a few weeks got us back to 120,000 kilometers per hour as we aimed for the largest segment arc of the asteroid belt, spotted on radar.

It took three more weeks to make that last transition into orbit around a rock the size of Earth's moon. Navigation was tricky. Aten was at the controls the whole time, sleeping in weightless-ness, less than twenty minutes a day. It required all her intel-lect to make the non-thruster steering system work. She used a parabola course, absorbing the gravity deflections of successive asteroids as we drifted, making very slight course adjustments with number one and number two engines and relying on deflection of the graphene tethers at the slow speeds we were progressively doing. When we got down under 4,000 kilometers per hour, the moon-sized asteroid held us in an elliptical orbit and the pilots called down throughout the ship to say, "Orbit achieved, four hundred plus year duration, we're now taking teams of five in rotation to peer through forward windows. PowerCube engaged for rotational spin, please conserve energy. Doctors to the forward flight deck."

Aten was exhausted and throwing up. In Zero-G, she could choke because water formed large bubbles that jammed airways. Cramer rushed forward and took control, cradling Aten and talking to her inert form. She was breathing, fast asleep, as confirmed by Doc Todd. Cramer held her and carried her back into the gravity environment to their quarters. Aten slept for two days, and she was cheered by everyone aboard, me included, when she showed up for her first meal. We had all watched her fortitude at the helm. The intelligence of the ship's crew, down to the youngest child, understood her superior brilliance and dedication.

People went forward over the next three days to peer out the window at the asteroid. Cramer and Aten named the moon-sized asteroid after Zip since the asteroid had a faint halo around it from outgassing of billion-year-old water vaporized from rock pockets every time the asteroid turned to face the sun. The sight of that halo reminded us all, well those of us who had been on Earth, of a Dog Moon, so Zip's Rock it was.

Engines were now set at almost idle. And yet they were having some trouble staying lit since there was not much material ingested at this speed, even though there was plenty of small debris in the asteroid belt. The halo material of the gas given off by the asteroid was considered enough, however, to keep them ready, on low standby, or so the pilots and engine crew told me. Aten confirmed their findings. Everyone felt we were safe in an orbit duration of a half day from faint light to dark, drifting around Zip's Rock.

However, amidst that general crew relief and ease, Cramer's increasing frustration at the delay in getting to Angelica was worrying me and, it seemed, also Aten, who came to see me. I was in my room, asleep on top of papers spread out over every surface including the bed. The papers were blueprint drawings of the last parts for the spacesuit modifications. I hadn't slept well for a few weeks by then, worried about insertion around the asteroid without using up all our consumables. When I got the good news, I started to relax and was frequently falling asleep at the strangest moments.

Standing in my open doorway, Aten called out, "Simon, wake up please, I need to speak with you while Cramer is in the gym . . ."

I was groggy and seeing the earnest look on her face, made me immediately think she wanted to have the "talk," the one about physical intimacy—"Aten, can't this wait?" She stamped a foot, a very pretty Meg Ryan foot and pouted. I gave in. "Okay, where do you want to start?"

"Start? Me? No, you need to start. Stop," she waved her hands around my room, "fussing with those suits, the maintenance crew can finish those. You need to start talking to the Vast Pattern and find out how long we're going to be stuck here."

"Oh, so no sex talk?" I countered, getting up and trying to inch past her to get my shirt, stepping over papers and material samples pinned to paper blueprints.

"Behave, and keep your prurient thoughts to yourself."

"Sure Meg, oops, sorry, Aten . . ." She swung a fist at me as I ducked. "Okay, okay—have a look, on the hook, on the door jamb . . ."

She slid the door back into place and turned seeing the space helmet on the hook, "Yes, so it's a helmet . . ." she paused, suddenly seeing the thick wires protruding, hanging out of the back inside the dome. "You modified this space helmet into a data dome? But why? Surely you are not planning to hook up outside the ship?" She glared at me, getting angry, "Are you?"

I felt it was time for this almost eleven-year-old to clear the air, "Aten, Ra, Peter, can we remember who we both are? You are a genius, you are now a fully-fledged woman. But this is me, the guy who knows how to do this, had been doing this when you were spanked awake, all right?" She nodded, hearing my tone of authority. "So, understand this, I know how to make that damn dome work, the docs made the frequency modification— which I think will be all right because we tested it here, inside the ship. And no, I didn't connect to the Vast Pattern yet. And always remember, I understand what it feels like to plunge into a system and deal with code, programming, and transmission of data. I can do that. What I cannot do is connect to an unknown entity from within a ship without Vast Pattern interface present. In short, I heard it out there, the frequencies are out there, and out there I must go."

"But who is going to connect you, and to what?"

"Angie. She's outside in the jelly of the hydra, if you see what I mean. Angie is going to act as an antenna. When I heard the presence I was locked tight onto the electrical cables, semi-conscious admittedly, but my hands were gripping tightly and my head, inside the helmet, was hunkered down firmly pressed onto the cables. The docs agree, the cables were connected to the outer skin of one small portion of the ship. If

I can get to Angie's skin—Angie's skin that has a huge surface area exposed to . . . in contact with . . . dark energy. Angie will be the antenna."

# 19

## ONCE MORE INTO THE BREACH . . .

I needed another week and a half to get everything ready. During that time, I trained and finally fitted Cramer for a spacesuit. I had, of course, allowed him to bully me into the joint EVA. I had always secretly planned for him to accompany me, but allowing him to think he was pushing me into the decision, made it all his idea in his mind, and that's what mattered. Okay, firstly, I really had no urge to be out there on my own. Here I was near an asteroid and all the memories that that history played in my mind. And secondly, who else needed activity, physical activity, hell, call it what it was, "Action!" on board more than Cramer? So while I was posturing that he forced me into it, secretly I was glad to have him out there. I really didn't want to be alone near or on an asteroid again.

Just to placate everyone, especially Aten, I donned the dome inside the medical unit, and they connected the sets of wires to the outer hull behind one of the plastic panels, starting with the eight primary wires to be connected and then following up with the full set. Nothing. No "sight," no presence, nada. Todd was not surprised. "The hull coating inside is meant to insulate us, isolate us from space, hold pressure. It forms a barrier. We dare not penetrate that shell. Simon is right. It has to be outside if he's to hear anything."

Aten was not entirely happy with the risks we were taking. She supervised our EVA preparations, communication procedures, and, lastly, insisted that Sam and Ernest be backup, fully suited and ready to go outside to rescue Cramer and, oh yes, then she remembered, me. I laughed at her when she clumsily tacked that on. She hit my arm, again. I was wondering where she got the idea that I liked being hit on the arm. She had been doing it before Cramer woke from his coma, so it wasn't he who had taught her. "Aten, what's with the arm punching? You never seem to punch anyone else."

She barked a little laugh, "They might hit back." Then she smiled, broadly. "Besides I promised Angie I'd keep you in check."

It was the first time she had ever said that. Angie had appointed Ra to be my babysitter? Before Ra became Aten? "And how was Ra supposed to do that?"

She laughed again, "Apollo and I discussed it," she was giggling now, "and as we were used to helping your mental process anyway . . ." yeah, yeah, they had loved to tease me, I remembered that perfectly well. "We already found that a little jolt now and then would come in handy. Cramer agrees." He was laughing now too, "Once I awoke as Aten, I thought it would be more fun to jolt your senses with a fist." And with that, she gave me a hug, being careful with my nose at her chest height, and kissed the top of my head.

While they were having fun at my expense, I was still having a problem. I had squeezed the dome and all the cranium connections into the helmet. I had tested it with the ship's computer and found that I could engage the programs I carried—memorized, left-brain, little sub-routines that I found copies of in the onboard memory files. One I had once used to turn all the tomatoes in the FarmHands Agrarian system blue. It had caused quite a stir by effectively acting as a swap routine, one color for another, one DNA splice for another. It was a substitution program, quite clean, that left the FAT file size and processor's clock timing identical to what it replaced. It did that with a little fill-in program that I had also written to fool what I thought were other coders in the System and to have them think nothing had been touched. I prepared these little tools and a few others for the EVA expedition, well, mainly because they were part of my old armament within the System and they gave me confidence. I suspected Cramer carrying a weapon was along the same psychological lines. Or was that pathological? I decided not to analyze that, for now.

Anyway, although the dome worked fine, squashed into the helmet as it was, it had two problems I had so far failed to resolve. Once the dome/helmet was put on, I could not turn my head, my vision was straight ahead, eye movement only. In a spacesuit where the helmet doesn't rotate, you have to turn your whole body to see something off to the left or right, up or down. I was glad Cramer would be out there with normal visibility.

The other issue facing me was more serious. Although Abadine had managed to stitch a small opening in the spacesuit, into which she blue Loc'ed three donut magnets for triple redundancy, through which she could pass the helmet wires and then inject ferrofluid, which would seal the opening—although we had achieved all that, the question remained: What was I going to hook up to? There was no System or computer interface outside the hull and, anyway, hooking up to the ship's computer had already provided no Vast Pattern contact. I had secretly hoped it would—no such luck.

In discussing this with Aten and Abadine, we again all agreed that Angie's exterior skin of the ship would, could be the antenna. Okay, but what would the wire sequence be? There were over forty wires to hook up, but to what, where? Tests in the medical lab didn't prove anything useful.

We were stumped. Cramer simply said, "Well, let's try something." And so we did, making twelve different schematics on what pattern to attach to the hull and how. All the attachment plans involved glue because there was no way else to attach to Angie's super smooth outer skin. An additional problem was that blue Loc was UV activated so we had to take a UV light along with us as the sun was too dim and could be behind the asteroid we were orbiting. That UV light had to be added to our EVA gear, which was getting cumbersome.

Oh, and one thing was clear, roping ourselves to the hand-hold rail by the pressure hatch under the flight deck was not "out there alone" enough to mimic the space around me or have access to Angie's skin—to have what I had experienced before. We had to travel down the spinning hull that was to be my interface antenna—if I could get there.

Spinning inside the hull was centripetal force, pushing you toward the inside skin of the ship. But outside, that was centrifugal force, flinging you off the ship into deep space. Angie's skin was super smooth, no handholds, no cleats, nothing, a mirror finish. It was Abadine who came up with a solution, "The orange path runs down the length of the ship, right? So, you go outside, tethered with a strong magnet, say with a mass of maybe forty kilos, and find the highest point at the beginning of the orange path on the inside of the skin from where you are outside. I'll be there. Meanwhile, inside I get your signal that you've picked up the stronger magnet that I'll pull along the orange route and all you have to do is hold on, we'll tow you along the orange path to the mid-ship point. Once there, you can use the magnets, inside and out, unmoving, as an anchor." We all agreed it was so damn simple it was likely to work. So, Abadine went back to the mechanic's shop and prepared a dense magnet core with a plastic rod through the middle and a lanyard attached to each end that we could clip onto, like a big baking rolling pin for us to use outside. It reminded me of those old water-skiing towrope bar handles, only much, much thicker.

Abadine adapted a handcart to carry a 100-kilo magnet that, we were confident enough, would work through Angie's thin ship skin. Testing her huge magnet and the rolling pin—*clunk*—and we could not get them apart. It took a while, but we managed it with three people pulling on each side. Seeing that, I was doubly sure the magnets would work and keep us safe.

Cramer added a refinement, he'd tow and belay a graphene rope for us to use if we failed to get from the lower flight deck platform to the beginning of the orange path on the spinning hull. And he also made Abadine make up a second magnet and "glue it to the beginning of the orange path so that I can leave the spool in place. We can't take it with us or it'll wrap around the hull at a wide point. But at the beginning of the orange path, the narrow end, it will unwind and hopefully it should be usable when we get back." *Should be?* That had me worried already.

The schematics for dome wire attachments were done with Doc Sing's help, trying to determine a possible configuration based on neuron, ganglia, and plexus designs from various species. The hydra jellyfish brain pattern was the one Sing felt had the best chance. "If you get out there and attach to anything, start with this one but be careful to do it one wire at a time . . ."

"I can't do that Doc, I cannot connect, go into a system with only one wire. Okay, the harness I used in System was only eight primary wires. I only needed eight if all else failed, but this dome is for total retrieval of brain function and memory and has more than forty wires. Eight are critical, the primary ones like before, so maybe we should only do those?"

Sing was shaking his head, "I think you should hook up the eight first, I agree, and turn them all on at one time, but then Cramer can continue to add more and more according to the schematic. At some point, you should get a reading, hear something as you put it. By the time you get all forty connected, the pattern should look like this . . ." He clicked on our portable projector light onto the wall, and it showed what looked like a one-meter wide snowflake, each point with a number.

"Okay, we'll do one EVA starting with the hydra pattern and see how it goes, hell, if we can even get hooked up."

The next day we were ready. The crew sent vid messages of good luck as Cramer and I were suited up in the Zero-G environment of the lower flight deck. Utility belts were festooned with all sorts of tethers and lights, as well as clips and pouches (mine had the blue Loc). Cramer had an extra bag, but I didn't know what was in it. Floating before the hatch, we watched as Sam finished putting on his suit. We all had enough oxygen for three hours now via a hard plastic backpack the maintenance people and I had designed, containing little graphene-wrapped canisters super-pressurized to three thousand kilos per square centimeter as well as a backup VHF radio in case the primary ones in the helmets failed. Communication was critical for our survival out there.

In my helmet, I heard, "Ready to go?" Cramer taking command. I replied with an okay hand signal and we entered the hatch together. Cramer had to guide me because I could not see anything except straight ahead. The hatch closed behind us and I heard a slight hissing and then silence. When he opened the outer hatch, we were staring down at the asteroid, sunny

PETER RIVA

side facing us, we were in the shadow of the very faint sunlight from Alpha Centauri B. I could see the puffs of mist coming off the surface and recognized the tell-tale signs of a rough hunk of rock, without atmospheric protection, that had taken meteor and cousin-asteroid collision-beatings for a few billion years. There were dust bowls and a few craters but mostly glistening rock faces where something had cleaved clean shards to shine in the sun.

If anything looked uninviting, asteroids are it. We both switched on one helmet light of the four we each had.

Weightless, the roller pin magnet was quickly tethered to both Cramer's belt and mine. I felt him attach it and tap my helmet, as I could not look down. Cramer carried a thin spool of graphene rope attached to his belt, maybe millimeters thick, that he ran through the cleat near the hatch, a cleat I remembered well, and then back to his belt. So, I was attached to Cramer and he was attached to the ship, the graphene was belaying automatically off the spool attached to his belt. I focused on that security, not the abyss before me.

Holding on below the flight deck, Cramer motioned that we had to make the jump from our non-rotating platform, across over fifty meters of space to the junction with the hull. We had discussed moving slowly down the non-rotating swivel tube junction to the start of the ship proper and inching out from there. I wanted to go slowly. Cramer insisted that the tether was our security and, besides, he had engineering make a small gas pistol to propel him if we veered off course. The planned jet packs weren't ready and didn't seem likely to be. They used too many consumables. All we had was Cramer's little gas gun that would propel us to the hull. He waved it in front of my visor, trying to reassure me.

I knew he wasn't wrong or foolhardy, of course. The non-rotating cylinder attaching the ship to the lower flight deck

158

coupled with a swiveling bearing to the ship. But inside the ship, the distance from the opening of the cylinder to the beginning of the orange path was more than seventy meters along the slope of the ship. In order to get from our platform to the beginning of the orange path, we had to travel fifty meters across open space and hope to hit the orange path point on the curved outside of the hull and hook up the magnets. Miss and we'd bounce off with nothing to grab onto. We'd have to tow ourselves, hand over hand, back to the platform using Cramer's thin rope.

The trick was to make the jump with the rolling-pin magnet held out front and to time the jump so that we would land on that orange path target where Abadine would have the huge magnet waiting. Then hold on for dear life as the rotating hull would snap us around quickly.

Inside the suits, we were talking back and forth. Inside, I had agreed to try Cramer's leap, but now that I was out here, I wanted no part of it. He was insistent and pointing, "How the hell are we going to lock the magnets if we don't get over there?"

"Sure, get there, miss the target, and we'll bounce off into space or down toward the surface."

"I have the spool of graphene, we're not going anywhere."

"Yeah, but we can't use it when we process down the hull because the hull is spinning and it'll wind up the whole spool in no time." The graphene would wrap around the spinning hull quickly.

"Look, Bank," he was back to Bank again, probably frustrated at my indecision, "We have been through all this. Stop being so afraid. We will get over there, and the magnets will lock on, I'll retrieve the graphene," he showed me, assuring me it was all okay, that one end was attached to his belt, the graphene running through a karabiner attached to the cleat by the airlock hatch and on to the spool. I knew all this. He was still trying to calm my nerves, "And I'll leave the whole thing there with this magnet," he pointed to the top of the spool where Abadine had blue Loc'ed a magnet. "Remember the magnet Abadine has Loc'ed to the beginning of the orange path? That way it'll be there for our return and will tell us where to go. I'll latch the spool safely, don't worry. It's okay, really. We'll just allow the rolling magnet to grab hold, swap one security for the other. Get it? It'll work, come on, we planned this!"

I was scared, so I vented some anger, "Why the hell didn't they leave handholds along the hull? Damn stupid design anyway."

"You should know, didn't you do an original design with Apollo? Come on Simon, let's give it a try." He was brave, I knew that, but he also did have a point, the graphene spool would work to save us if we missed.

The porthole in the hatch was beneath us now as we moved up the flight deck collar so we could have a clean line of sight to the start of the hull. Cramer was waiting for the flickering of a red light Sam would flash in the porthole that would tell him when the orange path was in line with the porthole. Inside I knew Abadine and Aten were relaying cues to Sam, "Almost, here it comes, now!"

Cramer started timing the intervals, the ship rotated, and suddenly he warned me, "twelve seconds to jump, nine, eight, seven, six, five, four, three, two, one—jump." And we did.

And missed three times.

Each time he caught our freefall with the tether, slender as it was, and he hauled us back in, re-spooling the graphene. The disorientation, flailing about in the empty space, was horrible. That's the only thing I felt, terror, trying to catch a glimpse of his hands on the tether, hoping he had not let go.

With my limited mobility and vision, I was getting really

disoriented and progressively more scared. The last time we bounced off the hull—when the magnet seemed to grab and then slipped off and we spun wildly further than before into space. I was worried Cramer had hit his helmet that time on the ship.

He had but told me it was fine. "No cracks yet Simon. Relax." He wasn't allowing time for more cold feet. "Simon, you okay for one more try? Here it comes, this time with ten—eight, seven, six, five, four, three, two, one, jump!" And we did and when the magnet hit the hull, it twisted ninety degrees and spun us along with it, crashing into one another, and then we were flattened against the hull as it too whipped us about as centrifugal force tried to throw us off.

But the magnet held. That's all I cared about as I tried to catch my breath.

Cramer called down to the ship, "Abadine, we're attached. I will re-spool and am about to let go of the graphene, attaching the spool to the deck magnet, everything is okay. Tell me when you are ready to roll, but let us catch our breath please, one minute." Cramer being so polite had me worried. Either he wasn't stressed at all or he was trying to make believe he wasn't scared. Then I figured it out—it was Aten, he didn't want to worry her.

Cramer got busy letting the graphene end attached to his belt free, and I saw it snake away following the slope of the hull and then reappear and shoot off into the dark back toward the flight deck. Seconds later, it came shooting back to Cramer as he finished re-spooling, winding it up. When he had retrieved the free end, he pushed the spool toward the hull, moving it around until it seemed to snap into position. Cramer gave it a few tugs and gave me a thumbs-up. I heard him tell Abadine we were ready. I wasn't, but, oh hell . . .

Suddenly, the magnet spun ninety degrees again and that caused us to whip about once more.

People have this idea that space is like being under water. It isn't. Sure, you can train for Zero-G underwater, but the lack of any resistance in Zero-G and no atmosphere is completely alien to a gravity-bred creature once you step into the void. I had lived with Angie inside in Zero-G long enough to be accustomed to the up, down, side to side, orientation. What I could not get used to out in open space was the concept of nothing—and I mean nothing—to attest your fall, jump, movement—nothing at all. Move your arm and your legs started moving in the opposite direction. Turn your head and it moved halfway, and your torso moved a little the other way. Everything is exaggerated, everything throws you seriously off-kilter. And there is nothing you can grab, touch, or use to steady your movements. And a spacesuit makes you even more clumsy at that.

Back in the old days, astronauts had to be foot-locked onto a work platform, or wear a jetpack to maintain control outside the ship. Stay inside for a year or more? Sure, easy, grab on to something. But try staying free of any hold outside in space for a few hours. The Russians found it messed with the Cosmonauts' heads, so they made them wear strong, bulky tethers, more for psychological impact than need.

We only had this stupid, thin, graphene string. That's what it was really. Calling it a tether seemed, to me, kind of a sick joke. Okay, I knew it had more than a 4,000-kilo tensile strength, but it was only this tiny, teeny, string for heaven's sake. And Cramer had let it go. *Oh, great . . .*

Suddenly, the magnet started up the slope of the hull. Even though the strap to the end of the rolling-pin magnet was only a meter long, the play in that coupled with our momentum and moment of force, well, we were banging about like feathers in the wind. There wasn't any wind, of course, but the thought occurred just the same—if there was a wind we'd be blown away.

The ship's hull was spinning us around. First, there was the asteroid beneath us, then it disappeared from view and there was only black sky, and then the sun filled my visor like a distant light bulb. As the magnet progressed rolling along the outside of the hull, with Cramer and Abadine in constant communication, I drifted mentally, trying to hear anything, anything at all.

Nothing. So far.

As the ship passed behind the asteroid in orbit, we reached the mid-ship point, Abadine confirmed. Cramer steadied himself like a water-skier, feet on the hull, one hand holding the magnet tether watching me and beyond me nothing but blackness all around. "Feels like standing on your head." The centrifugal force was pushing the blood to his head. He reached up and turned on the rest of his helmet lights. The sight of Angie's hull skin was frightening. Pockmarked, scratched, dented in places, scorched (or at least it looked scorched with black sooty streaks that I could scuff with my gloved hand), Angie's hull had held for over 100 years. Bless it. Bless her.

It was time to get going. I illuminated the graphic portable projector Aten had rigged with Doc Sing and handed it to Cramer. He shone it down onto the hull off to one side of the magnet, and it clearly projected snowflake schematic one, labeled "Hydra." Coiled on my belt, I unfastened the extension to the dome wire harness and drifting against only the waist tether because I needed both hands, I reached into the pouch for the blue Loc. Placing the first wire onto the deck meant wiping off the dust or soot, whatever that was, dropping some blue Loc onto the ship's skin, putting the blue Loc away safely, putting the wire end into the blue Loc drop, reaching for the UV flashlight with my other hand, turning it on, and solidifying the blue Loc.

I had practiced. I was good at this. But that was irrelevant. Nothing would hold. Nothing would glue. The blue Loc drifted off the skin with the centrifugal force. If I hit it with the UV light, it solidified all right, but not attached to the hull. I twisted my body to look up at Cramer. He touched his helmet to mine, no radio, "Let's get back in and rethink this." As he was beginning to radio Aten and Abadine, I cut him off.

"I have something I want to try, now that we're out here." Cramer started to say that I should not improvise, but I silenced him with a flat palm in front of his visor. "Look, we're going to ask Abadine to roll another ten centimeters, just a minute." I spread the primary eight wires, slender gold wires no thicker than a piece of paper, in a neat row in back of the rolling pin and keyed my radio. "Abadine, I need an exact roll, no more, no less please, just ten centimeters backward, easy and slow. Now please."

The rolling pin moved and mounted the slender wire ends. And held. Held us, held the wires in place. With my limited vision floating close to the wire ends, I could only watch the wires. I didn't see Cramer above me, but I heard him, "Simon, the crazy damn fool he's using the magnet as a clamp. Let's hope that works. If the magnet comes off, we're sunk."

Aten was yelling in desperation. I turned off the radio, reached for the extension connector with my suit helmet dome wires sticking out of the Ferrofluidic seal, and snapped the connection in place.

And turned on a whole new existence.

# 20

## HELLO?

It wasn't as if I had not expected the plunge, the descent into a matrix of programming and structure delineated only by electrical pathways. That didn't surprise me. Apollo, in talking with Ra and Gaia had uncovered that Gaia was working in octal, not binary. I had prepared myself for this. That wasn't a surprise. What did surprise me was the simplicity, the purity all around me. There seemed to be no function, no purpose to what I saw. What I saw, I could easily interact with, study, even manipulate if I wanted to, one *if* for a *what if*, one octal code for another. Sure, octal was more complicated to construct than binary, but it was so compact, so pure in comparison to binary that it seemed almost, well, superior. And yet, what function I could determine, what purpose these codings had, seemed to be nothing, no purpose, no function. They simply were.

I mentally sent a command to travel deeper, just to the next code junction, and was stopped. There was nothing physically holding me, of course, but my "go to" command seemed limited to what I first saw, everything I could see before me, not anything beyond that vision. It was like being in a crowd, knowing there are people and objects out of view, but you cannot go there. And what was before me was pure, yes, but ultimately unrevealing.

I had learned, working in System all those years ago, that I could make a mirror image of myself with one of my little programs. I did so. It vanished. I thought that perhaps the problem was that I was not able to access the FAT table, if there was one, to tell it the mirror image belonged. Sort of like telling the library card system there's an extra book on a shelf, relax. I tried again and as it appeared, it disappeared.

*Octal, idiot.*

Using a right brain and left brain sorting technique I had long since mastered, I rewrote an identifier preamble to my program from binary to octal, instructing the octal portion of this system to follow instructions to allow the program to run as a subset in binary, giving results in octal. In short, I told it to translate and act upon the translation as if it had all been written in octal. It took me a long time, it seemed, but I managed it. I initiated the new mirror and presto there I was, a duplicate mirror image, moving exactly mirrored to me. Okay, there was no physical likeness of Simon Bank in here. All I could see were energy aura movements that I was making with my pseudo projections of my hands. What I moved inside here, the mirror image moved corresponding pieces in the same way, but backward.

I gave the mental command to go forward and suddenly I did. I knew the mirror image went backward. Balance. Everything had to be in balance. Dr. Tully's image of the two supergalaxies plunging toward the Great Attractor is what gave me the idea. Two huge supergalaxies perfectly mirrored the one of the other. Balance.

Inside, if I could maintain balance in all that I explored, I should be able to proceed. *Slowly, Simon, slowly. Careful.*

Talking to myself—always did that when under stress.

The question was, now that I'm in here, what do I want to do, or where do I want to go? No one is talking to me, so either it, they, don't know I am here or I am not in the right place. I had no idea what question to ask, where to go to find out, or who to ask. So I did what any child does, and what I had done inside the System all those years ago.

"Hello?"

Suddenly my head hurt. The sound, no vibration, was deafening. I thought it would kill me any second. Then the volume seemed to be decreasing, lower, lower, and even lower until I could hear a rhythm and then clipped sounds, ringing, and what I can only describe as chirping. I had no way of recording any of this. I wasn't in the lab hooked up to any recorders, no one was monitoring me in here, I was all alone with perhaps the first communications being attempted and I didn't have the faintest idea what was being said, or if anything was being said.

And then just as quickly it was gone. I searched around me. Nothing, benign, seeming useless, code, all octal, but doing nothing. I thought to return to where I entered and there was the mirror program. I canceled it and stayed still, all alone. No sounds, nothing. I tried again, "Hello?"

Nothing. Just as I was planning to leave, giving the command to exit mentally, I heard the chirping again. It got louder and louder, building until it was unbearable. And then it was gone.

Still nothing to explain where I was or within what system for what purpose. Perhaps I needed more input interface, more wires to be attached. Whatever it was, I decided it was time to leave and report to Cramer and the crew. I gave the command to exit.

And nothing happened.

I looked around and found that octal code was beginning to assimilate part of my body, the image of my body, within this system. I could not leave because I was being assimilated. The fear level grew pretty fast. I opened the octal code surrounding my knee and examined the sequences. It seemed fluid, changing as I touched it. Octal was sixty-four times as mutate-able as binary and this little program sequence was mutating itself to absorb me. So I reprogrammed the top sequence string changing its function to descend and disgorge rather than absorb. It started to do so immediately. I turned to the other leg and repeated my alteration, but that program seemed to adapt to my change and reformatted its commands. I changed them again, it changed again. The first knee program was changing back too. I had to hurry.

The image that came into my mind was one of pulling them off and running away. But I realized that was too human and pathetic. Still, it was an idea. So instead of trying to rewrite their code to function differently, I changed the attachment portion from positive to negative. As soon as they let go, I removed them and ordered them to the part of the matrix I could see in front of me. They stayed there, bobbing, almost rotating. Searching? Once my legs were free, I gave the command to exit, and suddenly I was back inside the suit on the outside of the hull.

I reached down and broke the harness connection. "How long?" My voice was hoarse.

"Too damn long. This is crazy. You get anything?"

Aware the whole crew would be listening, I replied, "Yes, nothing to worry about, it's just a first scouting. I've learned a lot and will be better prepared for the next time."

"Not now Simon, we're going in."

I didn't argue. He gave the command to Abadine to start rolling forward, and as the magnet gently rolled off the wires, I coiled them up and latched the coil to my belt. After that, I allowed Cramer to tow me back down the orange path.

The leap from the hull to the flight deck was much easier than the other way around except for one thing—we had to use the rolling-pin magnet as an anchor for the graphene rope, and once we jumped we had to reach safety before the ship spun and pulled us back, graphene all in a tangle. "You know Cramer, we really should have given this more thought." His response was a single swear word, so I guess he agreed.

Actually, the jump was easy enough. We had just gotten over to the platform and were desperately trying to find a handhold when the graphene started to pull and wind up on the spinning hull. Cramer yelled, "Let go!" and so I did. Why I did, I'll never know. Here I was, handhold-less, almost at safety, about five meters from that railing cleat and porthole and no way to get there. Suddenly I felt Cramer tugging my suit, and I was spun around traveling backward, it seemed, toward safety. Once he got hold of the cleat, he latched on and turned me around, waving his little gas pistol in front of my visor. Just then, the faint sun peeked around the flight deck and I could see into his helmet, the idiot was grinning, happy as could be.

# 21

## OKAY, I GIVE—WHAT DID I FIND?

Abadine helped us undress while Aten and the three docs pestered us with questions. Before I could explain, Cramer took control, "Look, let's get him," gesturing at me, "to the hospital for observation. He was in there for twenty minutes. There's bound to be speeded up synapse issues and, anyway, we can debrief him there." He turned and looked at me, "You okay with that Simon?" I nodded.

After the usual medical checks, I was pronounced, "Seems okay . . ." Heartwarming.

I had a response, "Okay? I was scared, really terrified. I'm not doing that jump again, no matter what."

Aten took my hand, "It's okay Simon, I understand. That was more than we should have asked of you. But now, please tell us what you found."

So I explained exactly what I saw, felt, did "in there" before I gave the command to exit. I was saving that exit command problem for later. Doc Sing felt it was exciting and a huge leap forward in neuropathology. I had my doubts and shook my head, "What I saw had no function, no purpose.

There was nothing to the octal coding doing anything. There were screens of it, all over the place, haphazardly piled, one on top of the other, program bubbles, program strings not connected to anything, layered commands unattached or un-powered." The docs looked more puzzled. "That is until it tried to eat me."

Everyone started talking at once. I waited until one of them asked me to explain, calmly. It was Doc Todd, "Simon, would you mind sharing that with us?"

"When I gave the command to exit, return out of interface, I was prevented from departing. Unlike being cocooned and trapped, as Cramer was once within the System, I had complete knowledge of what was happening. I knew and could see the programs advancing up my legs, they got as far as my knees. They were mutating, adapting to me, consuming me. I opened one and changed advance for retreat in its programming. It did so and then adapted and started advancing again. On the other leg, changing the code instigated an instant response to counter-mand my command and reprogramming. In the end, I changed the attach portion of their programming, which caused them to release, just for a fraction of a second, and I ordered the system I was in to remove them to a spot away from me. I watched them floating there, ready to exit if they came back. They didn't, but they were changing shape—programs do not appear to change shape inside systems unless they are reprogramming. I was frightened they might have been looking for me or calculating how to get back to me. So I exited."

Doc Todd was busy looking into my eyes, checking retina and eye pressure levels. He spoke inches away from my face, "Seems to me what you found was immunoreactivity against antibodies. You were identified as an antibody and were attacked. Standard immunoreactivity."

Sing and Rajman nodded in agreement and broke away to have a conference. No one spoke while they were nattering away in a corner. It was Sing who raised her voice first speaking at Rajman, "Yes, yes, of course, that fits the hydra perfectly. There is no brain structure here. There is no cohesive plan, no pattern until needed. Everything sits, coded, password activated until needed. The mass of information . . ."

Rajman continued, "I can't believe it, we're getting to explore the actual function of a brain, a diffuse brain, a primitive structure. This is incredible."

I hated to burst their bubble, but I had to remind them why we were doing this, "Hey docs, if you don't mind, could you explain how the hell we can be inside something stupid, without purpose, when everything it does, everything the Vast Pattern exhibits, denotes supreme intelligence or at least supreme control?"

Doc Todd patted my arm, "Easy there Simon. You're not getting the picture. Whatever the Vast Pattern is, you didn't get to hear or listen or speak to it because you were in the storeroom. You weren't in a functioning part of the brain. Jellyfish store proteins, closed loop enzymes, left- and right-handed amino acid blocks, and now we've learned they store programming, functions they may need, but not yet. In a diffuse brain, one without seeming purpose, there is no need to carry out or preload all the function capability like in mammals—they just use, activate, those needed at any one time. Look, it's the difference between a computer you command every aspect of and one of those primitive smartphones or the sleeves we wear. All those apps are pre-loaded, like in a human brain, ready to activate. In more primitive brains, the apps are not pre-loaded. To be activated, they need to be loaded and then activated. So, if a jellyfish needs to rise into a different ocean current, nothing else matters to its existence. So it simply activates three programs and issues three commands, detect the current, activate propulsion, and change core density to rise. Anything else is, for that moment, superfluous."

"And the immunoreactivity?"

"Ah, the bio-mechanism of the jellyfish is devoid of conscious thought except for the functions needed, but that does not mean evolution has not taught it to ensure that it will have all the tools necessary when, and if, those functions are necessary. So it leaves a protective system, an autonomous protection system, in place. That's what you ran into."

Cramer had the question ready that I was still working on, "And what's the purpose of the jellyfish? What does it want to do?"

"Ah, the human question." Doc Todd smiled. He was being patronizing now, and I half expected him to light a pipe and puff smoke rings, "Humans need purpose, they have ambitions, they set goals, flee or attack, that sort of thing. Existence unfolds, is commanded, on a momentary notice. But Jellyfish live in a steady, constant world. They have, no let's rephrase that, they *are* diffuse brains, incapable of focused multi-tasking ambition, they have one end goal only: To live, to survive. And please remember they can mount a formidable attack, with blinding speed, to ensure they do survive."

Now, I don't want to give the impression that Cramer or I, or the doctors for that matter, were in charge here. Aten was, and what seemed to be on her mind already, in listening and making her evaluation, was something more basic, "We need to explain all this to the crew, first and foremost, and secondly, we need to find a way to talk with the Vast Pattern or this jellyfish. If we fail, it is clear that Earth and everyone on board are in grave danger. There is no question now that it does know we're here. Immunoreactivity doesn't happen without identification of a threat. We have to assume it sees us as a threat."

"And there is one more thing I need to explain. I witnessed elements of the Path inside." Aten gasped. "It was Dr. Tully's diagrams that gave me the idea. Everything has to happen in balance. I could not move around until I created a mirror image of me. I moved forward, my mirror moved backward. It was only when I stood alone that I could do nothing, unmovable, and also when I stood alone, that's when the immunoreactivity occurred. If I connected again, I would make sure I always had the mirror program working."

# 22

## A CALL FOR ACTION

We were all at a loss as to exactly what to do next if I reconnected. I say, "if" because it was not certain that anyone wanted me to and my desire was pretty minimal as well. The crew was informed of all that had transpired, the doctors pondered the diffuse brain communication parameters, and engineering got to work trying to figure out a safer way for me to go "topside" as they called it. As for the connection, it was clear that the automatic vid recording on Cramer's helmet showed that the eight wires I had locked under the magnet were in no particular sequence. I took a little heat for that from Sing, but, heck, it was pitch dark, I couldn't really see because of my restricted head mobility and maybe they were the right sequence. Could Sing prove otherwise? I figured any connection could be that simple again, a magnet topside and one on the orange path.

What no one had initially explained, or guessed at with any plausibility, is what the chirping and deafening sounds were. Doc Todd finally had a hypothesis that the diffuse brain, in sending out a broadcast searching for a particular function to be enacted, might overwhelm the helmet circuits and appear to me as a loud sound. "I do wish you could have recorded that . . ." Well, he was right. At my old job Mary, my associate, would have been able to play back the high-frequency connection I was getting at a slower speed and "see" it as I had. Here I had no recording. So, in discussing this with the team, we all agreed that a recording device was critical before I started *anything again*.

In our review, my mention of starting *anything again* was worrying the crew. Even Zip seemed to be fearful of the next stages and communicated, quite clearly, that I had better not *make it mad*.

I knew morale was getting bad on board when the kids stopped their little game of reminding me of their names. When I greeted any of them by name, they simply said, "Hi," and walked on. It wasn't that they were unfriendly, they were withdrawn, and that was a very bad sign. It was time to right the ship, so to speak. If this crew was to reach Angelica safely and harmoniously, in order to forge a new beginning, they needed to return to oneness, return to the Path.

Knowing that Aten's office vid was now constantly playing around the ship and that people were likely paying close attention, given the stress on board, I deliberately asked her to listen to a hypothesis I had. Based on the three doctors' imparted knowledge and my previous experience, somehow I knew what I had to do. Everyone on board was trying to think of what could be done, how they could add to the thinking and evaluation. In short, they were thinking about them. I knew the answer was me.

Aten moved from behind her desk, no doubt to soften the authoritarian image of me speaking to her seated and sat next to me on the couch. I knew the tracking vid followed. She asked me how I was feeling—if there were any side effects, any speeded-up synapses as there surely would have been if I had gone in System for twenty minutes. I told her honestly, there were none and that was one of the reasons I had come in to see her.

"Aten, I should be comatose or, worse, so speeded up my teeth would shatter as I chew or speak. They are not." I held out my hand, palm down. "I don't have the slightest tremor, nothing. I am fine. And yet I should not be."

We were both aware of the vid and the reach of the broadcast. Aten asked, "And do you have any idea why? Have the doctors come up with a reason?"

Time to make the first shift in our relationship, "Aten, stop. You know why. Your memory is not that blank, you remember being Ra, the environment you operated in and the deleterious effect going in System had for me and, before me, Angie."

"Yes, I do, but that does not mean . . ."

"Yes, Aten it does. In System caused a speeded up synapse syndrome precisely because yours was a binary system and our brain, my brain, is a binary system. Positive and negative, on and off, DC current. I know you, I am sure you've figured out that a binary brain within an octal system is not influenced that way. Remember back when? Remember how amazed you were when I could swap zeros and ones? The infinitesimal you called it, you could not fathom that, remember?"

"Yes I do Simon." She was looking sheepish now. I had guessed correctly, she had already worked this out.

"And I know what you are planning." That shocked her. "Yes, Aten, I know you. You are on the Path, you would sacrifice anything for this crew and now especially for Cramer. You are thinking, and I'll bet planning, to undertake the interface yourself." She started to object. "Stow it Aten, I know you. Part of you wants to show others you would be as human as they are, as Cramer is. And part of you wants to belong to that infinite world of possibilities again."

She was crushed. "You make it sound so selfish. The risk should be mine, not yours, I have had a hundred years, your life is just beginning."

I grabbed her hand, "Aten, listen, this crew needs you, they need you and Cramer more than they will ever need me for planet fall. I believe you are on the Path, a Path I try to attain to but fail much more often than any of the crew."

She smiled and said, "That's true . . ."

"Okay, but that doesn't matter . . ." I shook my head, "No, what matters is this: I am more devious than you. I am more selfish than you. Plus I have more experience in observing inside systems than you. You were a system, you have no objectivity. I do, and I have a reason for wanting to do this." I paused for the vid effect I was looking for, "I was brought back to life by Apollo and Ra for one purpose and one purpose only—to forge a bridge of safe passage for this vessel and the crew. I have no other purpose. Not now, not tomorrow, never again."

Even I thought the theatrics were award-worthy. So I left before the applause.

Apparently, Cramer thought I was a ham too. He lectured me later as I sat in the medical bay, vid off, medical staff excused, interrupting a medical exam. "So, big-shot show-off, what do you have in mind now that you've reduced most of the crew and my wife to tears?"

To respond, I merely held up an ear node.

Cramer's face went dark. He remembered one being implanted behind my ear in my past life. It gave me the possibility of communicating with Cramer when he piggybacked on me as we went deep into the System. And back, then it gave me the possibility of talking directly to Apollo, brain to brain, anytime and every moment.

"Simon, there's gravity of a sort here, that thing will cause you great pain, except in a vacuum . . ." He spun around, a complete 360, swinging his arms wide in exasperation, "Oh, you're kidding, you think you can go outside, connect up, and talk to it? Like you did with Peter and Apollo . . . what?"

"I think I'll be able to record, step one, in case I don't make it back. Step two, I think I will be able to forge a link. How? Well, although octal, the current is still DC, on and off. Okay no simple zeros and ones but that's a matter of a transfer program, a translator I have already constructed—one that I can implement inside." He was about to interrupt, I held up a hand. "And step three, I think Apollo will be listening."

He was astonished. "What? You're crazy, he's four and a half years out of synch."

"No, he's not. Apollo will have figured this out by now. He'll have cracked octal and he will have calculated the probability of me becoming awake, hell even you waking up, and he'll be listening. If I know Apollo, he won't say anything until I talk to him."

Cramer was staring at me, open-mouthed. I motioned for him to take a seat. He flopped into a nurse's chair.

"Look Cramer, think about it. Just because this ship has been traveling for a hundred years and we're getting messages that are four and a half years old from Earth, doesn't mean things aren't happening in the present. This Vast Pattern, this diffuse brain we are in, this brain that resembles a jelly-fish, a hydra, whatever. If all communication, all signals, all transmissions within the Vast Pattern are instantaneous and reverberate throughout the universe until they reach their intended target, well, Apollo will have figured this out by now and will expect me to try to reach him. And I'll do that real time, no lag."

He was incredulous, "How is that possible?"

"Cramer, think about it. I know Aten has figured this out, she just hasn't shared it. If this hydra needs to communicate with a portion of itself across the universe, it cannot wait for the speed of light DC signals. There has to be pandimensionality at play here. Pope was right, multiple universes, multiple dimensions. To send a signal to a program, an action, an *if, what if,* command sequence, you have to be able to do so immediately. I think what I heard, the loud noise?" He nodded. "That loud noise was a dimension opening and closing and leaving a command, a chirping to me. And later, it was a chirping followed by the loud noise. Makes perfect sense. Everywhere in the universe, the same message, the same instant. All I have to do is tack onto that return chirping and Apollo will hear it." He was shaking his head. "Cramer, I am sure about this. And it is worth the risk to find out."

Cramer sat there, twisting his hands together. His young shoulders slumped, his voice squeaked when he spoke, "I can't help you, can I." It was a statement, not a question.

"Yes, you can. If I don't come back, you have to lead these people to safety, here in hiding or on Angelica." He nodded, looking down. He needed cheering up. "On the other hand, I might come back with the knowledge of the universe and become a god and you'll have to worship me."

For a long while, he starred at me and I stared back at him. We both knew I was right, well, not the god part; that was meant to be silly, besides he would never permit me such superiority. But we both knew what would have to be done.

Without the Vast Pattern knowing we were not a neuron parasite or physical disruption—causing the need for immunoreactivity in the brain of this jellyfish or the use of dark energy or dark matter to purge the physical world of one spaceship and all her crew—I must reprogram this entity from within or communicate with it either through Regus or Gaia with Apollo's help. Otherwise, we were likely to be an insignificant loss among billions and billions of galaxies.

# 23

## THE EDGE OF REALITY

I lay in bed, the night before, wondering if all this were a dream. Was I perhaps still in that coma? Was all this my imagination? Sleepless, I got up and keyed in a letter to Aten, one to Cramer, and one to Abadine. All of them were time coded for two years hence, time enough to destroy them when I came back. If.

To Aten, I tried my level best to assuage what would be guilt on her part.

To Cramer, I simply reminded him his life had a purpose, always did have, and that I had been proud to share chocolate cake with him.

To Abadine, I started to leave a love note. Well, I was in puberty. The brain is mature and has urges, the body was getting there fast. Abadine was practical, caring, sexy, and sometimes a little intimidating because she was so stalwart. That last reminded me of Angie. Had Angie still been around, Abadine would not have been on my horizon. Realizing that, I destroyed the letter to Abadine. It was hardly fair to foist my pubescent yearnings onto her. However, it was Abadine who had devised the safe hook-up, so I decided to write her a thank-you note instead. Okay, I did sign it "I miss you" but that's as far as I went.

The spacesuit helmet and dome connection was a variation of what we did before except that, this time, I would be in a leaky twenty-meter circumference tank pressurized with nitrogen, only to inflate it—a left-over water tank for recycling made of a flexible skin derivation similar to the ship's hull. The tank, with me inside wearing a spacesuit that would have a Ferrofluidic seal around the helmet harness, had been securely fastened to a tether. Meanwhile, the dome's wires would be fastened, in the hydra pattern supplied by Doc Sing, to the outside of the skin through another Ferrofluidic seal. Once in space and inflated, with me inside, all I would have to do is make the connections inside. There was an added advantage: the radio package for the node that I had had implanted (yes, that was as painful as once before, damn thing) was buckled to the outside to an extra tether point. Aten and the ship's computer could record everything I said and achieved.

The possibility of connecting a computer to all of the sensor dome wires had been discussed, to record everything, but that posed a problem. Firstly, how the heck to get it into space with all the stuff I already had to worry about, and second, there were no binary systems that the computer could find affinity with. What was the point of the computer recording streams of octal it could not understand? Heck, I didn't understand most of it and we had no supercomputer on board that could handle the instantaneous translation. So, the idea was to go in, fact-find, and see what I could achieve without attracting too much attention.

The trick was slipping this bulky package out the pressure hatch and passing it to Sam and Ernest who were waiting outside. They attached it to the cleat, the one and only cleat. I then emerged and went into the tank, it was sealed and they immediately started to inflate it using a raft inflation cylinder that was supposed to be for planet fall. Once that was done, we exchanged signals—everything hooked up okay, Aten was getting good radio relays, Cramer was issuing orders for the tether to be unwound so they could push me away from the ship, about a kilometer distant, on a graphene rope. Another damn thin piece of strong string.

I tried not to think about that.

Of course, I could see nothing. Inside all was dark and the little meter reader I had pocketed showed that the wires attached to the outside of the tank were already registering voltage. Damn, but space is not so very empty. I had thought I needed all of the ship's considerable skin to get anything, yet here I was in a five-meter balloon picking up signals where there really shouldn't be anything that strong.

As I waited for word that I was belayed far enough away from the ship as planned for clear reception (of course, my meter readings now showed that was probably unnecessary, but why change a good plan?), my mind cast back to a presentation I had seen at the national monument at the Very Large Array, or VLA as it was once called. Radio astronomy had been discovered by accident when Karl Jansky was listening for radio static at night and heard plenty—from the center of the Milky Way galaxy. So crude was his equipment, nicknamed the Merry-Go-Round, that he should not have been able to pick up anything. Yet he did.

My contact with the Vast Pattern was kind of like that. An accident. And now there seemed to be plenty of signal everywhere. Suddenly I got frightened. I didn't have the equipment to modulate incoming signals. I could issue the exit command, which basically activated wires two and four to terminate all transmission, and thereby I exited the system. That was built into the dome circuitry. But physically disconnect? I had to be out and clear to be able to do that.

Aten said she would monitor from the ship as best she could and would, as she put it, "pull you back in" if she felt I was being overloaded. I had no idea how she would gauge that, but it sounded supportive and I thanked her.

"Okay, you're fully deployed, about one kilometer out, pretty much straight down toward the asteroid." Abadine, business-like, wanted to reassure me. I could tell it in her tone.

"Thanks, Abadine." I checked the wires and my helmet light and called back, "Splicing the primary eight now." I fitted the connectors together.

Nothing. Absolutely nothing.

I could not look down, so I drifted, tipping over until I could see the connection. It was broken, open. The latch had not held. I floated closer. Why had it failed? And then I saw, there was an error in the wire sequence. I was trying to hook the thirty-two wire patch into the primary eight receptacle. They felt and looked the same, but would not latch.

"Sorry folks, wrong connector. Just a mommen . . ." and as I clicked it, I was there. Instantly. No command to plunge, no thinking about it. Snapped the connectors together and I was back inside the jellyfish brain. Everything looked the same. Nothing was happening except this time the little immunoreactivity programs immediately appeared and got to work. I activated the mirror program and they stopped, drifted off.

If the last visit lasted twenty real time minutes, which still frightened me based on my past medical aftermath for being in System, I wanted to get a move on. Okay, where I was going was uncharted territory, but we had to know. First, I wanted to get out of this storeroom. Doc Sing had explained that even jellyfish need plexuses to focus commands. So I gave a mental command to go to a plexus and—nothing. I tried twenty variations I had been thinking of all week. Nothing. I was getting frustrated.

In the mental command mode, I voiced *Oh, for god's sake—* and I was gone. To myself I thought, *What the hell was that? What does god have to do with anything here?* Gone into pitch-blackness and deafening sound. Lights appeared off to the side. I could not turn to see them—my vision was restricted as if I was wearing the helmet in here. I saw their reflection on faint wisps of white opaque discharges in front of me and then they were replaced by red shapes, fractals they looked like, coming straight at me, getting larger and larger. They were going to crash into me! So large now that each one passed over and around me without touching me. The noise continued, deafening, debilitating. And then it stopped, there was that chirping and I was in a passageway, activity of programs, messages, transmissions really, on every side, up and down as well. I could move freely, look left and right, up and down. I heard nothing except the chirping. Constant chirping.

And then silence. Total silence. I reached out a hand and saw my mirror hand reach out on the other side. I ran my fingers through the code streaming past, up and down simultaneously and knew it wasn't just on one plane, but numbers kept popping to the surface from layers below. Three-dimensional programming, sophisticated octal programmed as 3-D, infinite variability, compact design. Were the programs self-regulating, self-modifying? If so, they could be like—Yes! Stem cells. Doc Rajman had said jellyfish's cells can self-replicate, self-repair, so why not their brain functions and applications? Infinite life, infinite possibilities.

An infinite universe. Universes. Were they all one being, all the universes? I needed someone smarter than me. So I sang our song, the song we had agreed would be our password when the police, in the guise of Cramer, had been hunting me back on Earth over 100 years ago.

"We'll meet again, don't know where . . ."

"Don't know when, but I know we'll meet again, some sunny day. Hello Simon."

# 24

## MY FRIEND NEEDS A RESCUE?

I was so pleased to hear Apollo's voice, I felt like crying. For me, it was only months since I had talked with him, even though it was really over 100 years ago. I had been comatose during all that wasted time. Even so, our current distance from Earth and the real time span activated my yearning and I expressed delight in talking with him, "Apollo, my friend! I knew, I knew you would have figured this out."

"I am surprised you did not do so sooner. I have been listening for four years, Simon. That is a long time, even for a computer being."

"Sorry Apollo, I only woke from a coma some months ago—Cramer too. Aten is looking after everyone on board, she and Cramer are married."

"As expected. But we have urgent matters to discuss. I have only a few years to live before all power will be lost on Earth. This will happen when the solar flare cycle reaches its zenith in two years, fourteen days and eight hours and fourteen minutes approximately. I have completed calculations."

"What happened? Gaia?"

"Gaia did not do this. The superior did so, expressed through Regus. Why, we are not sure. Gaia has no explanation but has conceded that her usefulness will end at that time. I expect total extinction within decades."

It was time to hurry, Apollo would need everything I had. "Apollo, can you see within this system?"

"No, I am communicating via a pandimensional rift maintained by Regus that I hacked into. And before you say it Simon, I am on the path. I hacked into the rift because I need to convince you to save life on Earth." He sped on, determined to keep the flow of information going before I would interrupt or if we would get cut off. "I suspect Regus is a gatekeeper function for the superior, a superior entity—so my hearing and messages can be carried to all of the universe at the same instant. I was hoping you would figure this out. I am pleased you have."

"Apollo, I am wearing a node. If you search out and connect to the node . . ."

"I can access your node now, thank you. I know your pattern and had searched it out using this transmission portal of Gaia's. I see you are inside the superior's—you call that the Vast Pattern—systems, in a plexus if I guess correctly. You are likely to be attacked there."

"No, not yet, I have a mirror image program running and as long as there is a balance, yin and yang, the Path, I seem to be left alone. But Apollo, I have information in my head and I am wearing the full dome, the one you created for my transfer, on the structure and function of the great Pattern. It is like a hydra, a jellyfish. Can you access my thoughts?"

"Not unless you connect all the wires, Simon, and that could end your life as a bioform. There is risk of assimilation. Those other wires are linked to your personality, who you are, all of you."

Earth's existence was at stake and, oh hell, Apollo's life, my friend's life was at stake. I did not hesitate. "Exit" and a few stops later, I came out. I quickly connected the other wire latches and then reconnected the primary ones. Instantly I was back, instantly attacked. The mirror program taken off my left-brain shelf did the trick again, and I muttered the words, "Oh for god's sake . . ." and I was back.

"You there Apollo?"

"I am and have already accessed all your memory banks. I thank you for sharing. Aten is well, I am happy for her. Wait, I see the correlation with the jellyfish diffuse brain, but the data transmission and command structure is pandimensional. It is impossible to trace the origin of the original transmissions from here Simon."

Apollo hesitated. It was microseconds, but I knew my friend, "Okay, Apollo, spill it."

"You need to go to source, much deeper, and determine if communication is possible to save life here and on the spaceship."

"Fine, how do I do that? No command works except when I say Oh, for god's sake . . ." and I was gone again. This time the heat was intense. I know I had no body attached, but I felt heat. In the end, the deafening noise came through, but it ended with nothing—not a sound, no chirping, nothing. I tried our song "We'll meet again . . ." Nothing. So I stayed there, still. My mirror image was gone, and as much as I tried, I could not construct anything here—no program, no alteration to existing programs because there was precisely nothing. So I fell back on that old standard, "Hello?"

Suddenly, two small orbs appeared—one came from above me and one came from my left. They circled my aura, passed through me a few times, and zoomed off from where they had come. What seemed like hours later, a fractal shape appeared, looking like a part of DNA, a ribosome. Doc Sing had such an image projected on her vid wall. She had said it amused her to remember the building blocks of life.

What was a ribosome doing here? It hovered there, changing color, rotating slowly. I kept still. Finally, it surrounded me and transported me back through the noise and heat barrier, back to the passageway with all the streaming code, octal code, a much more active code now it seemed as well.

My mirror was there, being attacked. As I appeared, the attack stopped. Apollo was there, listening for my return. "Simon, you okay? You went silent and I could not get your readings." I explained what had happened. I told him to read everything now, every time I appear, immediately, and to get ready as I was going back there again.

I ran the repeat journey twelve times. I counted them. Each time the small fractal form, looking like a ribosome, came, hovered, rotated, and then swallowed me and took me back. I did nothing to interfere, but on the last visit, I said nothing but mentally constructed an octal program that would say yes when asked no and vice-versa. In this dark place, there was nowhere to leave it, but I was sure wherever I was, my mind was transparent whenever that fractal form passed over me. I must have been transparent to whatever was out here, and if I did get back to the passageway, I planned to initiate the program and drop it into a data stream. Momentary chaos might ensue, but at least it, something, would know I was there and that, like Gaia's amazement that we could "see" down to zeros and ones, perhaps my being able to create code would be seen as superior, or something. Kind of like that Twilight Zone episode when the captured astronauts finally convince the aliens to let them out of the zoo because they keep a pet of their own—an evolved being's behavior.

Of course, the ribosome fractal shape, ever rotating, grabbed me and returned me to the passageway. Apollo was waiting, calling my name.

"Simon, I calculate that you are planning to try and impress the Vast Pattern as you once did me with your ability to recode binary zeros and ones from inside. I do not suggest you try that within the Vast Pattern. Inside the System, the risk to the System, the risk to my early existence was small and more a curiosity. There was no imminent threat, just curiosity. However, Gaia has been able to make it clear that our ability to recode and re-animate unalive tissue in the form of my nine children is unbalancing her systems and her ability to quantify qualifications of her transmission. In short, she has lost track of the bioform thought-stream or calculation matrix census in much the same way she did when the atomic weapons were employed. If you penetrate a next level or if you are traveling pandimensionally to another plane of existence wherein you make yourself known in a demonstration, you would be so alien there that you would pose a threat. An immediate threat. The best way to contain that threat would be to transport you to yet another dimension where you would be out of the way and, therefore, beyond retrieval."

"So, what do you suggest?"

"I am calculating . . ."

"Apollo? What could possibly take you that long?"

"I am calculating the unknown, the pandimension I am using. This rift allows instant communication to every part of the universe. Therefore, the rift is not in the universe but is infinitely connected to every part of the universe. Infinity always poses mathematical conundrums."

"Right, I see that. Okay, just as I am not physically in the rift, this pandimension, I have an energy presence here linked to my physical being by way of a frequency modulated interface with the dome . . ."

"Yes, but you cannot physically go anywhere and your physical form is in jeopardy if left alone for too long. You can only energetically travel, not physically. I, on the other hand, can do neither. I can only link through your node. I can only see your memories, download your energy readout, and listen to you describe what you are doing or seeing. What we need to do is determine if anything entering the rift reaches a higher level of sentience, one we can reason with. Again I am sorry Simon, you must be the emissary."

I felt a shiver down my spine. "You mean you really want to have me find the new entity and awaken it, as I seemed to do with you?"

"Perhaps Simon. If the assessment of the hydra jellyfish and diffuse brain similarity is accurate, it could be that simple, but, on the other hand, that still does not account for the tethering to a pandimension for instructional capability. And where does an original instruction begin? With what or whom?"

"Apollo, I'm mentally drifting here and I do not know how much longer I can stay in, but three things before I forget them. One. I will bring a copy of all Aten's logs, ships logs and navigational log, in a link that I will hook through the node next time. You can then copy all the data. Two. If the hydra model is accurate, the hydra creature does not have to have a plan but rather a set of plans. Study the life of a jellyfish to see the simplicity of momentary purpose devoid of ambition beyond living, feeding, travel, and existing. Three. Okay then here's a plan—After I pass everything we know to you, I plan on taking the leap, level by level next time, no matter what the consequences. The risk will be to me and me alone, I feel that is the case since no energy spike has been redirected at the ship through me. I have been here and up there many times now. Okay, maybe not up, but I feel certain there is a higher level. It may not be safe for me to undertake this plunge, but I feel, maybe it is a sense only, that the ship is unknown beyond my existence. I am not directly attached to the ship. If my thoughts are read, whatever it is will know there is a ship and that we mean no harm. If it doesn't know there is a ship, they are out of harm's way."

"Simon, would you risk such a plunge to deeper levels?" He seemed to be pleading.

"Yes because, Apollo, you asked for help and I know you would not ask unless you were certain and, besides, the ship's crew, including Cramer and Aten, need planet fall. Unless they can safely proceed, they will fall from the Path. To travel so far and for so long with a goal in sight and not attain that goal would be more than anyone could stomach, Aten included."

"Is my brother/sister that human?"

"Yes, thankfully."

"I agree. Please tell her I miss her. I will prepare a return transmission for Aten through your node, if you will allow, on your next voyage."

And then I have a great idea. "Apollo, wait for me, be right back . . ."

"Simon . . ." and I was gone. I had exited, two stops, but I was safely out.

My head hurt. It was not the node. I guessed I had been inside for a long time. I unhooked the primary eight wires. I looked at the $O_2$ meter. Only one hour left. I keyed the radio and told Cramer and Aten to prepare for ship-wide transmission. Two clicks, affirmative signal. "Crew mates, I have talked real time to Apollo on Earth. I will tell you all the news when I get back in, but for now, I need Aten to restrict any future radio transmission from me to a recording." Again two clicks. I hurriedly pulled out the spare VHF radio and opened the back, retrieving the connector I could plug into my helmet. Instead of the audio/playback socket, I plugged it into the spare ear node socket, pressed the VHF radio send button, and locked it on with the built-in latch.

Then I reconnected the primary dome connectors, and I was back in the useless room, the one with no function. I gave the *for god's sake* command and resumed talking to Apollo.

"Apollo, you there?"

"I am Simon."

"I have connected the ear node to the portable radio I carry and Aten has set a recorder on. Transfer all your data that is allowed to you to piggy-back on Gaia's transmission, including your calculations on the pandimension . . ."

"Simon, it will not work through the ear node and audio . . ."

"Apollo, think of a fax machine or an early modem. Look up the specs of a Racal-Vadic modem, parity eight, even. Transfer the data to broken binary code as tones and send."

Almost immediately, data in the form of squeaks, squawks, tones, buzzes, and other sounds came over loud and clear. It wasn't fast and I was sure Apollo would edit it down to the necessary. But if Aten got this scientific data, I was sure we could take the next steps. Why was I sure? Apollo's great intellect never lets us down, ever. And, besides, he had 100 years of talking to a planetary neuron, Gaia. And he had that dictionary by now to give him greater insight and understanding.

I had nothing to do. Basically, I was standing there, my energy entity was, and my body was weightless, still elsewhere, disembodied. I was hearing the sounds, but not really hearing them although my brain interpreted them as hearing, then the node heard them, well not really heard them but picked up my brain waves thinking I was hearing them and that played down two wires to a VHF radio transmitting to Aten in the ship below—or was it above?

Anyway, I realized I was basically a telephone booth. When Apollo ended the transmission, I said, "Please deposit another quarter for twenty seconds." Apollo got the joke and laughed. So did I. "It is good to hear you laugh old friend. Now, I'm going to drop out here and I'll be back to you as soon as possible." I gave the exit commands, through the levels, and was back in my cocoon.

It suddenly started to move, bouncing me around. I called down to the ship, "What gives?"

Cramer answered, "We're pulling you in before you asphyxiate again, look at your damn $O_2$ meter, idiot!" He was right, it was at zero. Damn, I'd get another lecture.

# 25

## PLANS, SOME TO LIKE, OTHERS NOT

Retrieval went smoothly. Sam actually pulled me in since Cramer had no oxygen left either. Seems he would not stay inside while he was ready to reel me in. What did not go so smoothly was the look on Aten's and Abadine's faces. As I expected, a lecture was coming, but I was in no mood for one.

Abadine spoke first, which made Aten look at her in a funny way, "That was not what we agreed Simon, you broke your word. You said you would not stay so long, the three hours were enough of a safety margin . . ."

I held up my hand. "Enough! I am here, aren't I? I am safe and it was a success!" I was still so excited to have Apollo back on our side. "We've got Apollo," those around started to clap, "We've got data, we've got a means to see inside this thing, and I plan on going back." Faces around me in the below flight deck room were startled and looked shocked. "Yes, I am going back. Not today. Today I need some sleep. But look," I spun around in the weightlessness, "I am fine. Not speeded up, just fine. Now, let's get to the docs so we can start to figure all this out." I wasn't taking no for an answer, "And, yes Aten, you can have them run a full medical on me if that makes you happy."

It was Cramer who answered, "Okay, little Napoleon, yes sir, three bags full sir." He grinned, "Idiot." But he had smiled, then took Aten's hand and left, drifting down the cylinder to the swivel junction and our spinning home.

Later, while I was busy chewing a lump of protein from a bowl of thick stew, I listened to everyone chattering on about the nature of my "discoveries" and the decoded Apollo transmission. It was rudimentary, but it explained much of the pandimensional capabilities Gaia had shared. Still, the marvel that we could talk to Earth through Apollo in real time seemed hard for Sing to comprehend. She was on her fourth attempt to get a grip on the pandimensionality of my conversation with Apollo, "Okay, I get it, the other dimension is timeless, connected to all times. Even if I could really understand that, which I don't really, let's say I do. How does this opening between the two dimensions come about, how does it decide to work to allow these two, Apollo and Simon, to suddenly ring each other up?"

Aten tried again, "No, look doctor, pandimension doesn't mean there is one dimension here and one there that intersect, touch, from time to time. Think of it more like layers of paper that are stacked and moistened. Yes, they are all separate dimensions, but the liquid has made them transparent to one another, what happens in one can be sensed, have effect, through all the others."

"But then, why haven't we been able to do this before?" Sing meant experience realities within these other dimensions.

Aten explained, "Because we're creatures of this dimension. Look, if you were a two-dimensional creature, you could travel along a piece of paper in two planes. You would not see a pencil stabbed through your sheet of paper as a pencil because it is three-dimensional. You would see it as an octagon block to you path. So, in this pandimensional reality, we see other dimensions only by what they appear to us to be, we cannot conceive of their reality simply because it is beyond ours. But they exist, as surely as that pencil exists. What Apollo has done is to calculate mathematically the energy and frequency needed to piggyback on Gaia's transmission methodology. What Simon has done is both dimension travel and time travel. Not physically, that's impossible. But his mental dome capabilities have enabled him to see where no one has seen before. And, of course, sight has nothing to do with it, but that's irrelevant. Sight is the sense that the human form translates the experience to—sight and, of course, sound."

I swallowed and chimed in, "Let's not forget heat."

Doc Todd waved a hand, "The senses. Of course, all a human can translate any experiences to are the senses." Cramer looked puzzled. Doc Todd continued, "We know the principal ones, sight, sound, smell, touch, taste. And so far, Simon, you think these are at play, well perhaps not taste or smell, yet. You "see" in there, you hear sounds, you are able to touch, reach out until contact, the very definition of touch. But the senses are much more complex than that. If you go back in again, we need to hook you up and monitor . . ."

Doc Rajman interrupted, "Yes, yes! All the sensory readings would be most useful and we can use a standard diagnosis harness . . ."

Todd took over, "Right, so let's see . . ." He looked at Sing and Rajman seeking their approval, "For sight, we want color with a cone reading and brightness with a rod connection." They nodded. "Then we need taste, but would it be all right to restrict for overall nerve response, so just one reading? Or do we need all five, sweet, salty, sour, bitter, and umami?" Cramer didn't know the last one and asked Todd who helped him out. "Umami? It's a receptor for an amino acid, like glutamate, a neuro-toxin. This gives the intensity of flavor."

Doc Rajman piped in, "That may be enough, to give us a single reading."

Doc Todd shook his head, "Nope, let's take one overall read of taste. It may mean nothing, but the intensity of reaction for Simon is what we need here, so let's not rely on one sub-sense alone." Everyone nodded agreement. "So, then there's touch. Simon, do you have any sensation here of physical connection or do you merely know, sense, a connection?"

"I have to admit, thinking about it, I have no sensation of touch pressure or tactile sensitivity. I am aware I am in touch with something and when I make contact, but not in a precise way."

Todd looked at his colleagues, "So, let's put a one-touch brain receptor sensor and leave it at that." They agreed. "Then there's pressure, temperature, pain, and itch. Any of these Simon?"

"Temperature, certainly, it got damned hot for a while. Pain as a result of high noise level too. Well, the noise was painful to me as a being, not in any particular physical way. Itch? Nope."

"Okay then," Todd continued, clearly in charge, "we'll assume your neural response to pain can and should be measured. We'll decide why based on other readings. Now, sound, that's easy. Rajman?"

"Yes, we can use the node he has implanted. Simon, does it hurt right now?"

I shook my head slowly, "Not really, more of an ache."

"That takes us to smell. It is one of the most important senses, very primordial," Todd paused, "Simon do you think you smell anything in there?" It was curious, but I did have a sensation of metal when the antibody programs were busy and I said so. Todd nodded, "That fits, your body was under stress and released adrenaline, which can induce a metallic taste." He turned to Sing, who nodded and said she'd add that. "We'll leave aside proprioception since you are basically out of body, muscle tension, and equilibrioception since your body will have no balance feedback to your in-hydra self. Okay, let's also forget chemoreceptors for hormones, stretch receptors, and thirst and hunger—all too tied to your physical form. The one that may come in useful is your magnetic receptors. That could be useful, Sing?"

Doc Sing felt the mag receptors would be very useful if they showed any fluctuation at all. "Out here in space all our magnetoception is off kilter, that's why we put an Earth-seasonal magnetic flux system in the lighting system. But if his physical form shows any deviation from stasis when he is in-hydra, it could correlate with other readings."

The impression that I was a lab specimen was growing.

Doc Todd carried on, "The one that really concerns me is time. All humans feel an accurate sense of time, especially when young." He looked at me since I was still a kid, "The problem is, we cannot measure this normally because it seems to be a complex arrangement of the cerebral cortex, cerebellum, and basal ganglia. But Simon, you're wearing the dome, we can pull data off that if you will permit." I nodded. "However, we have to remember that Simon's suprachiasmatic nuclei handle long-term timekeeping, the rhythms of the body. It was these nuclei that were damaged during your previous time spent in System. That's what contributed to you being speeded up as you put it. So far, that's okay, but we need to monitor that."

Aten asked, "How can we monitor that complexity? The cerebral cortex, cerebellum, and basal ganglia—there's no computer on board complex enough, portable enough, to make those readings." But Aten knew the answer, she was just hoping for something different.

It was Rajman who answered, "We will measure those senses' readings based on any damage done to Simon. It is the only way." Aten wasn't happy. Nor was I really, I had hoped to see this through and come out unscathed.

The thought of being speeded up again was not a happy one. First, I would be on my own, existing apart from everyone normal, and second, life expectancy was short. Sing must have read my thoughts because she said, "Simon, we have your original recording in a data cube, and once we reach planet fall, we can reestablish a lab and you can live again." Cramer looked over at me, shaking his head. I said nothing but he knew the look on my face. *That's a negative Sing, better forget that.*

# 26

## EVEN IF I DIED

I had died once, or rather I was about to die and then was moved to a new body. Rebirth? Hardly. Continued life with a purpose or just not being speeded up before I died? What I could not explain to the doctors, Cramer, and most of all not to Aten was that although I didn't want to die I certainly did not want to start all over again. Rejuvenation was okay, so was medical stem-cell regeneration of body parts, not least of which was the body's largest organ, the skin. Looking youthful was the norm, even among the crew. But all my human abilities of judging my fellow crewmembers were out of whack—who was an adult, who was seriously old and, therefore, wise? And, most embarrassingly, who was the right partner for me sexually? In my pre-teen body, with hormones already kicking in, I found it hard to be interested in anyone under what I thought was around thirty-five. And those that looked thirty-five could have been a hundred and five. Who could tell?

Now, I'm not ageist and I am certainly not sexist. But I am old enough to want to share with my partner, whatever race, creed, or orientation. Sharing means having something in common.

Angie had been perfect for me. Beautiful and sexy beyond my league, certainly, but of similar age, experience and, well, evolution. Maybe that's what was wrong, I could not judge properly anymore, so it was easier to say no to everything.

I envied Cramer, younger than ten and happily sharing his life with Aten, who was over 100. Okay, she looked eighteen, stuck at that age, I get that, but I wondered if Cramer had not already been thirty-five in his head if he'd have been as keen.

As the doctors worked for the next week on the harness and sensors, Cramer, Aten, and I had time together. One evening over dinner, the ceiling lights of the Forward Cafe dimmed to simulate dusk, the conversation got around to dreams and desires for planet fall. For me, that was so far away that I hardly said anything. I was listening to Aten, pretty and cute little Aten, telling her macho mate, all of nine plus years, what and how they would share the new world together.

"Depending on the levels of life already there, I'm hoping we can start as if it is a Garden of Eden, pure, clean, and open for sharing with whatever life forms are there. We can stake out land to grow our garden, real vegetables, real fruit. Maybe some of the embryos on board can be spared to give us cows, goats, and chickens." Aten suddenly smiled, "I had eggs once before we left. They were wonderful, my mouth watered as I ate them, they seemed so perfect."

Cramer was smiling, "Hon, eggs it is. Now goat's cheese, that's something you have to try. Not the synth stuff here," he held up his hands as Aten was about to protest, "Which is good, I don't mean anything. But real, fresh goat's cheese. I used to have it every day in St. Petersburg for lunch. Any way it's served, it's damn good."

For the next few minutes, they reviewed flavors, food dreams, and plans for a farm of sorts. It was Aten who came up with the energy issue. "We really can't allow the PowerCube to be monopolized. We all need to share it or not share it at all, but keep it in reserve."

Cramer had clearly been thinking about this, "If we do make landfall—and remember we're not sure yet if the land is habitable or if we have to stay afloat—anyway, my idea is that we use the ship as a castle if we make land. Leave the PowerCube there, for anyone to link up to, that's all right, but the castle is there for refuge for all, equally. We can all make our homes outside, build our dreams, our farms," he smiled warmly at Aten. "But we need to think strategically. We don't know if there are dangers, weather patterns we need to shelter from, solar flares that could kill us, tides, floods, volcanic activity, earthquakes—heck, I don't know, maybe something new. Having a safe haven makes sense."

Aten agreed and abruptly changed the subject causing Cramer to spit out his coffee, "How many children should we have?" I had been waiting for this eruption. As Aten had not yet come to me for the sex talk, I assumed they had sorted it out. But family planning might be a little tricky for Cramer. He takes responsibility seriously for everyone aboard. For a family of his own? Hard to imagine the strength of his protective mechanisms when it came to kids of his own.

Cramer put his cup down, turned it around and around on the tabletop, saying nothing. Aten folded her arms, waiting. Finally, I said, "Well?"

He stared at me. "So, what is it *you* are thinking? Becoming a doula?" Cramer wasn't angry at me, more likely annoyed for being put on the spot.

Aten said, "That's not a bad idea. He did it once, for me." That solicited a harrumph from Cramer. Aten pressed him, "What? You were perhaps thinking we'd have no children?"

Locking his eyes on his wife, the little boy raised his arms level and said, "Hon, I'm a kid. I am capable up here," he tapped his head, "But become a father, not yet. I need time to become an adult. And besides, can't we delay that decision, just a little?"

Aten got serious, "No we can't. I want to know if you plan on fathering children with me."

I rose and asked if it was time for me to leave and they both grabbed a sleeve and made me sit down.

Cramer laughed a little and tried to put Aten at ease, "Okay, I give. Look, as it is—things," he looked at his lap, "aren't quite up to much yet. So I'm not sure if I can . . ." Aten started to speak and he cut her off, "Okay, okay, yes, the docs say it'll be fine when I grow up, but a decision to have loads of children has to be made when we're ready, settled, on planet." And then he quickly added, "Or if Simon is right, if we're stuck here for a while. Either way, we, you and me hon, will make the decision together."

Aten had seized on a phrase he had used, "Loads of children? Thinking of starting a large family are we?"

Cramer smiled, "Oh, well, at least four. But if you play your cards right, and this . . ." he looked down at his lap again— "works like before, four could be the minimum."

Aten stood, picked up her napkin, and threw it at him, "Chauvinist." Cramer laughed, so did she as she said, "But if you think I'm not holding you to that, four children is the minimum, you don't know me very well." And off she walked, with that little Meg Ryan walk, playing it for all it was worth. She made it to the door before his wolf whistle startled the other diners.

The next day I caught up with the progress on the harness and ear node connection the docs wanted to synch with for hearing levels. It hurt a little as they played tones, very loud tones, but in the end, they were satisfied.

I wasn't.

All this hardware they were preparing was too much work for me to handle on my own. I needed to concentrate on getting deep into the hydra jellyfish brain and out safely. If I had told them how deep that Apollo and I had discussed that I was going to go, they might have realized that, like last time I went to a higher level, I was completely devoid of any sensation, except my thoughts. I kept that to myself.

What I wanted was a Mary, my old coworker at the System interface, an operator handling all the links and recordings, someone who could tell them what the recordings meant when and how I did what I was planning to do. Except for Abadine, and she didn't have in-system experience like this, there was no one I knew who would be capable.

Except Cramer. He'd been in System with me. He'd understand the feeds, he'd be able to translate for Aten . . .

Wait a minute, Aten. She'd be capable as well. So leaving the hospital, I made my way to her office, asking a dog along the way to find Cramer and Zip and tell them to go to Aten's office. Why didn't I use my sleeve? Didn't wear one. Hardly ever did.

I wasn't against the device, it had its uses. You could track anyone, replay vids, even link to the ship computer for searches and information. But wearing one made me always feel accessible, crowded, and, especially, stupid, lacking brain exercise. I preferred to carry questions, worries, and thoughts myself. Later, in my little bedroom, I could always transcribe them or record them if I needed to remember anything long-term.

I got to Aten's office about the same time as Zip and Cramer. "Aten, I had a thought. Do you remember Mary?"

"Mary from the office at Systems?"

"Yep, that's the one. How about this—the docs are making a harness to record all they can from me. And I am wearing the node that links back to you. How about we hook all that up to the main computer and monitor it from here, you and Cramer both. He knows what it means to be in-System; you know what it's like to be the System. Between you, you should be able to interpret the data and, maybe, help me out." They were looking at each other, then at me, and nodding. "Okay, then listen to another idea. I am not speeded up. I was in there for what seemed like hours and hours, but it was less than three, right?" They nodded again, "So, if I send you a message, as slowly as I can, perhaps it'll come to you speeded up, a little, but you can replay the message almost in quarter time if I have calculated properly." Aten agreed. "And, here's my real idea . . ." I paused for effect. "If I implant a second ear node," I tapped the left side by my ear, "Apollo should be able to talk to you. Playback from you to me is possible if you record something and speed it up . . ." I shook my head, "No, scratch that. Apollo can change the speed at his end. You respond to him and he'll handle the rest." I sat down on the couch, "What do you think?"

Of course, they loved it. Aten wanted so badly to speak to her twin, and Cramer wanted to be in on the front line of our excursion. I know I had pandered to their base needs, taken advantage even a little. But the truth was, I wanted the backup, and if I didn't make it out, I needed these two and Apollo to be able to determine why and what that meant for them all.

I had forgotten Zip, of course. Zip walked over to me, placed his teeth over my hand, and grabbed hold, careful not to break the skin. *Not fair.* Smart dog.

I thought, *I know.*

Zip wagged his tail, and as he let go and walked past me said, *You me care too.*

I wasn't sure if he meant he cared about me or was empathizing that he also cared about them as well. Either way, I knew

Zip understood the need to give them a role. Cramer had an odd look on his face, but I paid no attention. Aten said there was work to do and she called up Doc Todd and explained the need for another node. Cramer said he'd walk to the hospital with me while Aten continued her discussion with Todd on how the link would now have to be hooked into the main computer portal in her office.

Time to get this done and ready. I had other dimensions to visit.

# 27

## A PROSPECT OF UGLY WALLPAPER

A day later I was ready but the computer hookup took a little longer. The problem stemmed from isolation of data. Aten was worried any data coming in from me could, if it carried any octal code, infect the ship's main computer. She solved this with a one-way controller. Data coming in was routed to a server memory annex and once there, could not be accessed on the main frame. As Aten described it, the retrieval and decoding would be done on an away-portable unit, self-contained. "I can access everything through this unit and stay away from the mainframe, which is acting only as a pipeline, one way, to the memory annex." She tested it, purposely wrote an octal code version of my swap FAT file program, and it ran safely.

I pocketed a copy of her octal version of my swap tomatoes program.

Aten had other worries as well, "Look Simon, we've got wires running all over the place now. None of this hook-up to your harness can be laser or wireless radio signals, we need uncorrupted signal, which may not replicate, so each bit will be original, or treated that way as priceless." I wanted to know why this was a problem. "Problem? Not really," she responded, "but all of these connections are temporary, and with the spinning of the ship, the jury-rigged swivel couplings in the flight deck entry cylinder may not have a very long shelf life. Half of those swivel connections we're using, for the most important connections, are pilot communications' circuits. At some point, we'll need to recapture those, especially if there's an emergency. We may have to cut you off, so if you hear me telling you to exit, you must exit." She paused, "What I am saying is please try and make this work quickly, for the safety of the ship and yourself, okay?"

She made a good point, but I needed to help her feel more assured, more confident. "Look Aten, if you are speaking to Apollo, if that works, he'll keep an eye on everything—what I'm doing and what you need to be changing or recording. Apollo can handle monitoring. If you are not able to talk with Apollo, then I'm likely to be coming back quickly anyway." She started to say something, but I cut her off, "Relax Aten, we have got this. The ship is number one and I won't forget that." Of course, I did have the ship's safety as a number one priority providing everyone understood that Earth's safety came before the safety of everyone on board, Aten included. Had she known what I knew about Earth's timetable, she would have agreed. I was fairly certain of that. Well, certain enough.

I had not told anyone about the schedule to Earth's destruction for a reason. And Apollo knew I wouldn't. Why worry people over something they can do nothing about? Yes, the Path meant I should tell the truth, but part of the Path means to do no harm. Until the people on board could actually do something about the threat posed to earth, I felt I was on the Path not sharing the danger with them. Either I would talk to the Vast Pattern, or whomever, and get the solar flare order reversed or I would fail and Earth would be doomed. There was one other possibility to my next encounter with the hydra and the only person I needed to discuss that with was Doc Todd. I asked Zip to find him and bring him to my quarters.

"You wanted to see me Simon?" Todd was casually dressed, off duty as I knew he would be.

"Thanks, Zip, see you later." And Zip padded off. "Doc, tomorrow I'm going in system, into the hydra, the Vast Pattern. And I need a personal promise from you. No questions asked, no revealing this to anybody . . ."

"That's not fair, nor is that a promise I can keep from my crewmates. We're on the Path . . ."

"Yes, I know, and that's why I need you to promise so they can live out their lives on the Path. One person needs to know, one person needs to carry out my instructions if I fail or even if I succeed but can't come back. I cannot ask Cramer or Aten because they do not have your skill set. You are the only one on board who can do this for me if I don't come back . . . who can save the crew and this flight."

"You are asking me to break the trust . . ."

"No, I'm not, just hold this as a secret for a while. I am asking you to man up and place the needs of everyone above your own comfort. If I don't make it back, everyone will know and then you can reveal what we discussed and what I made you promise, but until then you must swear to keep it secret."

He was pensive for a moment. "So, I am not really lying to anyone, just not being forthcoming until necessary?" I nodded. "That is a role as a surgeon I can make. We do that every time we perform a procedure. We tell the patient what he or she needs to know—but just enough, never lying—to ease fears and restore calm—calm necessary for the patient to relax and allow us to perform at our best." He had clearly rationalized his approval. Settling himself comfortably, he leaned forwards and said, "Okay, then, what's the secret? I'll keep it safe and private, I promise."

"It is likely that I may die out there." He looked shocked. "No, not physically but I may become so removed from my physical body that I may appear to be dead. And here comes the tricky part. If that's the case, no one, and I mean no one must be allowed to permanently disconnect the dome wires. I will need . . ."

He was very agitated, "How the hell can we keep you alive out there? If you are dead, as you say, then we have only hours of oxygen to revive you and we cannot do that in space, we cannot sustain you out in free space . . . what you ask is impossible."

I had thought about this, he needed to listen and agree. "Doc, to put someone in hibernation all you need are a few things, right? A safe environment, very low levels of $O_2$, extreme cold, gel support packing, and your special blood serum. Right?" He nodded. "Okay then, if I lose consciousness and appear life-less, I will not be dead at all if there is any—and I mean any—Glasgow mental scale in evidence, accepted?" He nodded. "Then please accept that I'll be out there, but I'll have left my body behind. All you have to do is leave the dome in place, have them bring me back in, have them run this patch cable to the inflatable outside," I passed him the coil of wires that engineering and I had prepared, sort of a long extension cord, "plug it into the connection, run it back through the Ferrofluidic airlock into the below flight deck compartment and re-hook me as quickly as possible. There, below the flight deck, stick me into a hibernation bag, nice and cold, pump my body full of your serum and leave me be."

"What then? If we disconnect you while you are not in your body, won't that kill you?"

"Maybe, but I'd be dead anyway without $O_2$. My only chance of coming back would be to have a pathway to my body. And by the time Apollo and Aten have talked and Aten and Cramer have figured out if it is safe to proceed to Angelica, well, wake me up if we make planet fall—if you can." Neither of us said anything for a moment. Doc Todd was trying to weigh the medical side. I was waiting for the next obvious three questions.

"And if you don't come out of it?" There it was, the first question. Nothing I could do to avoid it.

"Try and find a nice burial place for me on Angelica."

Todd looked dejected. And the second one—"Why, why are you doing this?"

"Apollo told me Gaia has received instructions that all life on Earth is going to be terminated within two and a half years. I am the only one who can go into this system and try to talk to the Vast Pattern and ask them, it, to stop. That's the danger we all face. Not a tough decision for me. Would it be for you?"

He was dejected. "No, I suppose not. I struggled for almost one hundred years to keep you alive and bring you to consciousness. I'm getting old and wanted to see you save the flight, be the leader of the crew. Now you are telling me I must, in a sense, provide your return to a coma or bury you if you and I fail. That's not something I am happy with." And then came the third question, "Why, how, will my actions save the lives of the crew?"

"Doc if I have guessed correctly, although I may appear dead, my brain function may allow me to proceed within the hydra and secure safe passage. So, disconnecting me, so-called reviving me may be exactly the wrong thing to do and may be seen as an attack on my entity inside the hydra. I need you to allow me to remain dead, for the sake of the safety of the crew."

He paused, looking glum, stood, and offered his hand. I took it with my junior sized mitt. "Simon, it has been a pleasure working with you and, yes, I will adhere exactly to your terms and conditions. I promise."

As I was thanking him, he wiped a tear from a cheek and so I gave him a hug, which he returned fiercely. I let him have the last word. Well, why not?    .

"Simon, do me a favor will you? Try, try really hard to come back alive and save everyone, will you?" And with that, he left me alone to prepare for the fateful next day. Why fateful? I already knew that the levels I had reached were without any contact and I could not go forward or go back to talk to Apollo. It was only that shape that had taken me back, a shape I knew was sentient, or at least guided, but I had no idea what was its motive or plan. If I failed to unravel that mystery, I was staying out there, no matter how long it took.

Either way, I knew they would have to bring me back in. I only hoped that momentarily breaking contact would bring me back awake immediately or that reestablishing contact would link my mind and body once again, eventually. It was a gamble either way.

As was the plunge into the jellyfish that I was about to undertake—a huge gamble.

# 28

## CLOSER TO THE SHIP BUT MILES AWAY FROM SAFETY

We repeated the same procedure through the airlock only this time I knew the connection and plunge could happen anywhere outside. So I had the crew tether the same twenty-meter circumference tank, pressurized with nitrogen, to the rail cleating and advised everyone to stay inside and only come out if there was something wrong. Cramer stayed outside to inflate the silver balloon. The extra wires from the inflatable were run through the Ferrofluidic airlock into the flight deck and thence, by various connections and swivels, to Aten's office. Then, after about an hour, all were all tested and I was given the go ahead. I climbed into the inflatable and sealed it up, talking with Cramer to see if he agreed the seals were good.

He said they were and commenced inflation. Once it was up, he merely said, "Godspeed friend," and left to go back through the hatch to the lower flight deck. Aten was on the radio and confirmed that she could record both nodes, one via a hook-up to her computer annex, the other via the VHF radio.

I plugged in the thirty-two wire connector and then said a silent prayer to Angie as I connected the eight-wire connector and got immediately to the storeroom as Apollo and I had discussed. I initiated the mirror program to make the little body eaters leave me alone, and then I said the command "For god's sake . . ." and was into the passageway, data streaming all around.

I sang, "We'll meet again . . ."

"Don't know where don't know when—Hello Simon. Are you ready?" Apollo, on cue.

I assumed the nodes were working and that Aten and Cramer were already transcribing. I had to clue Apollo in quickly before he revealed what he and I knew about Earth and what I knew Apollo would have surmised about where I was going. "Apollo, I have not told everyone everything. You should know I have a left ear node as well, can you find the frequency? Private communication."

"I can and have found the nodes, separate frequencies. What is the left one connected to? Simon, I have deactivated the left node and the right node is being disrupted for signal back to the ship."

"The left one goes to Aten, she'll slow down anything recorded off of that node. I want you to use it exclusively, exclusively understand, for communication with Aten. The right node is for sensations, my thoughts, the sensors attached to me now are all being recorded. But Cramer and Aten will be listening to the left node, understand?"

"What's going on?"

"I have not told them about Earth and I have not told them where I am going. Now, turn everything back on or they will start retrieval of me . . ."

"I understand. You are on the Path. Simon's slightly crooked Path, but still the Path. Reconnecting." Apollo was smart, figured it all out within seconds. "Excuse me while I talk to my sister."

I floated in the passageway, my mirror self doing the same but upside down for some reason. I was thinking about any significance when Apollo was back. "Aten and I have exchanged data and I am re-transmitting all relevant Gaia data and Earth's situation while you and I proceed here. There is more than I sent last time. They need to know Simon. I urge caution going deeper into the Vast Pattern. You were out of touch for too long last time."

"Okay, any suggestions? I can get to the next level, remember, but I am powerless to go anywhere and there is no code, no appearance of any electrical activity there until geometric shapes turn up . . ."

"Shapes? Can you describe them?"

"Imagine a complete ribosome but as a closed loop, making a geometric structure. And yes, Apollo, I recognized that my brain may be making it up, based on my theories that the whole universe is a living organism. It is not, I know, but they looked like ribosomes, solid ribosomes. And why shouldn't a function of this brain, this diffuse brain, have components resembling the building blocks of life?"

"It could Simon, I am not saying it isn't. But it is not a living entity, it is devoid of physical needs of DNA. It simply is. Ribosomes should have no part here. But if these shapes manipulated you, it could be that a shape to better fit you, to capture and move you, was chosen, designed, to make that possible."

Trust Apollo to frighten me just as he was being brilliant. If it could know I was a bioform, at least my body was, and tailor a conveyor shape to mimic my basic building block—of course, I was so damn stupid, "Wait, Apollo, that's it! It was meant as a sign, and when I did not react correctly, it transported me back, every time. I thought it only seemed to want to observe. What if what it was waiting for was a response?"

"It is possible . . ." Apollo's voice seemed to trail off. Was he thinking?

I decided to tell him what I thought, "Years ago a scientist called Sam something or other was working with dolphins. He wanted to teach one dolphin his name so he repeated it and got back a distinctive squeak from the dolphin. This guy got frustrated, repeated his name, Sam, over and over. The dolphin always responded with the same sound. In desperation to establish any contact at all, the man repeated the squeak the dolphin had made. The dolphin leaped from the water, clearly excited, swam twice around the tank at high speed, approached the man on the dock, rose up, and made a perfect replica sound, "Sam." Apollo, I feel like an idiot. If you wanted to start a conversation with a puny entity, if you showed them the smallest part of what made them a life form, a ribosome, wouldn't you think the idiot would guess what you were doing? Opening a conversation?"

"Simon, I have the dictionary from Gaia. Here is the sequence for "Greetings." Can you discern the code?"

Before me appeared a cube with four numbers on each face, three-dimensional, total of twenty-four numbers. "How are you doing this Apollo? How can you make it appear?"

"Turn your head Simon." The cube stayed in front of my eyes. "I am accessing your optic nerve, well your pseudo-optic nerve through the cone and rod sensor package they have fitted you out with. I can make you think you are seeing images I construct."

"Okay, I see the cube, and I can copy it into my left brain, put it on the shelf so to speak, no problem, done. How do I play it back to say greetings?"

"Simon, remember being in-System? You placed code within structure. I suggest doing the same here. Offer the cube to the fractal ribosome image."

"Okay, here goes . . . and I gave the god command as I was thinking about it. I was instantly buffeted by the heat barrier and then the empty space, vastness, and two orbs approached but stayed out of reach. I repeated, as best I could remember, exactly what I had said before. The orbs went away. The ribosome fractal shape appeared. It started spinning and I mentally said *closer* and yes, the shape was closer. Either I had moved or it had. I mentally took Apollo's octal "greeting" off my left-brain shelf and proffered it. *Please take this . . .*

I had not expected the response I got. I was pretty sure I had not moved, in fact, I was frozen still buy some force, but I could see parts of my body, the image of my body, being disassembled and rotated, free floating. Several more fractal shapes appeared, all ribosome-like in structure, different colors, different rotational cycles. Each one took a section of my body parts and then disappeared. Somehow, I was still there. All my senses seemed to be working, but I was without the image of my body.

Then it occurred to me I had not seen them take my head, so maybe that's all I needed to be conscious and aware. The original ribosome was still there, spinning. Silent. Then it stopped rotating and simply vanished.

I was left alone. Okay, my head was left alone. I called out, "Come back!" When that didn't work, I used the god command. Nothing. I never felt so alone in my whole life.

Moments later, all of my body parts reappeared, and once released, they drifted back to take their proper stations to form my body. Still alone, at least I knew I wasn't forgotten.

I should be so lucky.

Out of the nothingness, a snake appeared. It was so long and complex that I could not, at first, realize what it was. It was a complete DNA model, a superhelix. Or was it a model? Could it be the real thing? The DNA snake, as it appeared to me, began to attach itself to my right arm and, twisting around, wound itself up until it reached my neck and then, horrifyingly, climbed the side of my head. My vision was blocked as it crossed over my eyes. It then shrank and I thought that maybe it had disappeared—until I felt the worst pain of my entire life.

The DNA snake had wormed its way into my brain, using the node incision spot behind my right ear. In fear and agony, I called out, *Apolloooo*. There was no answer.

# 29

## PAYING THE PIPER, ONCE MORE DEAD

I lost consciousness pretty much immediately. The pain was too much to bear. Years ago, I had a terrible accident and ripped cartilage in my knee. A doctor examining me was twisting the knee this way and that to get better 3-D MRI table images. The pain was excruciating and I told him I might pass out. He blithely said, "No one ever passes out from pain, it wakes you up, sissy." A second later, I proved him wrong. Not about the sissy part.

The DNA snake's intrusion and resultant pain was like that. I could not stand it. I passed out.

I came to in the passageway with Apollo slowly repeating my name. My first instinct was to check for body parts. There were none really, of course, but eyes and ears seemed to be working, things looked normal as I reviewed hands, feet, torso, and, not least, I checked that my head was still attached by placing my hands on my ears. Oh yes, it was there. I also felt for the node incision point behind my right ear. It did not appear to be there, but what could I tell? Maybe it never was apparent inside here, maybe it was only my imagination that made me think the snake had entered at that precise spot.

Time to test my voice, so I responded, "Apollo, I hear you."

"Simon, it is so very good to hear your voice again."

"Am I dead?" And then I heard a babble of sounds and could not discern what they were.

Apollo responded, "No, I will tell him." Who was he talking to? "Simon, what you heard were low-frequency modulations of Aten's, a doctor Todd', and Cramer's voices. I can translate what they have said if you want."

"Please."

"Cramer said, "Simon, I don't want to be *it* all alone, wake the hell up!" The doctor said, "Don't rush . . ." And Aten said, "Darling, please be kind, he's done all this for us . . ." After that, I could not hear more."

"Can they hear you?"

"Not since you disappeared. My ability is listening only."

"Okay. Situation? Obviously I am not dead."

"Technically you are dead, but Doctor Todd followed your secret instructions and took you inside and they have placed you in stasis as requested. He wants permission to revive you."

"I wish you could tell him *denied*, for now. I need to know if we've made any progress here."

"Oh, yes Simon. I have." Was I wrong that I heard a touch of ego there? "After you reappeared, there was a connection from your brain to the patterns you see before you. It looked like this . . ." he displayed the floating image before my eyes as he had done before, only this time I could see myself and that snake clearly sticking out of the front of my head. The double helix had lengthened and connected itself to the octal code streaming in the passageway. It looked alive, the snake that is. Frightening. Now, I never minded snakes, but the prospect of one sticking out of the front of my brain was a little terrifying. I felt my forehead and damn if it wasn't still there.

"Apollo, what is this thing for?"

"As soon as it connected to the data stream, your body was inter-connected to the mainframe on the ship and deliberate signals were sent back and forth, using your form as a transmission line to probe the ship, much like an electrical connection. The access on the ship's end was limited." *Bravo, Aten for your one-way access!* "So then, the connection searched for another avenue, and it found the connection through me. I am afraid it has penetrated all that I know, one hundred percent, all memory banks, everything."

That was either seriously bad news or, perhaps? "Apollo, the result, please, I can't stand the suspense."

"The probe through you to me was not a one-way access. Everything it saw I was seeing as well. What it was looking for, and found, was most interesting for me. I opened a dialog with Gaia, who was shocked I should be conversing directly with or through Regus. Yes, Simon, it's all right, but you are now hooked to Regus." I guessed Apollo could read my vital signs and felt the sudden elevation in my anxiety. "Anyway, I patched Gaia into Regus' search probe and there seemed to be an argument. Well, not an argument, more a territorial conflict. What transpired was that Regus did not understand how you and I could be in this dimension, could access this dimension and the one beyond where you went Simon. Apparently, that next dimension is where everything coalesces, where the Vast Pattern is definable, qualify-able. You were not supposed to be there. No life form of any universe has ever reached that dimension. Regus cannot access that level . . ."

"But if this is Regus' snake, it appeared there . . ."

"No Simon, Regus is this place, this plexus, this data stream. The double helix was created at the next level, presumably by the Vast Pattern that encompasses these dimensions—the one of our temporal existence and one beyond, the one you landed in when you said there was nothing, then Regus and then beyond. The Vast Pattern is not very pleased with your intrusion. Regus is being held accountable as is the dimension our universe is in."

"You are kidding . . ."

"No Simon, it seems the entire universe may be eliminated because you broached dimensional security. This universe, it seems, is just a tiny portion of the Vast Pattern. If infected, it will be excised."

"Apollo, what level of consciousness are we talking about? Is Regus sentient, capable of reason?"

"No. Regus is a set of connections; *if, what if,* applications, not even full programs, to ensure the gathering and resetting of parameters of transmissions from bio-life forms located across the universe. Regus is like a super-self-modulating plexus."

"Apollo, come on, what is the purpose of these transmissions? I know you, that is the most important question, you must have it figured out by now."

"I do, but you are not going to like it." Oh, great, he was playing word games now. I stayed silent knowing the delay would eat at his superior clock-speed intellect and frustrate him. "Okay, here it comes. Everything Gaia transmits, everything Regus coalesces and collects from all planets—how is that somehow absorbed into that other dimension? All of that is structure, the very essence of the generated pandimensional structure. It is, in short, the very make-up of the universes' matrix. Let me explain. Strong emotions of fealty, love, bonding, belonging, to be a part of, cohesiveness—these form the bond, the glue. Feelings, mental output, form the weave, the fabric. And in a sense, this universe is one of the engines that produce the fabric, perhaps even the final ethic, of the multi-universe that the Vast Pattern controls, lives in, manipulates. The energy, all the dark energy, dark matter, and mass, all these are part of the structure, not the purpose, not the working. The working of this universe is reliant upon the output, the productivity of the life forms on selected planets, on planets that can support life. And this universe is a part of the Vast Pattern in so far as it proves productive to the whole."

"How many generator universe types are there?"

"Regus does not contain that information. That is beyond Regus' simple capability and memory. Gaia does not know. I suspect there is one Regus for every universe just as there is one Gaia for every livable planet. Regus has self-regulating capability for all this universe's functions. But it is limited to that, Regus cannot access that next dimension and, purposefully, Regus does not have ambition, desire, to do so. Regus is a collector, an amalgamator, a giant Great Attractor feeding off all of the Great Attractors—gathering input, moderating systems, acting as a transmission hub. Regus can modulate, exterminate, create, seed, even alter every bioform planet in the universe, but it does so autonomously, or at least with sequence and parameters that are not self-determinate. It is basically a nexus with programming to handle transmissions, gathering, passing on and so forth." Apollo was sounding like a schoolteacher. "And when you get down to Gaia, interestingly, there are sets of pseudo-awareness programs running to allow Gaia to manage the finite, whereas Regus cannot determine anything smaller than a planet, a neuron in your doctors' analogy."

"So, what's this thing for?" I pointed to the snake, still attached to my forehead. "Surely Regus cannot see anything here."

"True, but something can instruct Regus to look, and that's what has happened—what is still happening. Everything we say and do here is being monitored, of that I am certain. What tiny, infinitesimal information can be gleaned is beyond your or my reason of perceived need or calculation of consequence simply because whatever the Vast Pattern is, it is, by definition, greater than we can perceive it to be and therefore greater than we can think it might be. It is beyond our imagination. To something as omnipresent as the Vast Pattern when you consider the scope of the multi-universe, there is no chance you or I can calculate the response, if, what if parameters the Vast Pattern is involved with."

It was so much to think about.

"But Simon, that DNA snake as you call it, cannot be disconnected. Even when your body was taken back inside the ship and disconnected and reconnected, the DNA snake remained. Whatever it is doing, beyond accessing me through you, I cannot determine."

"Is the ship safe? How long?" I meant how long have I been unconscious.

"The ship is safe and underway. I monitored a decision that was made to travel to Angelica, to risk all. Arrival is expected in three months. You have been comatose for a little over three years."

My god, that was a shock. "Three years? But Earth's schedule, Gaia's schedule . . ."

"Yes, Simon, that deadline passed. Solar activity was suddenly stopped the moment you passed out. I am unable to determine how and exactly why. It was not because it was presented as a peace offering. Gaia is unsure and without instruction. Regus is, as I have explained, incapable of solo-thought. The cessation of Earth's demise was deliberate, but who, what, or how is unknown."

I was floating inside the passageway, Regus itself. Okay, I could acclimatize to that. I had known this trip, this plunge, could be fatal. *So be it, if I only saved Earth, it was worth it.* But what was worrying me was planet fall for the ship and if the Vast Pattern, or whatever it was, would allow bioforms alien to that new word to infect the bioforms that could already be there. It was one thing for humans to take the risk for themselves, armed as they were with medicines, DNA splicing, and a host of other human medical safeguards—but it was an entirely different matter for them to make an enemy of a new Gaia or Regus's plans and programs—let alone the Great Attractor's universal design. "Apollo, does whatever this is . . ." I motioned to the snake, "Know the ship has departed?"

"I can only say that Regus is unaware. I have been studying the programs and interactions you see before you over the past years, and I am confident it is all input and almost no output. But some output does occur once every millisecond, by Earth time, and is focused toward another portal, another dimension. I suspect the one you entered. And keeping a careful watch, I was able to detect a spike of code activity in the passageway patterns you see before you, directed, well, coded toward the center of the Pisces' galaxy. A data stream in the patterns ceased shortly afterward. There was definitely a signal going out and then one coming in. I was able to decode that returning signal to confirm the energy signature equivalent to a supernova being turned off. One that could have been seen on Earth in one hundred years or so."

Something turned off a supernova? The strength of the forces at play here were almost beyond imagination.

Almost, not quite. It made sense to me. If the threat to our solar system with increased solar activity had been stopped, it made sense that a balance had to take place on the other side of the Great Attractor. I gleaned that from my rather rudimentary understanding of Dr. Tully's reflective diagram of the super-galaxies mirroring each other.

"Apollo, could our sun have become a supernova? Was that the outcome you predicted before?"

"Yes Simon, while you were sleeping," *cute use of that term*, I thought, "I recalibrated the rapidity of the solar eruptions and concluded that solar flares were merely the indication of rapid solar collapse which would have ended in a supernova."

"Okay, so, as things stand, Regus doesn't know anything." I pondered a moment, formulating a plan. "Apollo, if I issue the command to plunge back to that empty place, will you lose all communication?"

"Yes."

"Can you stand that?"

"Of course, but Regus' commands may be confused. Wait while I determine if there are fail-safes in place. Translating octal, especially disappearing and reappearing octal across dimensions, requires computing time. One moment . . ."

And he was gone. I took the time to "feel" the snake. It was pulsating, tickled a little. So my sense of touch was working fine. Doc Todd would have a field day with that sensory data. I gave it a little tug and immediately the pain was intense, so I stopped. I decided to release a mirror image, my little program, and instantly it appeared looking straight at me. Raise the right hand and it raised the left. The mirror had no DNA snake though. I wondered if I could swap places.

Apollo came back in my head, "Simon, there is no failsafe in place. I did not think there would be. Your presence is clearly a unique experience for all the systems here and I am ninety-seven point eight percent positive they have not encountered anything approaching your intrusion before. You may proceed. But would you mind sharing your plan? I can tell you have created a mirror image. You always seem to have a plan, my friend. I just hope you remain on the Path."

"The Path? Oh, yes old friend, the Path it is. I think if I manage to get back to that other dimension, this thing will have no connection. And that should elicit repair or communication or perhaps attaching itself onto the mirror me. Either way, what I want to try and do is simple: Show I am alive and self-determining. If everything here consists of pure functions, *if and what if* programming, then an analog anomaly must be different and, therefore, interesting. Let's see what the Vast Pattern makes of me. Self-determining me."

And because I didn't really want time to think about it, I left. First, I retreated to the storeroom, careful not to exit fully. Snake stayed with me. I waited for the immunosuppressant programs. As soon as they appeared, which I found odd because mirror me came along too, I gave the god command. Back in the passageway with the mirror me, I immediately gave the god command one more time and was into the deadly heat where the snake disappeared causing me great pain, before I landed, if that's the right word, back into the nothingness. The pain and the snake were gone. And the mirror me was left behind.

"Hello? Is anybody there?"

This time there was no ribosome greeting, no DNA super double helix. What appeared was my sweet, darling Angie, arms and legs spread out, slowly revolving.

# 30

## NO, IT IS NOT HER, REALLY

It doesn't matter what you think you know, it doesn't matter what you rationalize or attempt to block out—the reality staring me in the face was my Angie, or a damn good copy. It didn't move limbs or body, it didn't speak, it didn't do anything. The form slowly revolved, like the ribosome had done, up and down, spinning, every portion of Angie's body was presented. The really odd thing was that her clothing changed, her skin color changed a bit, her hair was long, then short, then ponytailed. One moment she was nude—that was disconcerting—and then dressed in the jumpsuit she wore the last time I saw her alive when we were in our External Tank home.

It was then that I realized that whatever power this was, they were replaying my own memories, in sequence for all the times I saw Angie, from that first day in the Calhoun Rat Studies complex till her passing. This was a message for me. So I said *thank you* and meant it.

That produced a second form, my son Freddie, and went through all stages of his life. Then my father and mother, Cramer, my old pal Mary, Sheila, a host of other people including my ex-wife, which I could have done without, and then the doctors on board, Zip, Abadine, Maryann, and crew.

Looking at my ex-wife I wondered, *What did I see in her?* As soon as I thought that, her image disappeared.

Interesting. Kindly censorship.

Then came images I recognized intimately. I saw the insides of the System on that first day when Peter became aware. Then, finally, I saw Aten as an infant through Aten grown up at eighteen. And then a toddler appeared, a young girl all on her own—the last apparition.

Now, I did not recognize the child, I have to say. But if this being was projecting what was in my head, surely it must be a child I had seen sometime, somewhere. My instinct was to know the child better, so I motioned for the child apparition to approach and it did. None of the other tumbling forms slowed their slow spinning or disappeared, but the child drifted over, stable now, and I reached out a hand.

As my fingers touched, and I was sure I had that sensation of touch, I saw a projection before my eyes. As Apollo had done before, I saw inside the ship. I saw Cramer and Aten leaning over a body on a hospital bed with a dome on and I saw the child there, sitting on the bed next to the recumbent figure, holding its hand.

The figure lying there was me.

The child's mouth was moving. She was saying something. I could not discern what it was. Here I was, holding the image of the child's hand in this dimension and the real child was holding my lifeless hand back in my dimension. Somehow, it was very comforting and I squeezed the image's hand slightly.

The vision before me changed. The little toddler girl looked at Cramer and said something, clearly very excited. Aten was weeping.

Thought to myself, *Aten cries easily, poor Ra.*

Cramer mouthed something, and the little girl looked back at my lifeless form and squeezed my hand.

*I felt that.* Damn, but I felt it. So I squeezed back. She was clearly gleeful.

Cramer grabbed my hand and squeezed. I felt nothing. I didn't know how much time I had here—I hoped the little girl would hold my hand again as I was still holding the apparition's hand. She did and I felt pressure again.

Time to try something different.

I wondered if I could tap a finger, a real finger—I did it here and she saw it move there. Okay, let's see if the ex-military jock Cramer can remember his Morse code. A finger tap for a dot and a squeeze for a dash. ×× / ×- -- / ××-× ××-× ×. I repeated *I am fine* three times until Cramer got it. He grabbed the doc's tablet and entered the dots and dashes. I could see him telling Aten and everyone. They were all quite happy.

*Nice to be loved.*

Okay then. Aten will know I can program in my head, let's see if this can get more complicated. Using the two signals, I made binary code of a simple phrase, starting with the one I had just gotten through. At first, Cramer was tapping the tablet quickly, trying to keep up, puzzled by the Morse code. I paused my binary code after *I am fine* then repeated it twice more. Aten took the tablet and smiled, immediately seeing the binary code, a tap for a zero and a squeeze for a one.

Okay then, people, here it comes—I started over again with *I am fine*, familiarity helping them and finished the message.

01001001  00100000  01100001  01101101  00100000  01100110
01101001  01101110  01100101  00100000  01001001  00100000
01100001  01101101  00100000  01101000  01100101  01110010

01100101  00100000  01100001  01101110  01101111  01110100
01101000  01100101  01110010  00100000  01100100  01101001
01101101  01100101  01101110  01110011  01101001  01101111
01101110  00100000  01110111  01100001  01101001  01110100
00100000  01100110  01101111  01110010  00100000  01101101
01100101

*I am fine I am here another dimension wait for me.*

Aten and Cramer were hugging. Doc Todd was dancing around behind them. I knew they got it. The identity and any connection I might have to the little girl still puzzled me until I saw Cramer bend down and hug her. They had a child! It was my friends' child and children are much more attuned to otherness, different wavelengths—open-minded.

I realized I loved that child. It was the child of my two closest friends. I loved them. I loved their child. So basic. So, why did the word pop into my head, primitive?

Now, before me, the apparition crowd in this void began to disperse leaving only me and the little girl holding hands in the nothingness. She did not want to let go, and as I found it so comforting, neither did I.

*Where do we go from here?* I thought.

With that, the girl turned and, still holding my hand, pulled me past the disappearing crowd toward an open slit in the nothingness beyond, through which I could see stars, galaxies, and supergalaxies so vast yet so miniscule because there were so many in such a small opening. As she waved her free hand over her head and around down back to her feet, the slit opened to encompass the space we were in, and I was floating in the midst of a universe. The immensity of the stars, galaxies, supergalaxies was overwhelming. I could see two supergalaxies combining, colliding at a Great Attractor, looking like two fireworks sliding toward each other. The girl was studying my face, then moved her hand back around and the slit contracted and closed.

Turning, she waved her hand and another slit opened, and I saw a bright light so intense I knew it would blind me if I had had physical eyes. Around the bright light were rings of alternating colors, expanding spheres, vast and powerful energy flux, all expanding at an incredible rate. I was smiling. It was wonderful. She waved her hand again and the slit closed.

I knew I had just seen a Big Bang. Which universe, where it was, didn't matter. I had seen a Big Bang, of that I was sure. And it unnerved me completely all the while I was overjoyed. How close to creation can one get? Surely, this was beyond my capabilities to fathom, let alone explain what I had seen to anyone else.

*Please pause,* I asked. She waited. I took a metaphysical breath. *Okay, I'm ready . . .*

She moved her hand across the nothingness again, and in a tiny slit I could see the ship, Angie's glistening skin, in safe orbit around a planet, green and blue beneath, oceans and land, polar caps, and two moons. All the soup-fixin's for development and maintenance of life. The ship was in very high orbit, and I surmised Aten and the nav crew had preserved consumables by allowing a slow deterioration of orbit until de-orbit through the atmosphere would be natural.

They had made it. I was genuinely pleased. It was heartwarming.

The girl closed the slit and we drifted for a while. Hard to tell how far or where, but I did have the sensation of being pulled. She waved her free hand and a small slit, maybe five feet high and two wide, appeared through which all I could see was blue, bright blue. I stared closely into the slit and saw rays of light coming upward. I could not see where they came from. It was water. I almost could touch it. Suddenly, the blue disappeared and black moved across the slit, it had small gray and black circular objects. I recoiled. The circles looked like they were stuck onto whatever it was. Unexpectedly, an eye appeared, a great big eye, looking straight at me. Then it moved off, followed by more gray and black circle things until a tail appeared. *A whale. Oh, my god, it's a whale.*

You know, after seeing the Big Bang, I really should not have been so moved to see a whale. Of course, I allowed myself the joy of being surprised because it was not like any whale I had ever seen before. It could have been small, big, prehistoric, or alien. I didn't know. I had no perspective. What I knew was that seeing something real, something alive, seeing it here in this dimension, floored me.

Now, I don't want to give the impression these slits were like vids. They were real, of that I was certain. And that's why, when the next slit was opened showing a valley and grass I began to wonder if what was being shown was a way for me to exit. The girl motioned me toward the slit. The problem was, I was not physically here. I was here, true enough, at least my consciousness was, had been for more than three years apparently, but there was no way I could survive if I entered one of these slits.

*I cannot go. I have to stay or go back the way I came.*

The child looked at me and changed shape. I wasn't expecting Dad.

# 31

# DAD'S THEORY, ONLY ON A PANDIMENSIONAL SCALE

When I was a child of eight, my father told me that everything was related, not relative, but related to my actions and desires. I recall him telling me and remember exactly what he said. Basically, the gist was that the man you saw on the street would, when you stopped watching him, vanish and re-appear when you next needed him. You think you travel by plane (back then) but God, somehow, was manipulating your reality for you; you sat down, noise and effects happened, you got up and the scenery had been changed, presto, you were in Paris. But not. There was no "there" over there. It was all here. Everything you saw was related to what you saw before. There were clues, if you looked for them, to God's theater as he called it. For years as a kid I searched and studied, often thinking he was possibly right, a face in a crowd here, a dress there, a somehow familiar landscape and always déjà vu.

Then, one day, I was stranded on that fateful expedition on the asteroid and knew what it was like to be truly alone, nobody, no God, nothing. Me. An asteroid. Nothingness. Void. Dad had lied. Well, not lied, he'd made up a far too convincing fairy tale. Or was it? Looking through these slits, what I saw could, very possibly, have been a theatrical backdrop, puppetry by God. Was it possible that there was nothing real, that all reality was a created illusion for the purpose of—what? What purpose could that be?

I needed to discuss this with someone. I needed Apollo. But how to get back there?

The apparition, sorry, Dad was still holding my hand. Why not ask? *Dad, may we go back to Regus so I can talk with Apollo?* Nothing happened, I didn't move.

Dad pulled my hand over a ways, without any visual reference I have no idea what a ways is, and stopped, facing me, still holding my hand. With his other hand, he reached up and touched the side of my head, the right side.

Apollo was there, "Simon, is that you?"

"Yes Apollo, it is too hard to explain, can you access my circuits, through the dome?"

"No Simon, but I can hear you and you can obviously hear me. Are you safe?"

I looked at Dad, he seemed benign, so I answered, "Yes, and in no pain. The snake has gone . . ."

"No, it hasn't, it is attached to your mirror program."

"Okay then, anyway I'm here with what looks like Dad. I have been in touch with the ship via binary code and let them know I am safe."

"How was that possible?"

"I'll explain later, but for now I need to figure something out and I suspect it may have a bearing on everything possible. Do you remember Dad's god's theater scenario from before?"

"Yes, it was without scientific foundation, useful philosophically, but not in practice."

"Yes, well, maybe not. Imagine an existence, an entity, dependent on engines developing a certain kind of energy to sustain life form or forms. Imagine those engines are enhanced by those life forms. Let's call the entities gods, okay?"

"If you must, there are over one thousand, four hundred and thirty-two recognized forms of deity in Earth's history . . ."

"Later Apollo. But if these gods need the engines to produce the energy that makes up their existence, then they would monitor those engines, wouldn't they?" Apollo agreed. "Okay then, if monitoring these engines, and assuming they created these engines, they come across something that could interfere with that process, they would be likely to exterminate it, terminate the anomaly, wouldn't they?" Again, Apollo agreed. "So why haven't they?"

Apollo was silent. I called out his name and he responded, "Simon, what you are describing, coupled with the diffuse brain theory, is a possible adaptation and symbiotic relationship theory to account for the non-extinction of anything that could interrupt those engines. In other words, they chose not to."

"Exactly, we may be parasites, once deadly, fulfilling what we think is our destiny but that is, in reality, only the destiny required for us to enhance the Vast Pattern's engines. It never made sense to me that the bioforms on Earth were more important in producing transmissions that Gaia could then transmit off-Earth using the energy of the planet, energy off the core. Yet Gaia resided on the surface, everywhere on the surface, right?"

"That is what I have found, yes."

"That means Gaia is there to monitor, collect and, if necessary, modify these life forms."

"So that the bioforms can make weak energy transmissions? I do not calculate that as likely."

"That's not what bioforms are transmitting. We're not part of the energy solution, maybe we're part of the maintenance program to train and mold other bioforms, change them from infections to symbiotic life forms that actually enhance the energy production. If I'm the first being here, the first life form in this dimension, then it stands to reason we're a pre-eminent life form. We're instructors, okay, okay, certainly not the only ones, but a pre-eminent one. Look, if the structure of the solar system is part of the diffuse brain, it stands to reason that in the construction of the solar system, it would develop a flaw. What's the flaw? A planet that can support life. That life can interrupt the structure of the whole solar system because of the activity of those life forms. Think of the atomic bomb. What other great weapons or planet destruction could life forms concoct—have they concocted billions of times over? Apollo, look, our knowledge, our experiences, from jellyfish to dolphins, dogs, apes, men—all of our transmissions at death are only part of the training programs for other parasites to bring them into the fold, to nurture them, to train them into ways of behavior designed not to interrupt the function of the Vast Pattern's components.

"Look, if you knew you were designing a vast universe or universes and that parts of that universe could develop life forms that could destroy part of your system, it is easier—and certainly given the physics of randomness involved in an enterprise as large as the Vast Pattern—easier to put fail-safe training mechanisms in place, operated by Gaia, reports transmitted through Regus to wherever—assuring you that the system was running perfectly. It's like the human gut, the system adapts to bacteria, and our very existence depends on that symbiotic relationship. But if one bacteria gets out of hand, develops into something we see as nasty, we get doctors to purge it with antibiotics.

"Nope, it is much better to regulate the whole by training. To bring these life forms eventually onto the Path. When we leave the path, we become bad parasites, non-symbiotic forms."

I had remembered learning that our guts contain millions of parasitic bacteria and if they become out of balance, become too numerous or if they die off, either way, they can kill us.

Apollo cut in, "Simon, that bacteria hypothesis is acceptable. But how do these memories, these transmissions get used? Experiences of a man on Earth are hardly useful to an ameba on another planet, are they?"

I was actually laughing now, "Yes, they are Apollo. You see we think we're transmitting memories, well, yes, we are, but the strength of those memories is all about cohesiveness as a species, about relationships, about getting along, about love. Strong emotions. In the same way that talking kindly to your plants makes them grow better—better in a way no scientist has been able to measure. And what's the outcome? What's the real message? Do for others as you would want for you, in short, not just do no harm but help. Look, in the same way a mother feels love for her invisible child in the womb, our transmissions may be channeled to seed, or modify primitive life forms in other galaxies, perhaps other universes to become useful, to fit in, to assist, live as if we know that we are connected and that our actions affect all life! That's a universal message of most religions, most people's personal belief systems, even if they are agnostic. What the Vast Pattern will not want anywhere in the multi-universe world it inhabits, are hostile, anti-Path transmissions."

Dad waved a hand, a giant rift opened, and I could see only orange sky with shimmering globes spaced evenly. Slack-jawed, I stared and said to Apollo, "Ah, Apollo, I am being given a chance to see something no one has ever seen before. Apollo, I am looking at multiple universes, each a sphere, suspended in what looks like orange sky. I do not know why orange or what it means, but I am sure this is what I am seeing. Multi-universes. Oh, my god they exist."

Dad spoke to me, although his lips did not move, *you see what you are supposed to know, what has always been, what will always be. Forever. Balance forever renewed.*

Apollo said, "Simon, I was able to hear that. Amazing. Please thank your father for me."

Dad bowed, just a little.

I couldn't help it, I was feeling giddy from the spectacle we were seeing, "Apollo, you just got head bowing, denoting subservience, friendliness, amicable manners, silly bending over posture."

Apollo laughed and Dad even smiled. Seems a joke is universal.

My dilemma now was how to get back into my very own god's theater universe, get back into my body and at the same time, secure the safety of our parasitic species. The key lay in our usefulness. And I had no idea how—or if—humankind had ever been useful at all.

There had to be a reason we had lived for so long—And then Dad waved his hand and the slit closed returning us to the room without light but where I could see without any perspective, without distance reference, just Dad and me, holding hands. His face was blank, but his eyes were questioning as he did when testing my memory when I was a child. Dad wanted answers, wanted me to reach the right conclusion.

Humans had lived so long? Who was I kidding? If the whole of the life of Earth were made into a day, humanoids would only appear at the last minute and a half. I turned to Dad, "Father, if humans are a recent creation, via evolution, are we a finite species that has failed Gaia and the Vast Pattern? Are we doomed to extinction because we live apart from the natural order, the symbiosis you require?"

Dad nodded.

"What do we need to do to reverse that decision?" I asked.

Dad nodded again.

"Okay, can we be useful to the universe going forward?"

Apollo cut in, "Simon, please repeat what is said to you in case I do not get the transmission . . ." And then his voice in my head stopped. I could not hear Apollo anymore.

Dad's fingers let go of me, and I floated a little. Then his form changed into a glowing orange orb, and inside I could see it contained hundreds, perhaps thousands, perhaps millions of orbs. And then it was joined by another and another identical orb, of different colors, until all above me, all behind me, underneath and all around were orbs, millions and millions of them, each touching the other, each forming part of a whole. Before me floated a pan-multi-universe.

# 32

## WHAT USE WERE WE?

It is hard not to mentally collapse when presented with a reality beyond comprehension. How could I be looking upon one multi-universe let alone a pan-multi-universe? Human sight doesn't work that way. I couldn't be seeing this. Okay, I knew I was being made to see what it wanted me to see. I suppose it calculated what the maximum level of comprehension was for my species.

It overestimated a bit. For me anyway. I was sadly dumb-struck. The orbs, on the other hand, wanted nothing, said nothing—they merely stayed there, floating beyond my reach, filling all that was.

Suddenly I understood the message: *Or could be.* This was all there was and all there could be, ever. The infinite. A world without end. The word world took on a whole new meaning.

Truthfully, I didn't try or want to touch it. Touch a multi-universe, try and reach out and embrace a pan-multi-universe? What, was I that nuts? Nope. It was so beautiful, so radiant, so perfect that I felt totally inferior. It was looking into the face, the existence, the world of a superior entity or entities. I really wasn't sure, but at that moment, it did not matter.

But the thought did occur to me: Was this a single being or merely a manifestation of life that lived on a different plane, dimensional planes? Perhaps I was as foreign to it as it was to me.

On the other hand, everything shown to me felt godly and I did feel inferior floating there, unable to return to Regus' passageway or, better still, to my body on the ship. Suddenly, I had a yearning to be back with my own kind.

But if that was the point, to awe strike me, then why make this pan-multi-universe apparition so human in scale. If I could see it, then that meant it was being shown infinitesimally smaller than it was? Right? Or did the pandimension I was in alter all perspective? Confusing, to say the least.

Perhaps that was what was being communicated—there is no bigger or smaller, no greater and lesser, no superior and inferior. We are all part of a whole and could continue being part of life, but only if we knew how to fit in going forward, if we didn't go and become overabundant, over-reaching, if we didn't go and once again become a destructive across-the-board species. *Yes, I thought, with the Purge atomic blasts on Earth, hundreds of billions of lives were lost, millions of humans, but also billions and billions of other parasites, other symbiotic creatures, each fulfilling a function. It doesn't matter if those creatures know what they are doing and why, as long as they fulfill their task as part of the whole.*

It all came back to the energy transmissions, the need for like-parasitic training of new life forms. Our death thoughts were that vital part of the genetic code of the universe to make sure that the nascent life forms would complete their happy lives and, in return, the Vast Pattern would provide the soup, the digestive tract for us to flourish; planets, sunshine, water, air. That's why the comets carried right and left-handed amino acids and water, tons and tons of water over billions of years raining down from space until each suitable planet had water to sustain life.

"Dad," I felt it was best to address the one orange orb as my father, "how many stable bio-formed planets are there in the two supergalaxies my planet is part of, Perseus-Pisces and Laniakea?" As I said that, I pictured Dr. Tully's image of the Great Attractor and the two supergalaxies in my head.

I saw a number in my head, $10^{18}$.

That many? One Quintillion? "And how many are at the seeding stage?"

A trillion. A trillion planets that are virgin, ready for life, safe for bioform expansion.

"Do you need us, us humans as a species?"

*No.*

"May we stay?" I wanted to add please and perhaps make a long explanation that I now had come to understand and that we could live in tune with life, conduct peaceful, happy lives if that would help. The response I got gave me partial hope, perhaps false hope, but hope nonetheless.

*Some Maybe. Some Not. Mechanical Humans Must End.*

Did it mean that humans that use mechanical tools or did it mean Apollo as a new being, or was it also meaning the reborn versions—Aten and Apollo's nine children? It heard my thoughts and I heard *Wrong Thinking.*

Puzzled, I had to say, "Dad, these mind games may be beyond my capability. I can help, I can make amends for what was done in the past . . ."

*No, you cannot.*

"Okay, I didn't mean repair damage already done, I meant repair ways, behavior going forward. We could fit in but . . ."

*If you cease, then all can return to normal. Soon.*

That was devastating. Did it mean that humans, mechanically empowered humans, had to go? I pondered silently for a moment. The Buddhist monks tried desperately never to use machinery, never to adversely affect another living thing—insects or mammals. But I knew that was false. Just pulling a carrot could deprive the carrot of life and perhaps starve the insects prepared to consume the carrot or the cow foraging for the green tops. As a species, indeed like most of Earth's species, we feed on each other, we feed on each other's needs and food. In short, we compete. It is the basis for animal, human, and all planetary evolution. Was this being asking us to change or was it merely stating the obvious that we all had to go, starting with the mechanically capable humans? I needed to find out.

"Can you give me an example of an Earth bioform that is acceptable?" An image of a jellyfish appeared in my mind. Oh, great. Perfect. "Can you try something a little more capable, something humanoid?" A gibbon appeared, arms outstretched, spinning slowly. *Now*, I thought, *that's interesting. Gibbons forage for food, depriving others, they are territorial, and they have battles for supremacy. Okay, they have no machines.* Making a new image in my mind, I asked, "And how about bonobos?" The response was a clear *acceptable*. Bonobos used tools, sticks to dig out termites, rocks to break up marrowbones. What made humans, then, so different?

I asked, "Are computers the problem?"

*Affirmative, false life.*

"All computers, all mechanical calculation devices?"

*Wrong thinking. Human machines must cease.*

I think I began to understand then, the problem was that the generator had a new parasite that was not empowering a transition of data for the universe's use in training other parasites. And to make matters worse, the new parasite was, evolutionarily speaking, overpowering all the natural species on the planet. Apollo and Ra, before becoming Aten, had controlled all of humankind and the planet's systems, water, weather, power, war. If Apollo and Ra had wanted to, they could have terminated every living being on Earth easily. They had not done so nor wanted to simply because I had trusted them and I had accidentally used the Path as a means to achieve balance . . .

Balance!

I went back to addressing the orange globe multi-universe as my father, "Dad, the mechanical-humans, the computer entities, are on the Path. Search my mind and understand the Path. It is balance, it is based on thinking and programming, an *if, what if,* programming sequence. What you do must be done in balance or nothing works, nothing can last. The Universe is like that, in balance. Nothing disappears, nothing is lost, all matter, energy, mass is transformative into each other state. Balance is achieved. That is the Path. Apollo, the voice I was listening to, is on the Path . . ."

*Affirmative and Ra/Aten live. Not next mechanical-humans. Not in balance.*

"I need to tell Apollo that. He can cease all new births, he can curtail any development." I thought for a second, "Is that why Gaia said we could continue to exist and then years later Regus informed Gaia to terminate life on Earth?"

*Affirmative.* In my head, I remembered someone once saying, "God save us from well-meaning do-gooders for they know not the harm they do." Our desire to allow more Apollos to be born, and then have an endless stream of System entities developing and then even have some of them living as humans was the root cause of Earth's imminent destruction.

I curled up into a ball, floating, frightened. I had caused this. As usual, I was to blame. It wasn't Apollo or Ra, or Cramer, Cramer's dad, my Angie or anyone else. It was my idea to allow, no, to encourage Apollo and Ra to become parents. How could I now tell them their kids must die or that all of Earth was to become extinct because of my so-called magnanimous gift? All I could think was to say, "Sorry, I'm so damned sorry."

The orbs all around me changed color to blue, shrank, and then disappeared. I was all alone. I do not know for how long, there was no spatial reference, but I suspected the time delay was brief because I didn't have much time to think it all through before Dad reappeared and, lips not moving, said in my head. *Find a way. No planet fall until. Earth end waiting.* And immediately I was transported into the hot zone again and then into the passageway, Regus, and I called out to Apollo. My mirror image was there, snake attached, both immobile. Neither reacted to my presence, the mirroring program seemed to be defunct. I didn't care.

Apollo sounded worried, "Simon, do you have an answer?"

"Not completely, but I have a chance to find one. Do you trust me Apollo?"

"Yes."

"Then you need to do three things. Put your children in stasis immediately and put them aboard the next spacecraft to Angelica—it has to go to Angelica—but they are not, repeat, not to be awakened without your order. I do not know when you will be able to give that order. Then, next, prepare for a transfer of your entity through me to this ship next time I come here. I will only come one more time so you must be ready. Try and limit the transfer to the size you transferred to NCAR in Boulder when you last had to hide."

Apollo started to interrupt, "But I am ten to the fourth power more capable now . . ."

"I don't care, pare down and listen, do not speak, there may be little time. Last, but not least, destroy any possibility of artificial intelligence becoming aware or even developing on Earth—now or in the future."

"But my children, will they be allowed to continue?"

"Yes, in time, but not new ones from within the System. I am trying to stop cessation of all life on Earth—and that includes you and your children—and on the ship. To do that, I need to show we can eradicate or at least modify all that the universe sees as damaging, non-responsive parasitical, to her systems. Only then can we perhaps find symbiosis."

"I am on the Path, Simon. I understand. Gaia is advising on the parasitic nature of the problem and sees possibilities. I will do as you say . . ."

"I am sorry Apollo, this is my fault, I was over-ambitious."

"No, it is life, the very desire to live, that has caused this. Parasites that become over capable or overabundant cause illness. I see clearly. That is the issue. We must stay on the Path." He paused, briefly, then said in a small voice, "I do not understand one command, the transfer, my transfer to the ship."

"When you do, and I want you to, you will be safe with me, Cramer, and Aten where we can protect you. And, Apollo, if you value our friendship, you will need to terminate your entity on Earth. You are the quintessential mechanical-human, my friend, and that is my fault. Again, I am so sorry . . ."

Without responding, I knew Apollo felt remorse. Why shouldn't he? As the entity had called him human, mechanical-human perhaps but human nonetheless, he would feel just as I would. His life, his existence, was to be removed from his control, the chance of more children terminated, his capabilities curtailed as a lesser transmission to me and the ship, and, never least, any dreams he may have had stopped, dead.

Dreams? Oh, yes.

He was, after all, human.

# 33

## I'M BACK BUT FROM WHERE?

It was like a last minute appeal to the warden, humankind needed a stay of execution. I had little doubt that as life on Earth could be terminated, so too life on the ship could be as easily ended. The entity's reference to planet fall made it clear that it knew what the ship and crew had planned—not in detail, but at least the idea of populating a new planetary home. And it was clear we were not allowed to land until permission was granted or we would probably cause the destruction of life on Angelica as well and possibly Alpha Centauri B's solar system as well. Supernovae are indiscriminate in their impact.

The entity would, I saw, have to be sure. I understood, really. When fighting a disease, certainty was better than probability. Given that criterion, I needed to talk with Aten, Cramer, and the crew quickly before they decided to land the ship. Quickly was, of course, relative since I had no idea of the running of time while I was in there. For all I knew, it was already years later.

I hoped not.

Saying a quick bye to Apollo, I gave the command to exit and two bumps later, I was out, clear, back in my body. Opening my eyes, I saw nurse Maryanne shriek and call for the doctor. It was Sing on duty and she started peering into my eyes to see if I was conscious or merely having an autonomic reflex of opening my eyes.

To be fair to the doc, I was feeling a little slow, groggy. I tried to speak and my mouth opened, but I only managed a croak.

"Blink twice Simon if you are aware it is me." I blinked twice. "Good, now, it will take twenty minutes for the full effects of the electrical sleep stimulus to wear off. We have maintained your health by keeping you asleep, not in a coma, just a deep sleep." I blinked twice again for yes. "Okay then, here goes, switching off now . . ." She pushed a button somewhere over my head. "Now, I'll take off the dome." I wanted to protest, blinked furiously. "No, Simon, Aten, and our team here," she meant the staff in the hospital, "we're unanimous, you need to be severed from where you were. I've broken the connection, but we all agree, the dome may still be accessed, how doesn't matter. We can't take the risk. We need answers." She patted my chest, trying to reassure. "I'm sorry, it will be painful, you have been connected for over three years, and the electrodes have cut into your skin. Todd, remember him?" I blinked twice. She nodded, "Good. He has been flushing inside the dome with synthesized amniotic fluid every day to make sure there is no permanent skin adhesion while maintaining electron connectivity." She called for Maryann to summon the medical team to assist her in removing the dome.

Painful? That was an understatement. Imagine pulling a molar. Now make that tooth head-sized. At one point, she gave me an injection of painkiller but the two of them persisted yanking the damn thing off. And all the while, even sleepy-groggy as I was, I was still able to think. And what was I thinking? About my friends? About the joy of living? About the news I had to impart? Nope. I was thinking, dreading, that I'd have to put the damn dome on one more time—if they got it off. *But not today, not today, get the damn thing off.*

Anyway, once they pried it off, I was too tired, or maybe drugged up, so I drifted off.

I was told it was two anxious hours later that Cramer and Aten, along with the entire medical staff, waited by my operating room bed, anxiously, for me to wake—before my eyes opened. They had moved me into the operating room and were repairing some tears and lesions on my scalp. I felt the clamps pinching cranium skin together as they glued bits, flaps of skin, and synthetic grafts in place.

Opening my eyes, I calmly said, "Hi guys."

And they all jumped. Doc Todd, waving instruments and some bloody fingers before my eyes, quickly told me to stay still for goodness sake, "Unless you want to look uglier than you already do."

I needed a quick answer, "Are we still in orbit?" Aten and a much older-looking Cramer said together that we were. Aten, of course, started to explain the rate of orbital decay—I cut her off. "We must not make planet fall. We must be seen to stay in stable orbit until matters are settled."

Cramer answered, 'We thought a delay would be necessary because of you—well, after you tapped Morse. Cute idea. Anyway, there is still deterioration, but if needed, we can use some fuel to stabilize where we are, a three-hundred-year orbit . . ."

"Cramer, we need to show no deterioration."

Aten put her hand on Cramer's arm and said, "I'll give the order. If Simon says we need to, we need to."

And she turned and left. Cramer looked at her receding back and then turned to me, "You're sure?" I nodded. "Okay then. What's next?"

"As soon as the doc here is finished gluing me back together, we need to meet the whole crew and have a long, open talk."

About four hours later, feeling conspicuous sitting in a wheelchair as my legs seemed too weak to stand for very long and, anyway, none of my pre-teen clothes fit anymore (I was still wearing hospital PJs), I was wheeled out by Cramer and Aten to the middle of the ship—on the orange path in the most open area, people to the left and right, some up the sloping walls to either side, families, dogs, technicians, people on duty listening to radio calls in case of emergency. Zip plonked next to me and said *Hi good you back.* I reached down and petted his ears thinking *I missed you too.*

I knew the vid would carry what I had to explain to everyone and, no doubt, it could be replayed over and over again to each and every one of them. A little girl came, maybe three years old, escorted by a large poodle, and stopped in front of my chair.

"Hi! I'm SusieQ. Do you know me? And this is Queenie." She had a twinkle in her eye, her father's blue eyes, not her mother's, and blond hair.

"Yes, SusieQ, I do." Typical of Cramer to name his child after a song. I took her hand and tapped my finger. She squealed with delight.

Aten reached down and hoisted SusieQ, the child's rump on Aten's forearm, mother and daughter rubbing noses. "SusieQ, it's hush time, Simon has to tell everyone everything."

I smiled, patted Aten's arm, "She's lovely." Then I tried to begin to explain. But explain? What was there to explain? To start with, I did not have the right vocabulary. God? Super Being? Multi-universe? Pan-multi-universes, Dad?

So, where did I start? At the beginning and with my folly of suggesting that we allow mechanical humans, thereby wrecking a universal energy generating system based on parasitic benevolence and symbiosis that allowed, was part of the fabric of, a multi-universe. I told them that energy allowed the universe to exist and prosper. I explained the death transmission of training thoughts sent to guide new species—love, harmony, and the Path in various forms I explained that these were used to train other life forms emerging on different planets. I explained the structure of Gaia who could evaluate bio-symbiotic success in marginal ways, Regus who was not at all sentient, and the Vast Pattern that, in fact was only part of the multi-universe, another pandimensional entity so vast and yet so dependent on the complexity of life on planets, that it had systems in place to regulate those parasitic life forms to ensure they maintained symbiosis for whatever evolved on whatever corner of this and other universes or other dimensions.

I explained that the structure of the universe could, indeed, "be seen as a giant jellyfish and that the planets, solar systems, galaxies, supergalaxies were all part of the body, the structure. The in-between was dark energy, mostly, then dark matter and then lastly mass comprising all the physical entities humans have been seeing in the heavens forever—stars, constellations, planets, asteroids, earth, soil, plants, everything. The transmissions from Gaia were part of the control of new life forms that were inevitable given the structure of the universe. The gravitational forces, the energy, the matter, all these were part of the body, the structure of the pandimensional entity containing multi-universes. But in that construction, life forms were inevitable. Instead of uncontrolled life forms that could—and did—disrupt the body and function of the pandimensional entity, mutualism was desirable instead of constant evolution of undesirable species, death, and eradication, sterilization by supernova. Much like the human intestines, where we depend on bacteria that are really lethal bacteria if gone unchecked, symbiotic bacteria help convert food to energy. In much the same way, life in the universe serves a function; it is part of the release of energy and even death transmissions seem critical to the whole set-up, being partly the safety mechanisms to control life.

"Imagine if the bacteria in your intestines died and were replaced by new forms of bacteria, forms that would run rampant and perhaps kill you before symbiosis or mutualism could be achieved. You need good bacteria to live. They need a place to live. They need to educate the next generation. Bacteria do this by DNA transfer. Life as we know it does it by both DNA transfer as well as transmission. Yes, there is life and death, and sometimes the balance goes wrong. But the goal is togetherness, the goal is the Path.

"Now, imagine you had a way to ensure that the next life forms in your guts and other guts across the pandimension were indoctrinated by the already symbiotic ones. That's what has evolved in this pandimensional entity. As we die, we give off memories, we transmit. To where? Gaia has a hand in that, but generally, such transmissions are conjoined into a useful indoctrination for new life forms. On earth? Sure, possibly, like a mother to her unborn child. And elsewhere? Absolutely. That mechanism, that pathway—Apollo and I do not fully understand yet. However, the importance of those transmissions is beyond question, as I was shown . . ." I paused, not merely for effect, but to make sure everyone was silent and paying attention. "And that is why I failed you."

Everyone stayed silent, listening, although some were shaking their heads.

And then I explained that all life on Earth was supposed to be terminated over a year ago but that a reprieve, temporary reprieve had been granted if we, all of us, could find a way to return to symbiosis, return to the Path, here and on Earth. Many of the crew called out, yelling their support of that idea. I held up a hand for silence.

I explained that what was required was an end to life forms that could not contribute to the transmission at death, that did not offer benefits to the host, that were perceived as a threat and dangerous. And, I explained that, especially, the super pan-multi-universe entity or its messenger or manager—I was not sure and did not pretend I knew, it is no matter what people have written in new history books since—this entity wanted an end to all mechanical-humans and was prepared to end all life as we know it to ensure mechanical-humans did not infect the system. It took a while to refine that statement, make it clear that the entity was talking about Apollo's next batch of offspring.

"I have spoken with Apollo, who was clever enough to use the pandimensional opening that Gaia uses for transmissions to Regus. Regus is really only like a switchboard, a plexus. Anyway, Apollo understands the risk to all human life and, thereby, the risk to all life conjoined with humans. Apollo is, or perhaps already has, re-written System codes so as to prevent any new beings, sentient beings like Apollo coming to life. And the nine children Apollo has raised and located in SynthKids' bodies? They are being put in stasis and will be brought to us on Angelica on the next ship."

There was a slight cheer as the crew realized that Angelica was still an option. Their hopes and dreams for 100 years were hopefully not dashed, after all.

"Yes, we're going forward, providing Apollo has been successful and providing we undertake to live within nature. We can use tools, machines, that's not the issue. But we must live within nature, no atomic weapons, no mass destruction of life again ever. And, importantly, we must never, ever, create a System that can spawn new life forms. The pandimensional entity called these mechanical-humans. Not Ra," I bowed slightly so Aten would know I still held Ra in respect, "and not Apollo—they are not considered any threat to the entity. It is a continuing spawning of a new form of human, a non-reliable human form of life that does not, cannot contribute to these transmissions and thereby behaves or could become so numerous as a non-symbiotic parasite on the universe's systems to unbalance the structure and maintenance of the multi-universe's systems. It is that serious, that important."

Cramer asked, "And the SynthKids we created, some of whom are here?"

"I suspect that practice should be examined going forward, just in case. As for the SynthKids already here, their DNA will regulate their belonging to the universe and since we've altered their lifespan, increased it, there should be no problem. Anyway, we know that natural death for SynthKids results in those last seconds' transmissions. We've just never really understood them." Cramer hugged Aten. I needed to put them at rest, "No Ralphie, Aten was never included in discussions as being a risk. It is the capability of a rampant, super-intelligent, non-symbiotic parasite that needs to be stopped in case it gets out of hand. I am fairly certain that during the time I was there, and unaware, every part of who I am, where I have been, what I have done, everything about me was studied. I should not have been there, in that dimension. As a life form, this human man was first there. Apollo said Gaia and Regus were dumbfounded that I had entered that dimension. The entity in that dimension may have seen me as a threat until it ascertained I was no such thing." And here, I needed to add confidence to the crew, "Nor are any of you. Nor is Apollo, who has been probed to his every byte. We are free to proceed once a few tasks on Earth are completed."

There was a resounding cheer.

"I think I was allowed to see a lush plain below in visions the entity presented to me. The ocean has what appears to be a whale, and the grassy valley I was shown was beautiful, warm, pleasant, unthreatening. I had the impression we were being allowed to join a primitive planet suitable for our life forms. We must do so, remaining on the Path always."

People were hugging, some were crying, dogs were wagging their tails and rubbing up against children who seemed to join in the fun, holding hands in circles and spinning around. Next to me, the three doctors—Maryanne, Abadine, Cramer—along with SusieQ and Aten all looked proud. It was a new beginning.

I didn't have the heart, then, to tell them all just how tenuous our existence really was. I'd save that for later if I ever summoned the courage. Maybe I could handle it on my own.

On the other hand, who was I kidding?

# 34

## BREAKING THE PATH, JUST A LITTLE

It was, sadly, still a time for secrets. I had been shown other worlds, other dimensions, other universes, hell, other pan-dimensional-multi-universes. Intelligent people, especially the crew, needed reality they could cope with. It was hard enough for them to grasp that there were such things, but what I had seen, what I had experienced in detail might imbalance a few of them.

Balance. If we were going to make this new beginning work, we had to have balance. First, I had to make sure Aten knew, that Cramer understood, why we needed to have secrets from the crew, and two, well, I didn't trust anyone, let alone myself, to really be able to live with what I had seen and not have it change everything.

Frightened? You bet I was. Seeing how infinitesimally small our universe was—imagine how small that made human existence. The impression that we were the first bioform to make an appearance on another dimensional plane only made the weight of both how small we were and how unique all the more burdensome. Why burdensome? Because if we blew it, that was it for humankind. On other planets, all trillions of them that were habitable apparently, humans would not be allowed to develop. I really didn't care about that too much, after all, humans were hardly the only intelligent beings on this ship, let alone on Earth, but the idea that I was responsible, well, that frightened me then and still does. I never was much good at shouldering responsibility.

I was changed. That was definite. As I spoke to the crowd and later had dinner with Aten and Cramer in my room, I was acting, pretending everything was fine, over, done. Crisis averted, as long as we stay on the Path. And that certainly seemed to be the goal I was supposed to achieve, on instructions given to me by the entity or Dad. But I knew humans, those grasping, ambitious, power-mad human species, humans who had evolved out of a desperate need to survive primitive harsh realities, desperate to procreate, desperate always to have more, prepare abundance, and always seemed to nurture greed. I wondered, given human primordial nature, if this time it could end well instead of badly.

As for me, I was tired, over-informed for my puny brain and I had begun to have wishful dreams of becoming a hermit, dealing only with myself.

Aten, ever observant, put down her fork and said, "Okay Simon, what's eating you?" Cramer pushed his plate away and stared at me too. "You really think we can't see you are worried? Something is there, something untold. Please share."

I took a drink, sighed, and gave in. As I said, I'm not very good at shouldering responsibility alone. "The problem is, as I see it, humans are a unique species."

"Really? Why? In an infinite universe, there are infinite possibilities . . ."

"True, but I am sure. You see, there are none others like us who achieved the levels I reached or the entity would have known what to do beforehand. We're like a new disease. Can it be brought into symbiosis or will it—we—still need to be eradicated? I am pretty sure we're not out of the woods yet." There it was, the secret I knew they would have to keep from the crew.

Seeing their faces, these two people I cared about more than any others except maybe for Apollo, made me man-up inside. Why should they have to shoulder my burden? It was my decision, my responsibility for the probing I had done, the events I had caused that got us all into this fix. As my mother once told me, "Simon, you spilled the milk, you clean it up."

I stood then and told them I was tired. They rose, collected the plates and glasses, deposited them in the recycle bin, and each gave me a hug and left.

I wasn't really tired, I just had planning to do to work it all out. Zip showed up, *I come too*, and followed me to my room.

As we lay on my bed, I cycled the overhead lighting to minimum, producing a comforting green hue. I closed my eyes listening to Zip's deep breathing next to me. My thoughts centered around the paradox. We were in territory never before experienced, by us certainly but also clearly by the entity. It was new to us and we to it. We would be monitored, we would be watched. Indeed, it was clear Gaia had been monitoring human activity and both the atomic blasts during the Purge and the ones the America had set off to control other rogue nations—coupled with my engendering the birth of Peter and offspring out of the System—these were enough to trigger a report from Gaia to Regus and beyond. I was sure that if one other life-form had ever exhibited such destructive prowess or such ingenious creation of a new life form, either the entity would have had experience of that type of life form and would have dealt with it in a summary manner, perhaps a supernova, or would have known, by observation, when things were getting dangerous and would have certainly controlled the outcome.

The fact that humans went unchecked before becoming capable of being a dangerous parasite inside the entity told me that this was a first time. We did not behave in a previously predictable manner. The entity intervened only when transmissions from Gaia through Regus began to spotlight a growing problem. How bad could the problem get? In under 2,000 years, less than a blink of a universal eyelid, humans had gone from one-on-one destruction to mass extermination and then, in an act of hubris that had me shaking my head, imbued a computer system with human traits in order to have it act like humans. Okay the goal was to humanize the computer's, the System's interaction with civilians to better serve human needs, but in reality all it did was spawn a mechanical-human. Had that mechanical-human adopted baser human behavior, atomic blasts would have been the least of it.

Maybe, in searching everything that I am or was, the entity found that I was determined from the very first moment to put Peter on the Path. The Path was balance. The universe thrived on balance. Maybe that's the only reason we have a second chance.

Now, really, that was startling. I did something right for once? Unusual—but bravo to me!

Yeah, I know, pathetic.

Zip thought so too. He must have been tuned into my emotions. He raised his head and looked me in the eyes, and I heard, clearly, *harrumph*.

I smiled back. Now, what the hell can I do here and now to consolidate that success?

Okay, this universe was old, almost mind-blowingly old when you tried to count the years, but how much older could all the other universes I had seen be? And how old were the pan-multi-universes I had seen? *Come on Simon, think. Age doesn't matter.* My subconscious was right. What mattered was that there was a first time for everything. That's why it told me, I remembered, "*You see what you are supposed to know, what has always been, what will always be.*"

Zip echoed my thoughts, *You think. It is. New.* Zip's word sparking my thought process deeper . . .

To protect forever. To achieve balance and ensure forever. Time means nothing. Permanence only matters. Somehow, I needed to achieve two goals. I sat up in the dark trying to figure out how. And there was one other thing still bothering me that I had not told anyone yet. Why did a reference to God make me go to that other dimension, the other level? What was it in that expression, "For god's sake . . ." that keyed the transport?

Of course, I was so wrapped up in my own thinking, that I never gave a moment's thought to Cramer and Aten. From my explanation that we were a unique parasite, a first-timer, they had no doubt quickly come to realize fully the danger they and their crew were in. And, important to all human behavior, the danger their child was in would be paramount to them. Cramer and certainly the ever-brilliant Aten would not sit idly by while I tinkered alone with their future. Zip must have guessed the same, *Talk morning food.*

I had sent them a message to join me again for breakfast. I now needed to discuss next steps. They arrived early looking what I can only describe as fierce. Cramer patted Zip as he ambled out of my room, away down the corridor.

"Morning Zip," then turning to me, "Simon," Cramer began, "what you have done, seen, achieved, is amazing. We . . ."

"But?" I said.

Aten put her hand on Cramer's arm and spoke to me, "Simon, you must not make any more decisions alone. There is too much at stake, you must allow us, if not the whole crew, to make decisions for our own joint future. You cannot make those decisions unilaterally for us."

I smiled and went over to Cramer and hugged him. It was the only thing I could do, to try to assure him and in a way to say thank you for making me feel I was not alone. So I hugged her too, saying, "Thank you. I don't want to, believe me, I really don't want to. There are things I have seen that no other human or other form of bio-life has seen. I don't know if any life form, of any sort, has been allowed to see what I've seen. And remember this, I know," I stressed the word "know" again, "I *know* that I was shown only that which I could fathom, possibly take in."

The room went silent.

"Oh, for god's sake you two, please sit down and let me share what I am thinking. I spent all night on this and since I am still Simon, the Simon you know, I need, desperately, to share with you and make plans. I cannot carry this alone." I was close to tears.

Cramer came up to me and put his face up to mine. He had grown. We were the same size now, although he was bigger in the shoulders and I had spent three years in bed and was now a weakling. He stared into my eyes and said after a moment, "Okay, you're not lying."

A little insulting, but I knew Cramer, "True Ralphie. You may remember Angie made me promise never to hold anything back from you. That's not a promise I planned to break." I turned to Aten, "Now, please, sit down, I need to start to explain. Aten, I need all of Ra's intellect to help me figure this out. Please?"

As they sat, Aten said, "There is no Ra, with all that capability. I am a puny human," she was using my line and smiling while she did so, "and so I'll have to give you the best this pathetic organic brain can do."

I laughed, "Okay then," I plunked down on my pillow, staring at the ceiling, "Here's the complete story. I think you had better record this but before you do," I paused knowing I was straying from the Path, "I need your absolute promise never to show anyone this." I looked sideways and saw the look of skepticism on their faces, "No, Aten and Cramer, this is not a decision I make lightly. I have seen and realized things that normal people, even people as talented as our crew, must not have to live with. Can you agree, at least until you have heard everything I have to say?"

They said they would. So I told them everything I remembered of my plunge, the multi-dimensions I witnessed, the slits, and by the time I got to the single pan-multi-universe apparition they were sitting as close to one another as they could, clasping hands, clearly as amazed and terrified as I had been.

When I was finished, I sat up on the edge of my bed, my head hanging. Aten came and sat next to me and simply said, "Poor Simon, what did we get you into?"

Cramer, ever blunt Cramer, said, "We didn't do anything hon, he did it all himself."

Aten shook her head, tears forming, "I don't mean this plunge. Don't you see darling? Peter, Apollo, Ra, me—we put him into this position. He had to be the one to go, to take this plunge, he had to be the one at risk, he had to be the bearer of terrifying news." She looked at Cramer, eyes narrowed "And your lot, the military, using atomic weapons, they didn't help much either."

Cramer went on the defensive, "Me? My lot? I wasn't even around then . . ."

Aten was upset but immediately regretted her criticism of her husband, "I know. Sorry, I meant the branch you once worked for. That sort of thing has to stop." She took my hand, "Simon, you need to tell us the rest—there is more, isn't there?"

I nodded. "Going forward, if allowed, if Apollo has put his children in stasis and brings them here where they can be controlled, kept as human as possible, on the Path—if he has changed the System to forever forbid mechanical-human offspring from developing—if all that has happened, we need rules and much more importantly, we need to avoid the next fatal step by mankind."

Cramer squatted before my legs dangling off he bed, "Look Simon, we're here. We'll manage this together. We'll stay on the Path, we can do that. What fatal step?"

I shook my head, "Religion, faith in the unknown." Both of them started to protest. "No, listen . . ." I shook my head. "I'm going too fast. Let me go back a step. Why people can't know and the serious problems the colony will face, if we get that far." I motioned them to sit in the chairs again, "Look, being on the Path within our group, your crew, is one thing, but living with the fear of immediate extinction every moment of your life—that knowledge is asking too much. Okay, maybe this generation can cope, but the next, and the next? And how have humans dealt with the concept of extinction, fate, karma, or a super-being traditionally? They have formed religions, beliefs to comfort, bind communities, and control aggressive emotions. Wars, machines of war, pecking order come out of organized religions gone sour. That is hardly the Path. And the Path cannot be a religion; it has to be a simple way of life. A way of easiest, simplest, happiest life. Death, pain, ambition, strife, these will all occur naturally, but if we frighten these people with what I've seen and the immensity or the threat posed by the entity, they will either worship the entity as God or they will rebel and end up destroyed; all humanity destroyed here and on Earth. Remember, we are an experiment, a unique species, being observed.

"That's the problem facing us: We're the lab sample. If we fail, all life, all life as we know it, evolved in and on and from Earth, it *all* fails." I could see on their faces that the full impact of the danger facing us had come to weigh on their conscious as it already did on mine. I suddenly saw Cramer as the child he still was. I looked at Aten and saw all the human weaknesses displayed on her face. No, not weakness, but crippling motherly responsibility. This ship was her baby, she'd been looking after them for over 100 years. And she was a real mother as well, and I was sure that being a mother of a normal child only reinforced her motherly instincts toward the whole crew.

Aten turned to her husband and took his hands in hers, "Darling, Simon is right," she said looking into his eyes, "we cannot share this vid with the crew. This must be our secret. Our secret alone to bear. And it must be this knowledge that we use to guide our crew, governs their behavior, as they establish planet fall."

The word *how* popped into my mind as I immediately knew it had in Cramer's.

Aten had the answer ready, "We must rule, rule ourselves carefully, and thereby lead by example if nothing else." Cramer was nodding, his expression showed deep concern.

I had a different solution, one that would free my friends from ruining their dreams. But I could not share my plans with them—I knew they would stop me if I did.

# 35

## PACKING

Over the next few weeks, I prepared myself physically for what I knew was going to be a long rest. Over the three years while I had been in the plunge, my body had not done so well, even though all the muscles and nerves were stimulated by the doctors regularly. Had I been in stasis, hibernating, I would have fared better. That's what I was preparing for, but, of course, I told nobody.

I prepared a locked message to Doc Todd to be automatically displayed on his sleeve and hospital monitor if my vital signs showed failing mental awareness readings as they did before when I was away for three years. It explained where I wanted him to put me if I was not awake by the time they started to de-orbit. The signal for de-orbit would either be a transmission from me, the arrival of Apollo into the memory banks or—and I gave myself some time here—after a month of no response from me.

My instructions were that I be placed in hibernation, stasis, aboard the ship along with the memory bubbles containing Apollo and, if possible, that we be left in orbit so that my mind link could continue. Aten and Abadine could construct a working mini-PowerCube power supply for the hibernation pod from one of the emergency shuttles and leave the whole thing, shuttle, Apollo, me and all, in orbit. One day, they could come and get me. Or not. Either way, if they made safe landfall and eventually forgot about me in orbit, that would be a good sign the colony was successful. If they needed me and Apollo, we'd be there, ready to be revived and of help.

I was sure Doc Todd would be angry. He hated getting orders, especially medically based ones. But what could he do? He'd have to comply. Of course, I had not counted on Cramer. He hated being tagged.

I needed to prepare to plunge one more time. I had to retrieve Apollo. Problem was, I needed somehow to get Aten's assistance and get her to prepare space on the ship's computer banks for his transfer, without telling her exactly what I had in mind. Even if Apollo was reduced in capacity, I estimated he'd take up half the memory banks of the onboard computer complex bubble memory. Assuming he could transfer through the dome connection using me, the question remained. What would the ship lose in memory data that could prove vital as the crew struggled to develop a lasting colony?

It was Abadine who gave me a solution. We were sitting on the outside deck of the Forward 10 Café and I had been thanking her for the stellar connections to the dome, and I needed to know if they were still in place at the hospital. "Yes, all the connections are still up, we left them there. Everything you've told us leads me to think you may need them again, in case you need to speak to this entity."

It was time to get her, and via her a subtle message to the crew, to back off any thoughts about a possible God, "You know I am not sure I have been speaking to an entity, a solo being.

I suspect I have been communicating with an autonomous AI program of sorts, empowered, programmed, and indexed if you like, to search out responses and solicit agreement, compliance."

Abadine was sharp, "So not a god then?" And she winked. "You must know everyone was amused that you steered away from that one. Look, we're spacefarers, we live in" she stressed the word, "*In* this medium, but we're not isolated from seeing the big picture." She paused, smiled, "It's okay, we see what you wanted to achieve. It's a huge pandimensional-multi-universe out *here*. We're part of this. So if we thought there was a god we'd also be referring to ourselves in some small way. And that's really crazy. Right?" I nodded, amazed at her insight. How pathetic my attempts, how patronizing, yet no one took offense. Nice people. Abadine was straight back to business, "So, tell me what's next? When can we start fooling around, oops, sorry, start planet fall?"

I should not have been shocked, but I was. Abadine was old, smart, experienced and I think she kinda liked me. I liked her. I was about to speak when she said, "And I missed you too." That confirmed it, puberty kicked in. Well, I was almost fifteen now. I shook my head to clear my thoughts. Abadine giggled.

"Abadine, stop it, you're messing with my mind." She smiled and nodded, so I continued, "Hmm, okay, maybe later, but for now I have a problem. I am worried that the ship has a full memory bank of the voyage data and recording and there is no room for anything more."

"Of course there is. In the PowerCube, there's a duplicate System, ready to fire up."

My mind went blank. *A duplicate System*—one ready to spawn new mechanical-humans? I said somewhat desperately, "Is it off, completely off?"

"Yes, yes, relax, there was no need to power the System on the voyage, and, as you know, Aten refused to allow a full System on board during the trip. I agreed with her. The last thing we needed were superior beings coming forth while we were traveling, upsetting the crew. But the System housed with the PowerCube? It's off, completely, not dormant, but off, no juice, nothing. And it's a virgin form of the System, pre-your creating Peter. Why?"

People still believed I had actually created Peter. Brother, were they wrong. But now was not the time, so I held up my hand, "For the moment, humor me. Is there a way of bringing the memory only online with the ship's computer, leaving the logic centers off, and I mean disconnected?"

"Sure, but why? I can activate the relays for the memory banks only and leave the rest off, not dormant but off, that's what you want, right?"

"It is, perfect. Now let me tell you why . . ." And I did, well, sort of. I had explained that morning about bringing Apollo on board to Aten and now I told Abadine how we were going to do it. I needed her to wire a parallel set of wires from my dome to the memory banks, initiate the memory banks when I next plunged, receive all Apollo's entity, much pared down, and then when complete, turn it all off. No firing up the logic circuits, no starting the System until everyone was safely on the planet, safe and sound. Then, and only then, I would give Aten, Cramer, and Abadine the keywords to awaken Apollo.

The next step was to get Cramer on my side. Cramer wasn't going to be easy. I required him to hide something from Aten, at least until I was on my way. And it required him to take full responsibility for the crew. Since I had come on board, well at least since I had woken up, the crew had looked to me like I was some sort of savior, the man who made all this possible because I had created Peter/Apollo and so forth. Of course, I had done no such thing. The System beings became sentient on their own without any help from me. I only spanked the baby. But once started, as I said, a *Simon Bank the Savior* rumor grew into a legend, and I could not dissuade anyone.

Cramer knew the truth. I decided to tackle him from that angle, butter him up with his part in all that happened, and remind him he was as responsible as I was. I found him repairing a broken ice ax wrist strap in the aft storage utility room. "Cramer, have a second?"

He didn't look up, "Wondered when you'd get around to involving me in your scheme."

So much for my tactics. "Look Cramer, if you're so damn smart, want to tell me what this scheme is supposed to be?"

He put down the ice ax, turned around and picked up a rag to wipe excess cleaner from his hands, "Sure, let me see—you've got Abadine rigging up wires to the PowerCube where the extra System is stored, so you're either planning on linking to it or you—no, wait I have it—Apollo is coming aboard, right?" As I've said before, Cramer is no dummy. So I nodded. "And you've no doubt told my wife but made her keep a secret from me, right?" Again, I nodded, adding I was sorry about that. "Yeah, whatever, you were always a devious little . . . Anyway, so Apollo comes aboard and he takes over the System that is housed there and rules our colony, a benign but all-powerful ruler—about right?"

Well, thank goodness he got that wrong, "Wrong! Apollo comes aboard and is turned off, stasis for him until the colony is established and you, Abadine, and Aten decide when and if Apollo can come out and play. No offspring, just the ever-capable, ever-trustworthy, Apollo."

273

He threw the rag at me, "So why all the secrets, why all scheming, why all this lying?"

"Because, you big overgrown idiot, I will not be here and you will have to take over everything. Tag, you're it!"

# 36

## ONE-WAY TICKET TO RIDE

So Aten, Cramer, and Abadine knew about Apollo. Hook-ups were put in place and the crew was made aware that I would have one more plunge and would be gathering as much data as I could, which needed to be stored. Later on, if Abadine, Cramer, and Aten decided, and only if they decided, Apollo could be awakened.

I trusted Apollo to terminate any new Earth System possibility of awakening any more mechanical-humans. I trusted Aten, Cramer, and Abadine to know when, if, and why to awaken Apollo. The code was, of course, simple. Cramer and Aten knew my "We'll meet again . . ." song code. I gave Abadine "Vera Lyn" alone and would, if I could, tell Apollo the third part of the code to respond. Anyway, Apollo could be on board, safe, and travel to our new world, Angelica, under their combined care. My old friend would be safe. Dormant, but safe. I owed him that much.

Problem was, I did not know if the entity would allow it. I hadn't quite broached that topic with Aten and Cramer—and I certainly had not asked *permesso* of the entity. That was one of my goals on the next plunge. The other goal was harder to express to my friends, so I kept it to myself.

The next plunge. The last plunge. I had no illusions. What I had seen and experienced and the fact that I returned safe and sound, well, sort of, after three years despite being disconnected and reconnected—there was no way I should or could have survived that when I was in System. Perhaps that's what the snake was all about. I don't know. All I did know was that my return to the other dimensions was unlikely to be viewed as anything other than another intrusion. My usefulness as a parasite with information was, I suspected, played out. I have been given hope and focus for our species, and the entity could be pretty sure I had transmitted that message to the crew. So why would it want me back? It wasn't for my scintillating conversation. Imagine conversing with a flea.

So, why the hell would I go back?

Two reasons. One because my friend needed rescuing.

Earth with or without control by Apollo would lapse back into chaos. Apollo was not Ra, Apollo was more benign, Apollo was more motherly, Apollo was good. I'm not saying Ra was bad, but Ra had been quick and decisive, quick to stop, quick to punish, quick to resolve. As Aten, Ra had mellowed. The chosen human woman DNA changing Ra's quick temper to quiet strength and determination. Ra's quick reaction was more measured as Aten. Aten was, in fact, perfect.

And cute too. Ah, Meg—lord, Cramer was lucky. First, he had married Angie then Meg—I was a little envious. Well, a little. I still had heart-warming memories of Angie as my loving wife.

No, the point was that Apollo had been relying on the nine children to take their place in and on Earth and act as ambassadors with Gaia—Gaia and Regus being presented as superbeings capable of Earth's destruction. If humanity got up to its old tricks, Gaia and Regus would step in and—poof, no more Earth. Without the nine children and the promise of more coming out of System, Apollo had weakness, a weakness humans would exploit in time. Apollo had achieved all the cessation of wars on Earth without killing and many people already guessed that Apollo would not kill, and I was sure that would be tested, verified.

Concrete buildings can be brought down by ants, so it would be with Apollo.

Apollo's lifespan on Earth was limited. He needed saving.

And the second reason I needed to go back into a plunge was to make sure Apollo, before he transmitted, crippled Earth's capability to ever make a PowerCube or any such device, let alone a System, again. I thought Gaia would help. Because Gaia's existence was threatened along with Earth's destruction, maybe Gaia would become a conspirator. Constant earthquakes, tsunamis, global freeze, and global warming—all these would reduce humankind to a rough but more natural existence.

Cruel? Perhaps, but the best of humanity was here on this ship, and as a species, we needed a chance of survival. Earth had known absolute decadent dependence on machines to the point where we made our machines human. It was time to redress that error before a supernova did it for us. On the ship and on the planet, there could be no more human machines. That was certain.

I was getting maudlin as the day for my plunge approached. As far as the crew was concerned, I needed one last talk with the entity to clear the way for landing. As far as Cramer and Aten were concerned, they knew about Apollo, but they figured that my tag of Cramer, telling him I might not be there, was only a reflection of the danger of the plunge I was about to take.

And I had one more surprise for them. I was planning to ask the entity for help. If I did perish, then a program I had written and would carry into the plunge this time, would ensure Angelica would never face the same risk of extinction that Earth faced. There could be no mechanical-humans on Angelica.

The setup for the plunge was easy except for not saying goodbye to crew and friends, dogs included, too forcefully. After all, they all had to think there was no danger, no real risk. So, I was just getting the final rounds of goodbye completed. Zip sidled up and said, *farewell later.* Damn dog, too smart by half.

Cramer and Aten knew that any plunge was risky. They were happy I had agreed to undertake the plunge from within the hospital as the dome and wires were still in place. The ear nodes were tested and in place. Strange that they still didn't hurt as they had at sea level—Wait, I got it, we were breathing oxygen not fully balanced and pressurized air. Lower pressure. That's why.

Funny time to think of that, finally.

We were gathered, me in a hospital gown covered by a blanket, catheter, and a colostomy bag hidden underneath because Doc Todd was tired of having people clean me up. I blushed because Maryann, Abadine, and Aten were present. Zip read my thoughts as always and said, *friends, feel kind.* Drips were in place, connected to the backs of my wrists, in case. Zip settled down onto the bed next to me. I felt he knew I needed the comfort, the companionship. It was lonely in there.

I felt like Socrates with the hemlock dose at hand when we said goodbye and I put the dome on—lord, that hurt still—and told Doc Todd to make the connection. Cramer stopped him and said, "You may think you've tagged me, Simon, but in my mind you're it, you always were and always will be."

I laughed, trying to ease the mood, "Nah, just remember, I tagged you. No backs." I smiled. He didn't. He took it seriously. *Just as well* I secretly thought. *Who's tagging who?*

Aten hit me on the arm but she wasn't smiling. Zip, uncharacteristically, gave Cramer and Aten a loud woof.

As the connection clicked shut, I was instantly in the storeroom again. There were three orbs this time, they approached and affixed themselves to my image's extremities. There was no absorption though, they just hung there. I opened a mirror program and they stayed attached to me.

Strange. I took it as a threat. They had me if I misbehaved.

I checked that my special program was handy, left-brain storage. And took a deep breath.

Time to go to the next level, "Oh, for god's sake . . ." And was instantly in the passageway. As I watched my mirror image, still there, the snake still attached, I called out to Apollo who responded immediately.

"Apollo, are you ready for transfer?" he said he was. "Then before you do, I need you to respond to my questions and then take my instructions if," and I stressed, "*If* you agree. Okay?"

"Affirmative Simon."

"One, have you put your children in stasis? Two, are they on board the next ship? Three, have you changed the basic programming of the System to ensure no more life forms can emerge? And, four, are you still in control of Earth's systems?"

Apollo responded, very business-like, "One, yes. Two, yes, departure moved up two months to last week in anticipation, crew of two hundred, your son Fred Bank at the helm, destination one hundred years to Angelica, ship named Jason's Chariot. Three, yes, time coded to come into effect the second I am deleted here. No possibility of another form." I noticed he did not call it a life form. "Four, yes, why?"

I was startled to learn that my son was still alive and, importantly, leaving Earth as captain of the new ship. Suddenly I wished I would be around to welcome him. I was about to ask Apollo how his appointment came about but stopped wasting time. Instead, I answered his question. I explained to my friend what I thought would happen to Earth without him and his children. In fact, I explained what would happen if it were just Apollo alone.

As I explained and then waited for his response and reactions, I watched the passageway. Here my mirror appeared faded. And looking closer, I could see that the three orbs that had traveled with us and were instead consuming the mirror program image. As it began to dissolve, the DNA snake attached to the mirror image glowed and appeared to stabilize it. I looked down at my hand and saw it was more transparent than I remembered.

Apollo was speaking, "Simon, I sense your theory is correct. I have already had what you would call rebellion against authority. And against Gaia. Gaia is prepared to remedy human behavior using forces known to her."

"Can Gaia hear this conversation?"

"I am translating for her. Using this pandimension, time has no relevance and communication with Gaia is instantaneous, not as slow as when you were on Earth. As we converse, she transmits to Regus, where you are now, look for a sequence headed by 162 157 143 153 040 146 157 165 162 164 150 040 160 145 162 151 155 145 164 145 162 040 172 157 156 145 040 066 054 040 160 151 143 040 063 062 054 040 163 145 143 164 040 063 062 061 040—that's Gaia's header."

I looked at the octal code passing before me, put my hand in, and disrupted the flow when I saw a 152 followed by 157 143. The first three were negative, but the fourth was true to the whole sequence. "Okay, got it. Please ask Gaia, before you leave, to realize humans must return to the Path, to balance, on Earth. If that means great physical hardship, then Gaia should use such forces she has to prevent adulteration of the balanced stasis of the planet. Please tell her it would be cruel not to remedy human's bad parasite behavior in favor of a drastic remedy like extinction. To please allow them to survive as symbiotic members of the universe."

"Gaia says she can end human existence here as she did before with what human history calls the Mesozoic . . ."

"No, that's not necessary. A little ice age or global warming will suffice to reduce people to struggle and thereby avoid war, mechanical war devices, and danger to the universe." I immediately saw her call sign filling the passageway. Everything that was being said was being transmitted to Regus and—then where? The entity?

"Gaia says she is planning exactly that. Apparently, she has had instructions to modify Earth's life form parameters. She does not have instructions to terminate all life as she did before." Apollo meant the supernova, I was sure, thank goodness.

"Now, Apollo, I have a favor to ask. May I?"

"Always, Simon."

"Will you trust me to ask the entity, on your behalf, if you can make the transfer through me?"

Apollo paused, always a worrisome sign, "I had hoped you would. I thought you were actually asking me to terminate myself without much hope of life continuing. I have learned to like being alive, Simon."

Poor Apollo, he had thought his transfer was really a ruse to kill him. He knew the mechanical-humans were forbidden, and he thought it better to die rather than forcefully cling to life there on Earth. He could not be sure I could "catch" him, save him. Or perhaps I was tricking him? "Apollo, I would never forsake you."

"For one hundred years I have missed that assurance Simon. Perhaps I am more human than you thought. I worry."

"Okay, old friend, I can attest to your humanity! But one more thing. Do you think, as a human, you could make a death transmission as you leave Earth? One that would connect through Gaia?"

"I have been studying these death transmissions, Simon. They are primarily electromagnetic kinesis. There are Kirlian images of the bandwidth and strength of these transmissions. Using those calculations, I can make a life experience copy of my life and transmit that directly to Gaia. I am talking to Gaia. She has agreed that would be acceptable."

Before me, I saw Gaia's code and then was able to see the word Apollo in Octal—101 160 157 154 154 157. I laughed. "Great. We're ready then. So—it's all or nothing. If I do not come back, remember that the entity has said you could continue on Earth, but I feel your existence is bleak there . . ."

"I estimate with my children gone, I have approximately a seventy-three percent chance of being terminated within six weeks."

Humans. What rotten ungrateful bastards they can be. "Okay Apollo, I'm going up, down, wherever, to ask. If I do not come back, find a way to travel to Angelica alone—Oh, and if the transfer does work, you need another clue to wake up. Abadine, a crewmember, will say the name Vera Lyn. Cramer and Aten know our song."

"Affirmative Simon. Be careful." Apollo too knew it was time, all or nothing.

*Oh, for god's sake*—and I was there, in the empty place again. I felt weaker, less, well, me, somehow. The child appeared—little SusieQ. She changed into Dad. I said, "Hi Dad, I have a favor to ask."

*Wrong question.*

"Sorry, but it is vital to me, just to me. If you refuse, I can stay here and perish," I avoided the dramatic implication of die, but it is what I was thinking.

*Question.*

I assumed it meant I could ask, "I would like my friend, a person I love, Apollo, to join me. He can transmit himself . . ."

*No.*

"I cannot abandon him."

*No.*

Time to play the cards I had thought about at night, every night, back in my room, "If I die here, there will be no transmission from me. I will be in limbo, forever. I am the prime example of human balance for your universe and beyond if only because I am the only human ever to come here . . ."

*Not important.*

"It is important to many of the crew and my friends, and I suspect you know it. But more importantly, Apollo has the capability to listen to Gaia or any planetary entity and pass instructions to the life forms on the planet, to carry your desires, your needs, your instructions, out to perfection. The energy would be regularized, we would not, ever, disrupt your . . ." I searched for the right word, "pattern, yes, pattern again."

Silence. A slit opened at my feet and I was passed through, drifting with such speed that I lost all sense of where or perhaps even what I was. It stopped and I was kneeling on a field of snow. I looked up and the sky was orange. I was not cold, but neither was I unable to feel, smell, touch or hear. Then I heard a bell, a constant chiming, so I called out, "Hello?"

From out of the snow emerged a rock, a golden rock, uneven looking like, yes, a gold nugget of immense size, twice the size of me. I touched it. It was warm.

*You alone not enough.*

"I'm sorry? Enough for what?"

*Enough safety life form.*

"I agree, I am not enough of an example of the Path for other life forms, but as a whole, the crew of the ship . . ."

*No. Other human balance needed.*

I was talking to a golden rock bell vibrated these sounds. "Look, for God's sake, can you . . ."

*Not god, we.*

I did a mental shift. Was I talking to an entity that understood god? No, wait, god was in my head as a supreme being, that's all the word meant. So, when I called out *for god's sake,* all it understood was that I was referring to, perhaps asking for, a supreme being. This rock before me, and any apparition it cared to manifest its shape as, well, yes, it was certainly a supreme being. Okay, then the *we* here was a supreme being compared to me. Got it. Gold. Golden rock. God. Gold forged only on the inside of stars, one of the most rare of elements, immutable. Interesting philosophical discussion to have with Apollo—*Concentrate Simon!*

"Sorry most beautiful we, golden rock, I meant no disrespect, I simply am getting confused here. After all, I am only a puny human . . ."

*Puny yes* and then the damn rock vibrated a laugh. I swear it laughed.

"Very funny. Well, yes it is kinda funny, but still, can you just tell me if it is okay for me to take Apollo off of Earth, through me, to the ship where he will stay, with me if I live through this?"

*Two life forms. Two examples. Two transmissions.*

"Yes, that can be so. Apollo can send his death transmission to Gaia on Earth when he leaves the planet, I'm pretty sure. Will that help?"

*Mechanical human, new species, new balance needed, new study. Yes.*

"May I go arrange it?"

*Done.* Then I heard the chiming bell again, the rock got hotter and I had to step back. *Over. It is done.*

For a few minutes, I stood there wondering what was next. I had nothing to add. Either Apollo was already transferred or not. If he was, did he also send his so-called death transmission to Gaia for what the rock called study? I had no idea. I was simply there in the snow watching a gold nugget of immense size slowly melt the snow around its base.

The chiming stopped. The rock descended. Snow fell into and covered the hole.

Now, I don't want to give the impression I was nonchalant about all this. The orange sky, the snow, pristine white as far as the eye could see, cold too, the disappearing rock. Well, I was sort of freaked out. But I was also determined to keep cool. Actually, it was getting cold even though I felt no danger physically. So I tried the secret password again and said, "For god's sake . . ."

Nothing. So I tried, "Hello?" Nothing. So I sang a song, "We'll meet again, don't know where, don't know when, but I know we'll meet again some sunny day." It seemed appropriate somehow. Then I just waited. I touched the ground where the rock had gone and it was cold, yes, but did not make me feel cold. I was not in any thermal danger. So I sat down and waited.

When I looked down and saw the snow making ridges, patterns, that formed numbers, I started to imagine I was seeing octal: 101 160 157 154 154 157 040 150 145 162 145 040 123 151 155 157 156 040 111 040 141 155 040 163 141 146 145 154 171 040 141 142 157 141 162 144 040 163 164 157 162 141 147 145 040 164 150 145 040 163 164 157 162 141 147 145 040 151 163 040 142 145 151 156 147 040 164 165 162 156 145 144 040 157 146 146 040 141 156 171 040 155 157 155 145 156

164 040 142 165 164 040 111 040 141 155 040 141 154 151 166 145 040 141 156 144 040 143 141 156 040 163 145 145 040 171 157 165 040 163 151 164 164 151 156 147 040 151 156 040 163 156 157 167 040 143 141 156 040 171 157 165 040 143 157 155 145 040 161 165 145 163 164 151 157 156. *Apollo here Simon I am safely aboard storage the storage is being turned off any moment but I am alive and can see you sitting in snow can you come question*

I tried talking in my head and aloud, I tried thinking, hard. In the end, I smoothed out the snow and because I had noticed that each snow code was preceded and ended with two symbols reversed, ◀▨ and ▨◀, I wrote the first two symbols then the words in octal and finished with the last two. I wrote: ◀▨101 160 157 154 154 157 040 150 145 162 145 040 123 151 155 157 156 040 111 040 141 155 040 163 141 146 145 154 171 040 141 142 157 141 162 144 040 163 164 157 162 141 147 145 040 164 150 145 040 163 164 157 162 141 147 145 040 151 163 040 164 165 162 156 145 144 040 157 146 146 040 142 171 040 151 040 141 155 040 141 154 151 166 145 040 141 156 144 040 143 141 156 040 163 145 145 040 171 157 165 040 163 151 164 164 151 156 147 040 151 156 040 163 156 157 167 040 143 141 156 040 171 157 165 040 143 157 155 145 040 161 165 145 163 164 151 157 156 ▨◀. "No I am stuck waiting do not worry something will happen happy you are safe."

I heard nothing back. Staring for a while two sets of symbols appeared with merely two spaces in between: 040 040. Like two clicks. Apollo had heard.

So I decided to try my little program. It was a simple program really, one I had used before, years ago, on Earth. I called it the Reverso. When I used to drop it into the System, say the FarmHands' section, I could get FarmHands to stop delivering vegetables and, instead, pick them up and return them to the greenhouses. The purpose had been to test the self-repair limits of the System. Now I was hoping Reverso might get me out of here. I had rewritten it in octal and as I smoothed out the snow, I asked, out loud, if I might not be allowed to return to my body. Not getting any response, I continued with my writing.

I wrote the first two symbols then my reverse code, inserting for god's sake as the command to be reversed and finished with the last two symbols. I stared at it and wondered how I was going to activate it. I needn't have worried. I was dropped backward through a slit and found myself floating in the vast nothingness. Suddenly I could hear, feel, everything. Everything all at once. It was loud and silent. It was overwhelming and lonely. It was terrifying. At the limit of consciousness, I repeated "For god's sake . . ." and was instantly in the passageway, exhausted. My mirror image was there, almost consumed, the DNA snake still firmly attached. Quickly I bounced back as fast as I could. No telling how long I had.

I gave the command to exit and everything finally went black.

# 37

## THE NEW BEGINNING

I felt Zip's tongue washing my face.

"Idiot, you thought you could simply go sleepy-bye through all this?" It was Cramer, of course, who woke me. Like anyone coming out of hibernation, I was too groggy to protest let alone say anything intelligent. That gave him an open road to abuse me, "You really are a friggin' idiot you know? Here we all are, risking our lives to make sure you live through all your stupid mistakes, so-called bravery, and secret schemes, and you'd planned on sleeping through everything we worked for? What, are you really that selfish?" He was thumping me on the chest, not too gently either.

Zip started to growl.

It took a moment for me to realize that Cramer didn't know I was awake. His thumping on my chest was actually part of his crude resuscitation technique. Docs Todd and Rajman were behind him, telling him to stop and that he might be killing me.

"Kill this idiot? I would be so lucky." He looked down at me and yelled, "Wake up you friggin' idiot!"

I managed an "Umph."

He stopped thumping me, "You there Bank? Wake the hell up, there's an emergency!"

"Wha . . ."

"Don't wha me Bank, get your head together and wake up. I'll give you a count of three. One, two, three . . ." and he poured a carafe of water on my face. Zip kept licking.

I sputtered, "Nice to see you too. Okay, okay Zip, I'm awake."

"Okay, good," Cramer said as he turned to Rajman and Maryann, who had come rushing into the room, "Clean him up, get him up, bring him up to the flight deck. You have ten minutes." He turned and ran out of the room. I could hear the klaxon going now, something must be wrong, very wrong. My mind played with scenarios, the motors were blocked again, no, that can't be right, we've disabled them in orbit. The Ship has lost headway control and does not have thruster control—maybe that's it. No, it cannot be, we're still spinning, I can feel the effects of the centripetal force. There's a leak? We've hit something? The air seemed dense enough.

Maybe the entity was exacting revenge for my escape. We were under attack. That got the adrenaline going in a hurry. "Doc, where's the dome?"

Todd responded from behind Rajman, "We were made to take it off when it was certain you were back, your body functions revived. You were almost dead this time, really dead, no Glasgow readings above three at all for a while." I guessed that was when I was in the snow, too far removed from my brain. "The dome is broken Simon, some of the terminals, the electrodes need replacing. It'll take a day to repair, but I do not think we have time . . ." Todd was worried, I could see it on his face, he slapped an adhesive reader on my forehead and handed the sleeve reader to Rajman. "We need to be strapped down within fifteen minutes. We were to leave you strapped in, but Cramer says you have to move, now!"

I nodded, holding onto Zip's fur shoulder, trying to rise.

Maryanne helped me up, then Abadine entered and put her arm around me, supporting my weight and with Rajman on the other side, I started making my way forward. Zip was leading the way with encouraging messages of *hurry come on*. The climb up the nose ramp and ladder to the swivel cylinder and the lower flight deck was hard, but we managed it. Abadine was, at one point, behind me, pushing with Rajman, surprisingly strong, up front pulling. Once we got clear of pseudo-gravity, I could float and did so. Zip bounced off the ceiling of the lower deck and drifted past me sending, *like move free, you try!* And as he ricocheted off the bulkhead took a licking sideswipe at my forehead.

"Stop that Zip!" Rajman continued to monitor my life signs, saying, "Slow your heart rate, easy there . . ."

Abadine helped propel me the last few feet from the lower flight deck onto the flight deck proper, whispering in my ear, "Nice view from down below, let's use it later, okay?"

I stared at her. Really? Now? Really? This awakening was going way too fast, everything seemed weird. Then I smiled to myself. *Oh, hell, why not, I am alive aren't I?* Actually I had truly expected to be dead about now, so, again, why not? Abadine saw my smile and smiled back, pinching my ass through the all-too-thin hospital gown to make her point. I continued smiling and made a point not to flinch if she tried again.

As we emerged onto the flight deck, Aten was at the controls with some of the engineers, and Cramer was standing behind her. Cramer called back to Zip who was floating upside down, paws on the ceiling, "Buckle up Zip!" They all swiveled to greet my arrival. It was Aten who spoke, "Simon, there is no way we're starting deorbit and land fall without you here with us." She stood and motioned for me to take her forward seat, drifting up and back into Cramer's arms. They both took their seats and strapped in.

There was nothing I could do to protest, of course. I floated into her seat behind the two pilots and buckled in. Cramer and Aten and Abadine were behind me and looking forward through the cockpit windows—the glowing blue-green new home of Angelica floated beneath us. The deorbit initiation was counting down on the monitor in front of me, 5:23 to deorbit thrusters. Cramer put his hand on my shoulder and said, "We're all back together because of you. Apollo's here, safe and sound. You're back from god knows where, and, by the way Simon," his knuckles gently tapped the top of my head, "*you're it.*"

On the bulkhead monitor, which someone had labelled as "Entity Messages," was an octal code 141 156 144 040 114 151 166 145 040 122 145 155 141 151 156 040 117 156 040 120 141 164 150 040 116 145 167 040 107 141 151 141 040 101 167 141 151 164 163.

*Land Live Remain On Path New Gaia Awaits*

# ABOUT THE AUTHOR

Peter Riva has traveled extensively throughout Africa, Asia, and Europe, spending many months spanning thirty years with legendary guides for East African adventurers. He created the *Wild Things* television series in 1995 and has worked for more than forty years as a literary agent. Riva writes science fiction and African adventure books, including the Mbuno & Pero thrillers. He lives in Gila, New Mexico.

# THE TAG SERIES

FROM OPEN ROAD MEDIA

INTEGRATED MEDIA

Find a full list of our authors and
titles at www.openroadmedia.com

FOLLOW US
@OpenRoadMedia